DANGEROUS DAWN

Aleatha Romig

New York Times, Wall Street Journal, and USA Today bestselling
author of the Consequences, Infidelity, Web of Sin, Tangled Web,
and Web of Desire series

COPYRIGHT AND LICENSE INFORMATION

DAWN

Book 3 of the DANGEROUS WEB trilogy
Copyright © 2021 Romig Works, LLC
Published by Romig Works, LLC
2021 Edition
ISBN: 978-1-947189-58-4
Cover art: Kellie Dennis at Book Cover by Design
(www.bookcoverbydesign.co.uk)
Editing: Lisa Aurello
Formatting: Romig Works, LLC

DAWN

book #3 DANGEROUS WEB

"Night never had the last word. The dawn is always invincible." ~**Hugh B. Brown**

The Sparrow Web world is covered in darkness, yet the dawn is near.

The dramatic conclusion to the Dangerous Web trilogy is here.

The veil of safety protecting Lorna Murray's life has been ripped away by the actions of a stranger, or is there more?

Will Lorna ever see the light through the lingering darkness? Will the sun rise again?

From New York Times bestselling author comes a brand-new dark romantic-suspense trilogy, Dangerous Web. DAWN, the dramatic conclusion, is set in the dangerous world of the Sparrow Webs. You do not need to read Web of Sin, Tangled Web, or Web of Desire to get caught up in this new dangerous and intriguing romantic-suspense saga, Dangerous Web.

DAWN is the dramatic conclusion of the *DANGEROUS WEB* trilogy that began in *DUSK*, continued in *DARK,* and concludes in *DAWN*.

Have you been Aleatha'd?

NOTE FROM ALEATHA

Thank you for reading the Sparrow Webs. You're about to read DAWN, the conclusion of the final Sparrow Webs trilogy, *Dangerous Web*.

If this is your first trilogy of the Sparrow Webs, please know that there are other amazing stories in this same world, complete and ready to binge today.

SPARROW WEBS

Web of Sin
(Sterling and Araneae's story)

SECRETS (Free everywhere)
LIES
PROMISES

Tangled Web
(Kader/Mason and Laurel's story)
TWISTED

OBSESSED
BOUND
and

Web of Desire
(Patrick and Madeline's story)
SPARK
FLAME
ASHES

For a complete list of my books, please go to "Books by Aleatha" following DAWN. Thank you again for falling in love with the Sparrow Webs world. Enjoy.

~Aleatha

PROLOGUE

Dawn
**Book #3 of the DANGEROUS WEB trilogy in SPARROW
WEBS**
The conclusion of DARK, book #2 Dangerous Web

Reid

"*I* haven't seen her," Maples repeated as Mason's knife cut
another notch in his wrist.

"Next one will be deeper," Mason said. "Poor Zella, she's going
to find you dead. If she can find anything in this shithole. I wonder
if she'll be more distraught over your death or at not winning the
million dollars."

Maples was now bound to the dining room chair where he'd sat nearly fifteen minutes earlier, his arms tethered to the chair's arms and his legs secured to the chair's legs.

"Who is the rich guy?" Mason asked.

"Hernádez, Garcia, Roríguez. Shit, some brown..." His beady eyes came my way. "Not like you, boy. You know...a Mexican. Not sure what we're supposed to call them or your kind now days."

As the small hairs on the back of my neck stood to attention, this asshole's poor choice of vocabulary added fuel to the flames of rage that began when I figured out what he'd done to my wife twenty-five years ago. I worked to keep my expression statuesque though it wasn't easy to suppress my enthusiasm for what was about to occur.

"Nancy was getting payments from" —Mason hesitated— "a—"

"Mexican," I said, finishing his sentence using Maples's words.

Missy was Latina. This had to be the connection. It was the only plausible explanation. "Why was Nancy getting payments from a Mexican?"

"He don't live there...he lives here. But she made some deal with him. He paid until...well, eighteen."

Mason's knife went to Maples's neck. "What is his name?"

Maples stretched his neck, backing away from the blade. "I can't—"

Mason pushed the blade against his sagging skin until a crimson drop of blood dribbled to his dirty, worn collar. "Wait. It was Garcia. Yeah, I'm sure."

Mason pushed the blade deeper. "Tell me what this has to do with my sister."

Maples's gray eyes narrowed. "The brown one or the pretty one with red hair?"

My fist landed in his stomach. "What did you do to Lorna?" I asked as his coughs turned to gagging.

Maples spat as blood dripped from his lip. "The payments were for the other one, but oh, that redheaded one was downright sweet. She had the softest little hands. And her lips—"

My next punch connected to his jaw.

He spat more blood and this time a front tooth. "Don't know why you're mad. She wanted it. We were friends and she liked my attention. All little girls like to hear they're special." He looked at me. "Oh shit. Are you fucking her now? Damn, I wanted that tight pussy. Is it still tight or saggy like her mother's?"

There was no conscious train of thought. I didn't consider the ramifications. For once, I wasn't thinking steps ahead. Taking Mason's knife from his grasp, I plunged it deep in Maples's upper arm.

It wouldn't kill him immediately.

"What did you do to her?" I asked again.

His words sputtered as blood mixed with his oxygen. "Nothing she didn't want. Just like her momma."

I looked at the blade in my hand, dripping with deep red blood. "This is for my wife," I said as I pushed the blade through his ratty shirt, above his belt and sliced laterally, as deep as the blade would go.

Maples's eyes widened as he watched organs and tissue roll from his wound.

There were moments of consciousness before death. It was his only time to make amends with a superior being or beg for his life, not that we could save it now, but he didn't. The vile creature stared at both of us.

Mason's eyes met mine before he took back the knife, and buried the blade into Maples's upper leg. Blood spouted as his body convulsed. We both stepped back as the asshole bled out before us.

His time for amends had expired.

"I would have been okay with him enjoying more of the experience," I said. "You know, since he was such a good friend to Lorna."

Mason took a deep breath before disappearing into the kitchen and returning with two towels. He handed one to me.

"Call the cleanup crew," I said as I wiped my hands on the

towel. "After this is done, we're bulldozing this place. Too much shit happened here."

Mason nodded as he sent a text. Once he was done, he reached for the knife, wiped the blade on the towel, removed a leather sheath from his pocket, and reinserted the knife. Next, he put the knife back in his pocket. "What? It was a gift."

His casualness made me grin.

I took one last look at Gordon Maples. As grotesque as it sounded, the sight of him gave me my first glimmer of light. I would make this world safe again for Lorna. Killing this disgusting creature was only the first step.

Together Mason and I turned and walked toward the front door.

I'll bulldoze every last splinter.

The hinges creaked as Mason opened the front door inward and we stepped onto the porch. Scanning the scene, I saw our SUV across the street and one of our Sparrows nearby on the sidewalk.

It was as we proceeded toward the stairs to the walkway that the bang of a screen door hitting a house across the street caught my attention. I barely had time to register the chain of events that followed.

The first to step from the house across the street was Zella. She wasn't at the bank as she'd been told, but on that porch, her baby still on her hip. Next, a tall man came into view, exiting the house behind her.

Slow motion as in the movies was a cinematic illusion. In reality, the clock didn't slow, it accelerated. There wasn't time to register details. Things I'd been trained to recall such as the man's characteristics or identity were merely a blur.

"Watch out..." I began to shout as the man behind Zella lifted a long shotgun and pointed it in our direction. With my reflexes on high alert and without conscious thought, my hand moved, reaching for my gun, freeing it from the holster.

Out of the corner of my eye, I saw Mason crouched behind the porch's railing with his pistol already aimed. Our backup Sparrows flew into action. One on the street ducked behind a car and pointed his gun toward the man. Another stepped from the side of the porch, his firearm aimed.

Don't hit the baby.

That was one of my many thoughts as shots rang from different directions. The air filled with pops and bangs—multiple explosions —as if a pack of firecrackers left behind from an Independence Day celebration had been ignited.

And then...

It wasn't the impact of the bullet that I felt as much as it was the way its thrust propelled my body backward toward the open doorway. I reached for the doorframe. Crimson from my palm painted the jamb as my grip loosened, sliding down toward the floor as my knees gave way. Collapsing in the threshold of the home that had caused Lorna too much pain, my light disappeared.

"Reid." Mason's voice came and went.

Dark claimed another victory.

GORDON MAPLES

Over a year ago
Englewood, a Chicago neighborhood

Talking heads jabbered on and on from the television in the rear living room, competing with the television in the front room. The newscasters were arguing about everything, each one louder and more determined. Taxes were going down or was it up? The Bears were headed for another loss or maybe a victory. An ex-senator will have his appeal heard. There was another body found in the dockyard. And everyone had to weigh in on the newest scandal that would be forgotten tomorrow.

Snuffing out my cigarette on my plate, I swirled the butt in the runny scrambled eggs. "I can't eat this shit." I shoved the plate to the floor, the cheap glass bouncing on the linoleum as the eggs slid and landed in a clump.

"Zella," I screamed to my oldest daughter above the television's volume. "Get me some more coffee."

The creaking of a hinge drew my attention to the far corner of the kitchen—the basement door was slightly ajar. It wasn't much of a basement. Other than the old washing machine and dryer, the basement was mostly used for storing shit. That's all the attic was used for these days too.

Speaking of old shit.

The door creaked again, opening a little more. "Gordy?"

The basement was also where we kept her.

I let out an exaggerated breath. "Did I give you permission to come up?"

"I-I'm not up yet, not all the way. I heard you yelling for Zella. She's not feeling well with the baby. I can get you coffee."

Since I knew this waif of a woman had no maternal instincts, she obviously wanted something. I turned to the newspaper spread out on the table. She didn't ask again; instead, she waited for my permission just like the little bitch she was trained to be.

There had been a time when she'd looked good, with full bouncy tits, a tight ass, and painted lips perfect for sucking. She was a hot commodity—literally. That was years ago. There wasn't much left on her that was appealing. Maybe her ass. It was still tight, unlike her pussy.

Overuse did that.

"Clean that up," I said, pointing to the lump of egg shit on the floor.

Nancy opened the door wider and taking slow steps with dirty bare feet, she came to a stop at the mess of eggs. When she looked up, her dull eyes opened wide. "Please, Gordy. I'm hungry."

"Do I look like I give a shit?" I ran my hand over my belly. "You ain't paid rent in years. No rent. No food. You're lucky you have a roof over your head."

She looked down again at the eggs on the floor. "I-if you don't want that...I could eat it."

"You want that?"

She nodded.

My lips curled upward. "Say please."

Her slender shoulders bowed forward. "Please."

A chuckle bubbled in my throat. I could take this further, make her beg, but honestly, I wasn't in the mood. "Fine, eat it off the floor and you can have it."

"Gordy?"

I sat taller, lifting my brows. "You want it? Eat it. You have ten seconds and then it goes in the trash, where you belong."

Her legs and arms trembled as she lowered herself to the floor. On all fours, she reached for the cold eggs, scooping them into her hand.

"No hands. You know the rules."

Watching as she placed her lips on the linoleum and sucked the cold eggs reminded me that despite her uselessness, she was still okay at that particular skill set. I rubbed my hand over the front of my pants. "Lick it clean."

My dick twitched as she obeyed, her tongue running over and over the dirty floor until there was no egg left. Still on her knees, her lifeless green eyes came to mine.

"Pick up the plate and get me more coffee."

Nancy stood with the plate and wiped her lips on the back of her hand. After placing the plate on a stack of dishes in the sink, she walked toward me to get the coffee cup. Slipping my hand under her thin dress, I grabbed a fistful of ass and squeezed. "Bring the coffee over here, and I'll let you suck me real good like the little whore you used to be."

Reaching for the mug with trembling hands, she nodded.

Her too-thin form walked away. As I took in her ass and skinny legs coming from beneath the loose dress, I voiced my assessment. "Hard to believe you were ever a looker." I laughed. "Men actually paid to get in your floppy cunt. Now it's your turn to pay."

Her money was gone, and her only form of payment was what she'd always only been good for. Without a response, Nancy filled my cup with coffee, set the pot back on the burner, and walked the cup back to me.

I set it on the table. Spreading my knees, I pointed to the floor. After lighting another cigarette, I leaned back against the old kitchen chair.

Nancy Pierce didn't need step-by-step instructions. Hell, she'd been sucking cock since long before I met her.

Around twenty-five years ago, she had been worth the bother of housing her. That ended when her brats moved in here. The boy was a piece of shit. Last I heard he was dead, died in some explosion, something to do with human trafficking. I'm not surprised. I knew from the first time I saw him he'd never amount to anything.

The little one was sweet enough to eat, but I don't have a thing for darkies, even the light-brown ones. It was the little redhead who had a nice ass.

As Nancy loosened my belt, I imagined what the little redhead might look like today. After she quit working with my Anna, Lorna Pierce disappeared into fucking thin air. Images and possibilities came to my mind as her mother unzipped my pants and pulled out my cock. Nancy's cold fingers surrounded me. I wouldn't take responsibility for my flaccid state. Getting me hard was her job.

My fingers fisted Nancy's thinning hair. "Do you want to be my secret friend?"

"Yes, Gordy."

She gasped as I pulled her hair tighter.

"Mr. Maples," I corrected.

"Yes, Mr. Maples."

Nancy had played this role enough times. I shouldn't have to remind her. At least her mouth was warmer than her touch. With my eyes still open, I imagined a much younger version of the woman taking me between her lips. In my mind's eye, her hair grew redder, her skin softer, and her mouth more timid.

"Pretend you're eating ice cream." I laughed to myself as she licked real good like. The ice cream line always worked with the little ones. They all loved ice cream. "Now suck."

Using her hair as a rein, I pushed and pulled, directing and dictating Nancy's rhythm. The noises as she gagged and choked only made my dick grow. Hell, her discomfort combined with the made-up visions in my head did the trick. My circulation rushed to my cock, making my dick throb.

The feeling rose from within. Harder and harder, I thrust until I stilled and came. I'd have lasted longer if she were younger.

Leaving my dick out, I kept my legs spread in case I'd make her do it again. "You still know how to suck." I smirked as she sat back on her heels and wiped my come from her lips.

"Gordy, can I have some coffee?"

I waved my hand. "If you drink it from a dog dish."

Her dead green eyes came my way.

"Forget it. I feel generous. Use a cup, one from the sink." No sense wasting a clean cup on her filthy cock-sucking mouth.

As she walked to the stove with her thin dress hiked up, small circular pink scars showed on her upper thighs under the fluorescent lighting. I turned to the ashtray and my burnt-out cigarette. That was okay; I hadn't needed the glowing red end to make her obey, not today.

I'd lost count of the years since she'd shown up on my porch again.

No one outside this house knew she still existed.

Weekly hits of heroin and cigarettes made feeding her less expensive. The hardest part was finding good veins in her used-up flesh.

"Umm." The sound of throat clearing caused me to turn.

Leaning against the archway to the dining room with her arms crossed over her breasts and her complexion pale was my oldest daughter, Zella. Her hair was pulled back in a ponytail, her bloodshot eyes were narrowed, and a cigarette dangled from her lips. The kid in her belly was beginning to show.

I fucking hoped this one was a boy.

How many damn daughters could one man have?

Ignoring my exposed dick, Zella looked around the kitchen and narrowed her gaze at Nancy. "When you're done with your coffee break, clean up this kitchen. I don't feel good. I'm going to rest today."

It was obvious from the dishes piled all over and beer cans and pizza boxes stacked on the floor and counters as well as empty cartons and containers that Zella rested every day.

"Too much blow," I assessed as she moaned.

My daughter shrugged and rubbed her stomach. "I think it's the kid. Pregnancy sucks." She scoffed. "Just like our maid." Her nose scrunched. "This place stinks almost as much as her."

"How's the rest of the house?" I asked.

"Fucking mess," Zella replied.

I spoke to Nancy. "Since you're upstairs, it sounds like you have a house to clean today. Do a good job, get the house spick-and-span, and maybe we'll let you lick our dinner plates."

"Only if you're a good bitch," Zella said. "And after I spit on everything."

"You know, Nancy, if you're not happy with the accommodations or our bartering system, you could always leave."

"I want to stay," Nancy said. "I'll clean the house. But...first...can...when..?" The cup in her grasp trembled as she looked from me to Zella.

"The bitch wants drugs," Zella said. "Fucking pathetic addict. Earn it. Bathrooms need scrubbing."

A sound from beyond the back door caught all of our attention.

We all turned as a knock rattled the door, reverberating through the kitchen.

Though the window inside the door was covered with a sheer curtain, it was stained and yellowed from years of cigarette smoke. Yet the silhouette of a person, a short person could be seen.

"What the hell?" I asked, pushing my dick into my pants. "Find out who's at the fucking back door?"

No one should be at our back door. Our backyard was fenced. The gate was padlocked from within and the only other entrance was through an old detached garage that stayed locked.

"Make your pet go away," Zella said, tipping her chin toward Nancy. "Even if it's a neighbor kid, we don't want nobody seeing your smelly old bitch."

"Go. Crawl," I said, knowing Nancy wouldn't be seen through the window if she stayed low. When she didn't move, I added in a more determined hushed tone, "Get your ass downstairs. If you make a sound, you'll be sleeping standing up because I'll beat your ass raw."

Zella laughed.

As Nancy scurried on all fours toward the basement door, Zella followed, and after closing the basement door, she turned the lock in the handle.

Standing taller, Zella nodded and stepped to the back door.

"Wait," I said, reaching for a pistol I kept on top of the refrigerator and placed the barrel into the back waistband of my pants. "Ain't takin' no chances. Now, go ahead. Answer the door."

Unlocking the bolt and then the chain, Zella opened the door inward. From around her head and shoulder, I saw our visitor wasn't a kid but a woman dressed all in black. She wasn't much, short and puny with yellow hair pulled back too tight and red lipstick. She was wearing large dark sunglasses.

"What are you doing in our backyard?" Zella asked.

"Miss Maples?"

"Mrs. Keller."

"You're married?" the woman asked.

"Was. He died."

That wasn't true, but it was her standard answer.

"It happens," the woman replied with no sympathy. Her head moved slightly side to side, appearing to be looking behind Zella.

Truthfully, with the dark glasses it was difficult to tell. "This house still belongs to Gordon Maples."

"Yeah, my dad...What do you want?"

"I'm looking for information."

As I came up behind Zella, I scanned the woman up and down. The black sweater she wore fit tightly around small tits and she had a tiny waist. Not skinny like Nancy. This woman was well proportioned with curves, just small. She couldn't have been one hundred and ten pounds soaking wet. Her pants were pleated at the waist and hung to the exact top of her black shoes or boots with pointed toes. It was like they were made just for her—expensive.

"What kind of information?" I asked.

"The kind I'm willing to pay a lot of money for."

I noticed her neck seemed odd on one side, wrinkly.

"But if you're not interested..."

I reached for the door and opened it wider. "Show me the money, and I'll tell you what I can."

The woman removed her sunglasses. The side of her face matched her neck, weird and wrinkly. It was like she was half old and half young. The young side wasn't too bad to look at. I started to wonder about her pussy—was it half and half too—when she spoke.

"Mr. Maples, if you have the information I need, I will pay generously. I suggest you refrain from trying any bullshit on me. I know what I want, and I will get it. It's best to remember that I'm not a patient person."

There was something about her I couldn't identify. Even though she was small and disfigured, she had a haughty air, like she might have money. "How much money are we talking?"

"That depends on what you can provide." She peered around us. "Is there anyone else home?"

"No," I answered.

The woman nodded. As she did, a dark-haired man stepped from our garage. He was tall and big, as if he was a body builder, but his clothes were wrong for the neighborhood. They looked like he belonged at one of the fancy clubs downtown. Instead of wearing working men's clothes, he wore a cream-colored sweater, black jeans, and shiny black boots.

Zella and I both took a step back. "Wait," I said. "How did he get in—?"

The woman raised a gloved hand to silence me. Her speaking returned my attention to her face. "This is my associate. You will let us in and we'll talk."

"And if we don't?"

The man lifted a revolver as the woman put out her hand. "Give me your gun, Mr. Maples."

"I ain't got—"

The man moved his finger to the trigger.

My gaze met Zella's, mine silently admitting our disadvantage. Exhaling, I reached for my pistol and placed it in the woman's small gloved hand.

Once she had it secure, she replied, "To your question, Mr. Maples. If you don't let us in, you will both die—today." She shrugged. "If you do let us in, you could have a nice payday." She grinned, reminding me of the joker in DC comics. The skin on the wrinkled side pulled tight. "I'm all about choice," she went on. "What will you decide, Mr. Maples? I'll give you until five."

The tall man spoke, "Four, three, two—"

I opened the door wider. "Come in."

As they stepped into the kitchen, their eyes feverishly scanned the counters of trash and dirty dishes. The woman's nose twitched.

"I-I was about to clean," Zella said.

The woman lifted her non-gloved hand to her nose. "You may be used to this stench, but I won't spend another moment in this filth." She turned to the tall man. "Get the car. We're all going for a ride."

This was kidnapping 101. All the daytime talk shows said to

never go with a stranger. For the first time in my life, I wasn't confident that I was the perpetrator in this new situation.

Zella's eyes met mine. "I-I need to stay here."

"Come in the living room," I beckoned. "It's cleaner. We can talk there." I nodded to Zella. "Get them...water or something. Coffee?"

The man handed the woman his gun, its barrel still aimed our direction. "I'll have the car behind the garage in two minutes."

The woman pointed the gun our way and tilted her head toward the backyard. "We're all going." When Zella reached for my hand, the woman added, "Now."

REID

Present day

The unmistakable odor of ammonia assaulted my sinuses. My entire body flinched to get away, yet there was nowhere to go. Coughing and wheezing, I rapidly blinked as the world around me came into focus. "Motherfucker," I muttered as I tried to make sense of the ache in my chest.

Shit.

Shaking my head, I lifted my hand to the source of the ache as beyond the windows of the moving SUV, scenes of Chicago flew by at rapid speed. Even breathing hurt as I closed my eyes and laid my head back on the seat.

My scalp alerted me to the fact someone one was fisting the front of my hair and pulling my face upward. I blinked once and then twice as Mason's stern expression came in and out of focus. "Fucking stay awake," he growled.

I reached for his hand and pushed it away from my hair. "Let go. I'm awake."

I was.

I wasn't sure when I'd been asleep, but the ten-thousand-pound weight on my chest and vise on my temples, along with the green-eyed stare, told me I was definitely awake. Again, I rubbed my fist over my chest. "Did a fucking horse kick me?" I looked down, noticing my sleeve. No longer light blue, it was saturated with red. My opposite hand went to it, feeling the stickiness. And as I lifted it, the elbow refused to bend.

"Leave it alone. We're getting you back to the tower. Dr. Dixon is going to need her own fucking wing. Hell, along with the obstetricians Sparrow wants to move in, we'll need a surgery unit."

Surgery?

My gaze moved up to the man driving. I couldn't place his name, but I recognized him. He'd been on the sidewalk outside the house in Englewood. After...and then...the girl...a man...gunshots.

It was like a puzzle where each piece slid into place.

I sat straighter, the interior of the SUV spinning unsettlingly around me as a wave of nausea competed for attention. "Fuck, I was shot."

"You always have been the fucking genius," Mason said. "Yeah, you were shot. Your arm was grazed. A little more than grazed, but the slug didn't lodge, and we were able to bandage you up enough to stop the bleeding. It was the second slug that hit its target—your fucking chest."

Groaning, I laid my head against the seat. "I told you we wouldn't need vests."

"And you're damn lucky I didn't listen to you. Hell, Sparrow is already pissed, but there's no way I'm telling Lorna you were shot."

I looked up to his unsympathetic expression. "Good. Don't tell her."

"Man, you look pale as shit, and that's saying something. There's a chunk of flesh missing from your bicep, a few bruised or cracked ribs, and you're going to have a giant-ass bruise on your chest. My sister may not be the savant you are, but she's not dumb. She'll definitely pick up on the clues."

My thoughts were on the injuries he mentioned. Since I didn't respond, Mason went on, "I'm not telling her. You are. She'll take it much better coming from your not-dead lips."

A moan came from my throat as the SUV bounced over something on the roadway. "Slug," I repeated. "You said slug. The man, he had a long gun. Was it a shotgun?"

"Yeah. And at that range...we need to tell Patrick that his upgrade of our vests was a good investment. Thankfully, the slug didn't penetrate the vest, but it gave you a swift shock. Phillips" — Mason tilted his head toward the driver— "passed his CPR test. If you weren't going to the tower to get your ass chewed, your arm fixed, and your chest healed, I'd tell you to buy a lottery ticket. Today is your lucky day."

I rubbed my chest. "The vest is gone."

"Again," Mason said, "CPR is best performed on your skin. Without further tests, we think the impact of the slug caused your heart to get out of rhythm and the stress caused it to stop."

"You're saying I died?"

"I'm saying your heart stopped and was restarted."

I closed my eyes. "Shit, aren't you supposed to have life flashes before your eyes or visions or something when you die? A light or pearly gates?"

Mason grinned. "Speaking from experience, I'd take a shock to my heart over third-degree burns."

I couldn't recall seeing any rerun reels of the important moments in my life.

As my head ached, I tried to recall. We'd killed that piece of shit and then stepped onto the porch. It was then that the world went dark. Maybe my lack of 'life before my eyes' meant it wasn't my time, or maybe that my destination wasn't accessed through pearly gates with streets of gold, but someplace warmer. I had a twinge of guilt, knowing there were two women waiting in that paradise for me. Could there be a man too? *"Your father was a patriot in the true sense of the word.*" I hadn't been able to reach Walters again, but I wanted to talk to him more about my father.

"...I guess this is where you are meant to be," Mason continued to talk.

"Lorna. When I die, she'll be my last thought."

"Well, you're alive so be ready to face her."

"And tell her we went to Gordon Maples's house? She never told me what he did."

"He fucking confessed," Mason said. "I don't care what fucking bullshit Nancy told her." His green eyes went to the front seat as he lowered his voice, "Maples deserved to die."

"I'm not arguing. I just don't know how to tell Lorna that we went there without bringing up the memories that she won't want to face." I leaned forward and wheezed. "Fuck, I feel like I was kicked by a mule or maybe a Clydesdale."

"Like I said, you're going to have a nasty bruise, and there's a good chance you have a few broken or cracked ribs from the compressions."

My gaze went to the rearview mirror. The driver's eyes met mine. "Phillips, thank you."

"Doing my job, Mr. Murray."

I wasn't certain that saving people with heart compressions was part of his job description, but if it wasn't, we needed to update our Sparrow employee protocol. Pain shot from my chest as I exhaled. "Shit, so much for in and out of his house. My mind is still choppy. What the fuck happened?"

The SUV exited the highway and entered the city traffic.

"Maples is dead," Mason said.

"Yeah, I remember that. Gutted like a fat fish."

"In hindsight, we should have cut off his dick." Mason scoffed. "...If we could have found it."

I reached for my chest. "Don't make me laugh." My gaze met his. "We fucked up."

Mason shrugged. "There will be more cleanup than we planned, but it's getting taken care of. It will. Sparrow made some calls. The incident on South Morgan will go into the books as gang retaliation. Seems as though a shipment of over a hundred kilos of heroin was inadvertently delivered to the wrong house. Instead of being an upstanding citizen, Gordon Maples asked around, looking for the most lucrative avenue of sale. Word got around, the intended recipient wasn't happy. Soon the police will find half the stash in the attic."

"Attic?" I asked, recalling that was where Mason had said they'd slept.

He nodded. "Yeah. It was a lot smaller than I remembered."

Scenes replayed in my head. There was Maples tied to the dining room chair as he watched his insides become his outsides moments before he took his last breath. And then we were leaving. The girl was across the street and there was a man. "What about the girl?"

Mason exhaled as he sent a text message. "He gave her a code. When I tried to get rid of her and the baby, Maples fucking told her to take the baby to Mrs. Stephens. I heard it, but I was too focused on him and on wanting to make him suffer. I should have known."

"I was there. I heard that and I didn't think anything of it."

"It was a code. Now, I can see it. The way she responded. I fucked up."

"How would we know that?" I asked.

"We should have been paying better attention. We didn't. Neither one of us did for the same fucking reason. Sparrow is going to ream us out and we deserve it. We weren't thinking like soldiers for Sparrow or for any other regime."

"The Order would have left me."

"Be glad we're not in the Order," Mason said.

"You're right," I said. "We made this personal."

The SUV turned and began to descend into the tunnel that led to our parking garage.

"It's me—my fault," I said. "I'm the one who wanted to find him, to make him pay. Sparrow can be pissed at me. What is he going to do, fire us?"

Silence settled over us as the SUV continued underground toward the garage. It was a construction marvel that Sparrow had this tunnel created beneath some of the highest-rent towers in Chicago. It ran over three city blocks long, making it impossible to know from the entrance to which building it led.

Finally, Phillips came to a stop near the elevator and put the vehicle in park. "Sirs, do you need help?"

"No," we both replied.

But as I reached for the door handle and pain shot up my arm and more severely constricted my chest and ribs, I sat back with a moan. Without a word, Mason came around the SUV and opened my door. When he looked down, he grinned. "Do you want me to carry you?"

"No, asshole. I can walk. I just" —I let out a breath— "need to get out of the damn back seat." Turning slightly, I reached forward with my left arm, the one that wasn't bandaged.

Mason grasped my hand as he partly pulled and partly supported me. Once I was out, he grinned. "Watching you hobble around like an old man will make the ass chewing we're about to get worth it."

Step by step, we made it to the elevator where Mason pushed 2.

"Two?" I asked. "I thought the good doctor was visiting me."

"You're walking and talking. We have a command performance on 2. She'll wait at the apartments."

Because Dr. Renita Dixon had nothing better to do or any other patients waiting.

My thoughts went to Maples and from him to Lorna. "What does Lorna know?"

"Nothing."

"Do any of the women know what happened?"

Mason shook his head. "Cleanup is still happening in

Englewood, but we do have some loose ends that need tying. Remember what you said when we first got to Englewood?"

The doors opened to the cement hallway and steel door.

I did remember. "That Maples lived in the same neighborhood as Dino's liquor store."

"We are about to have a second dead body on 1, and something tells me we may have a connection."

Mason scanned his eye and the steel door opened.

All eyes turned our direction as they let out a collective breath.

Holding on to Mason's arm, I took a staggered step into our control center. It wasn't the massive bank of computers that I saw. It wasn't the set of blue eyes staring my way. My focus was on the kingpin of Chicago. He was still dressed in his Michigan Avenue finest, except now his jacket was gone, his sleeves were rolled up, and his leather loafers were about to pace a hole in the concrete floor. When our gazes met, he stilled. "Don't go rogue. It was the last fucking thing I said."

REID

"Technically," Mason began as he helped me to my chair, "I believe the last thing you said was to take backup. We did."

Sparrow glared from my brother-in-law to me.

"It wasn't supposed to end this way," I replied.

"With a goddamned gunfight on a residential street in my city in the middle of the day?" He ran his palm over his dark hair. "I fucking hope that wasn't your goal. What was?"

"We didn't plan the part of Reid getting shot either," Mason said as he leaned against a long table, crossing his arms over his chest and casually moving one ankle in front of the other.

"How are you?" Patrick asked, stepping toward me.

"Sore as hell. I feel like I was kicked by a horse or hit in the chest with a sledgehammer."

Patrick looked at Mason. "CPR?"

"Yeah, the good doctor wants to run some tests, EKG and shit. By the time I got to him, there wasn't a pulse. One slug hit his arm. The second slug hit him square in the chest, threw him back about three feet or more before he fell."

Patrick's eyes went to the bloody sleeve on my shirt and back to my eyes. "Glad you're all right. If we lost you, Madeline and I would feel obligated to name our son Reid, and well, Reid Kelly isn't our first choice."

My lips curled. "I guess I lost that bet."

"What were you two doing six blocks from Dino's Liquor Store?" Patrick asked. "Romero and I were leaving there when I got the text about the shoot-out."

"Did you learn anything?" I asked.

"No." It wasn't an answer from Patrick but a resounding declaration from Sparrow. "Do not change the fucking subject. Why were you on South Morgan Street in Englewood? Was this a lead you're following up from traffic cameras? And why did I have to call in a request for heroin and then to pad a police report? We have enough fucking unrest on our streets without you two adding more. Not to mention, shit is happening in Englewood. We've got capos working the streets for information on the factions and following leads on who's supplying them. The last fucking thing we needed was this."

"Boss," I said, "it is all my fault."

"Fuck no," Mason said. "Don't listen to him. He's delirious with some near-death shit."

"I'm not—"

"The dead guy," Patrick interrupted, "works at Dino's."

"Maples?" Mason and I asked together as Mason stepped away from the table.

"No, who's Maples?" Patrick asked. "I mean the dead one from the shoot-out. He's on his way to the Cook County Medical Examiner. We tried to intercept his body. Anyway, we know his name is Stephens, Darrell Stephens. He's been a clerk at Dino's for the last ten months."

Apparently, there wasn't a dead body headed to i.

Mason and I looked at one another. He was the first to speak.

"So the guy who opened fire on us happens to work at the liquor store that has been getting illegal firearms deliveries?"

"And he happened to live across the street from Gordon Maples," I added.

Sparrow looked at me. "Tell us who the fuck Gordon Maples is."

"Was," Mason corrected. "He was a sadistic son of a bitch who should have been dealt with a long time ago."

"And you know this how?" Sparrow asked.

Mason sighed. "He was one of Nancy's sugar daddies a long time ago."

"And maybe not so long ago," I added. "He admitted to seeing her within the last five years."

"You went to the home of some guy who screwed your mother and ended up in a shoot-out?" Sparrow asked.

Mason's green stare came to me. Taking a breath, I put my good hand on the edge of the desk and after a few winces and moans, I stood. "I need to talk to Lorna."

Sparrow's stare came my way. "She can wait. This is more important."

Mason stepped forward. "This and that are the same thing. We didn't go there because of Nancy. And why we went there isn't for us to share. Trust us on this." His stare went to Patrick. "We didn't know of a connection to Dino's. It was personal. I remember making a personal trip down to Florida a while back and Sparrow took one to California."

Patrick stood taller. The trips Mason was referencing had to do with people he and Madeline knew when they were young, people who profited off the young people they befriended. We'd all worked together without asking for details. Sometimes we righted wrongs. Other times we were the wrong.

Sparrow's eyes narrowed. "After all these years, at the same time we have this gun issue and we're still trying to find out who took Araneae and Lorna, you two decided to take care of personal business on Sparrow time?"

In our defense, it was never not Sparrow time. Now wasn't the moment to mention that.

"Lorna..." I took a painful breath. "The connections we made weren't about what is happening. It's more personal. The recent events, the kidnapping and finding Nancy's body, they have awakened some thoughts or memories that any little girl would try to forget."

"*Little girl,*" Sparrow repeated, straightening his neck as his fingers clenched. "How little?"

"Ten, but that's all I'm going to say. Don't use your imagination. Lorna doesn't deserve that. You can be pissed at me," I said, facing Sparrow. "I have just" —I winced again as I took a step toward him — "felt so fucking impotent." My voice rose. "Someone took our wives—my wife. It's been weeks, and I haven't done a damn thing to reassure her that she's safe in this world. I don't mean the Sparrow world, I mean the whole fucking sphere. And then last night, she remembered something. It didn't make sense so I asked Mason."

Sparrow took a deep breath and stepped back. "I hope you cut it off."

"Couldn't find it," Mason said as his lips curled. "It was pleasurable enough to let him watch himself bleed out."

"As he was disemboweled," I added.

"You know," Sparrow said, "growing up, I thought it was only the sick rich bastards that hung around my father who had fucked-up wants, ones they were willing to pay good money to exercise."

"There's no economic barrier to perversion. It's just that the rich can hide it better," Patrick said before he crossed his arms and paced a few steps. "My list was long—my personal shit. Are there others you plan to visit?" His lips curled. "I wouldn't mind working with Kader again."

I looked over at my brother-in-law. "Talk about a sick bastard, Kader fits that bill."

"Yeah," Sparrow said. "Glad he's on our side. Are there —others?"

"Not that I know of," I replied. "The thing is, the memories Lorna has had were what Laurel calls those flashes. I think some of them are recent. Like Araneae, she has mentioned a dark-haired man. But she said some other things and" —I gestured between me and Mason— "we put it together that it had to do with a man they lived with as kids. And when given the chance at redemption, Maples didn't deny it."

"What are the odds," Patrick began, "that the Ford truck from Montana with the dark-haired man—who may or may not be Andrew Jettison—who shows up on traffic cams near a liquor store where illegal firearms have been delivered is that same Ford truck that left Nancy Pierce on the verge of death to be found with her daughter, and now the clerk at the same liquor store ends up living across the street from where you and Lorna lived with this Maples?"

"Darrell Stephens didn't have an old black Ford truck, did he?" I asked.

Patrick retrieved his cell phone from his suit coat pocket. "I'll send Sparrows back to check it out."

I sat back down and turned to Mason. "What happened to Zella?" When he didn't answer, I went on, "And her kid?"

"Right now, they're in a halfway house guarded by some capos."

"What?" Sparrow asked. "Who is Zella and if she witnessed it and won't back up the police story, why is she still breathing?"

"She has a kid," I said.

"Three," Mason said. "New info. First two are adults."

"Adults?" I asked. "How old is she?"

Sparrow shook his head. "No. Definitely, without question, no."

We looked in his direction.

"I don't care if you're fucking long-lost siblings or some other shit, no one is moving into the tower."

"Oh hell no," Mason said. "I'm not confident of her continued oxygen intake right now. She was a bitch when she was fourteen, and I doubt that has changed. But she might have information."

"Is the kid with her?" I asked.

"Right now."

With a groan, I turned my chair back to the computer and moving my mouse to the other side, I brought my screen to life. "Darrell Stephens. What do we know about him? Or Zella? Is her last name Maples?"

"What the fuck are you doing?" Sparrow asked.

"What I do." Holding my breath, I forced my right arm up to the keyboard.

"No," Sparrow said. "You're going to your apartment, and Renita is going to check you over."

My head shook. "No, for the first time, answers feel close."

A large hand landed on my shoulder. When I turned, I saw a small cuff of colors coming from beneath his shirtsleeve. "We're going to your apartment now. Don't make me carry your sorry ass."

LORNA

"*R*uby said that?" Madeline asked as we gathered the ingredients for dinner, both of us walking in and out of the pantry in the penthouse kitchen.

Biting my lip, I stilled by the large island. "I'm sorry. I've been thinking about it a lot."

She stopped and surveyed the items we'd accumulated.

"Is this all we need?" I asked.

Madeline nodded as a smile blossomed over her lips. "I'm excited that I can teach you something, but to be perfectly honest, I never baked pirozhki before. I have enjoyed eating it."

I made a sad attempt at repeating the name of what we were about to make, my poor attempt eliciting a genuine chuckle from both of us. "I guess it's fair to say when it came to languages, Mason got the talent." I looked at the recipe Madeline had found online. "I'll just call them mini-pies."

"Yes, that works. And what's so great is we can make all different kinds. That way everyone can try different ones. Salmon is a typical ingredient, but we can make some without any meat and others with vegetables, and there's always potato." She took a deep breath, standing taller, and placing both hands on her lower back.

"Why don't you sit? I can make the dough." I looked at the recipe again. "I'm pretty sure I can handle yeast dough. Then you can show me how to make the fillings."

Madeline slowly walked toward the bar stools, her hand over her large midsection. "Thank you."

I handed her the glass of water she'd been drinking.

"You know, your hair is cute."

I shrugged. "I'm not sure why I decided to do it. I have never done anything like this before. I'm also a little stunned when I walk by a mirror."

"I hope Reid wasn't upset." Her eyes opened wider. "He probably blames me for giving you the hair dye."

"No," I replied as I began to measure and add ingredients to a large bowl. "He was a bit shocked, but then he said..." I felt the warmth creep up my neck toward my cheeks.

"Oh," she said with a giggle. "Let me use my imagination. It had something to do with cheating on his redheaded wife with his brunette wife."

I nodded with a genuine smile. "Something like that."

Madeline took a drink of water. "Can we go back to what Ruby told you?"

"It's up to you." I peered out the large windows toward the afternoon sky, wondering for not the first time why neither Madeline nor I had heard from our husbands. Arancae and Laurel had been missing since I came upstairs. Not missing. They were both in other parts of the tower, working on what they did.

Madeline scooted on the chair, pulling the skirt of the casual long dress she was wearing. "Ruby was right. When I first got here, I was drowning in memories. Mine weren't suppressed by a drug or medication. I suppose it was me who suppressed them. And once I allowed myself to think about everything, it was almost too much."

"And Ruby said Patrick helped you?"

"He did. If we want to stay with the drowning analogy, he was my life raft. But if I'm being one hundred percent honest, once he saved me or helped me save myself, it wasn't over."

"What do you mean?" I asked.

She ran her fingertip over the lip of her glass around and around. I was about to change the subject when she spoke. "I started seeing a counselor at the Sparrow Institute. Laurel recommended her. And then once I got a little more comfortable with admitting even to myself what I'd been through, I began attending survivor meetings there too."

Taking off my wedding ring and placing it in a little holder for just such an occasion, I paused before kneading the dough. "I didn't know that. I thought you were volunteering there."

"I am now. I guess I started volunteering. Even though I hadn't given Araneae or Laurel the details I'd shared with Patrick, I think in hindsight it was a group effort to ease me into what the Sparrow Institute has to offer."

After covering the counter in flour, I dumped the dough, watching a cloud of white flour poof. "I'm sorry we're all on lockdown. I bet you miss your time there."

"I do a little. I've gotten to know other trafficking survivors whom I admire."

"I only know you and Jana," I said as I continued to knead.

"Living the life we do" —she looked around the large kitchen— "our network is pretty small, but the thing I've learned from all the people I've met at the institute is that I'm not alone. There are so many others, ones who got out much younger, ones who barely survived, and ones who didn't even realize it had happened to them."

"How could someone not know?"

Madeline lowered her feet to the floor. "I'm going to try walking. This little guy isn't helping me to be comfortable." She took another drink of the water. "Things said in group are confidential, you know, like *Fight Club*?"

"Of course."

"But maybe I can explain it in the abstract? No names."

I didn't want to encourage Madeline to say anything she didn't want to say.

Before I could argue, she began, "We'll call her Cynthia."

"Ruby's middle name."

Madeline nodded. "It's not this woman's real name, but I knew a Cynthia. Anyway, this woman I met recently wasn't kidnapped or sold like people mostly think of when you talk about human trafficking. People envision women packed in a box truck and then made to have sex in the back of some nail salon, or something like that."

A chill came over me as my stomach twisted. "I hate that anyone would have that image."

Madeline stopped by the tall windows and peered outside. "Cynthia wasn't sold to a pimp or forced to perform sex acts in a strange, unknown place." She turned back, her expression solemn. "She didn't realize that what she had been made to do was wrong because it was all she and her sister knew."

"What?" I wasn't certain I heard Madeline correctly.

"Their mother had friends. The friends would visit."

I lifted my hand. "Oh, stop."

"It ended after their mother was arrested—manslaughter."

"One of her *friends*?" I emphasized the word.

"No, driving while under the influence."

"What happened to the sisters?"

"According to Cynthia, they went into the foster care system and" —Madeline smiled— "it worked for them. They ended up with great foster parents. Their mother had told them not to tell anyone, so they didn't. At first, they kept expecting it to happen because they thought it was normal, but it never did. And with time, Cynthia said, she'd buried it. Even when with her sister, they never mentioned it, and any memories went away."

Placing the dough back in the bowl, I set it on the counter and covered it with a towel. "So what brought it back?" I looked up. "Sex?"

Madeline shook her head. "No. She had the memories so repressed that it didn't affect her sex life. It happened when she found out she was pregnant with a girl. She started having nightmares and then flashbacks, but she didn't know what was happening. It was after her daughter was born that more details came back to her. She called her sister. Her sister flat-out denied it ever happened."

"And what helped her?"

"Thank goodness, she found the institute. She knew something wasn't right, and she worried about her daughter. Her doctor recommended counseling. Her counselor listened and sent her to the institute." Madeline forced a smile. "The Araneae we know here is carefree and fun. In reality, she's really quite the businesswoman."

"She was before she met Sparrow...with Sinful Threads."

Madeline nodded. "I never thought she learned *that* from him."

I chuckled. "I would imagine his tutoring has been more personal."

"Or" —Madeline tilted her head with a grin— "maybe she tutored him?"

The banter brought a welcome lightness to our conversation, reminding me of the camaraderie we all shared, one that came over time and with familiarity and even through times of darkness.

After all, how would the sun break free each morning if it hadn't been reined in the night before? To continue the metaphor: When all was said and done, the love we all shared made me believe that light would eventually win. Dawn would shine from beneath the horizon and cover our world in golden rays of sunlight if we waited long enough.

"Anyway," Madeline continued, "Araneae understands delegation. She also has a well-defined mission statement focused on helping anyone and everyone she can reach. With that drive, she's created an amazing center." Madeline shrugged. "I suppose being filthy rich didn't hurt."

No one in the tower was financially strapped, but it was true that Araneae came into a large sum of money that she never expected, nor had Sparrow.

"What about Cynthia's sister?" I asked as I washed the dough from my hands.

Madeline shook her head. "She won't speak to her sister, swears she's lying."

"Then how do you know she isn't? Maybe what she thinks happened and are memories are really bits and pieces of stories or movies that she's seen and she mixed up."

"Or she is telling the truth."

"You think she is, don't you?"

Madeline nodded. "I think that more people are affected in some way by the depravity in this world than any of us want to admit. I've seen Cynthia with her daughter. I've seen her with her wife. Cynthia has come to terms with what happened, understanding that she was not responsible. If you asked Laurel, she'd talk about the maturity of brains."

"Of course she would."

"Children can't be held responsible for the choices of others. I know Ruby thinks she's grown up, but she's still a teenager. Cynthia was younger than that. Not only wasn't she old enough to consent, she didn't understand what she was even doing."

"That makes sense," I said.

"She didn't ask for that to happen to her, and she was not in a position to defend herself, but today, after facing her demons, she can defend and protect her daughter."

"You're saying if I met Cynthia or others from the institute at a dinner party or a picnic, I would never know they'd been victims?"

"We don't wear neon signs. I think for me, once I came to terms with the memories of what had been done and what I'd done to survive, I had to also accept that the responsibility for what happened to me isn't mine to bear. I am no longer a victim, but there's no shame in admitting that I was. That admission gives me the courage and strength to vow to never let that happen again."

"And Araneae's center is helping others too."

"It is. She has the funds, the will, and the passion, and she's taken all of that to get the right people." Madeline walked closer. "Now, let's work on the fillings."

I reached for her hand. "Thank you."

Her sparkling green eyes met mine. "Like Ruby said, if the dam breaks and you remember anything, swim like hell and reach for a life raft. Reid, Laurel, me, or once we're out of here, consider the institute."

"I know I wasn't raped."

"It's still okay to reach out." She squeezed my hand. "I've been thinking about it. I can't imagine how I would have handled it if they'd taken me, not after what I've been through."

Tears came to my eyes. "I'm so sorry that happened to you."

"I know without a doubt, being here with Patrick, Ruby, and soon" —she grinned— "this little one, here is where I belong. I may have walked through the fires of hell to get here, but if that's what it took, I'd do it again. You know what they say—it's darkest before the dawn. We can't give up."

"Hey, what are you—"

We both turned as Araneae entered the kitchen, her eyes open wide. She was all dressed for business from the waist up—hair, makeup, blouse, and jewelry. Comically, it didn't match her soft maternity leggings and sock-covered feet. I supposed it was a perk of working remotely. She could stay comfortable while appearing put together for virtual calls.

With her mouth agape, she came closer. "Fuck, Lorna, what did you do?"

I looked at Madeline, smiled, and turned back to Araneae. "I guess you mean my hair."

"I heard Aunt Araneae say—" Ruby said, entering from the

same archway Araneae had come through. She stilled at the threshold to the kitchen. "Shit. Lorna."

"Ruby Cynthia," Madeline scolded.

Before I could explain again why I was now a brunette with a shoulder-length bob, my phone buzzed. Pulling it from the back pocket of my jeans, I said, "I hope that's Reid."

The screen read *Mason*.

A bit disappointed, I swiped the screen.

"PLEASE COME TO YOUR APARTMENT."

I looked up at three sets of eyes.

"Is everything okay?" Madeline asked. "I haven't heard from Patrick either."

Araneae shrugged. "I haven't heard from Sterling, but that's not unusual."

"It's Mason. I hope everything is all right," I said. "Madeline, can you do the fillings by yourself? He wants me downstairs."

"Oh, are you making pirozhki?" Ruby asked. "I'll help."

"You pronounce that much better than I do," I called as I left the kitchen.

"I want answers later," I heard Araneae say as I passed the large staircase and headed toward the elevator.

REID

Dr. Dixon's arms crossed over her chest as I settled onto the couch in my apartment. "Reid, this is not up for debate. You need to listen to me. You need rest, and I expect you to get it."

Maybe the reason I hesitated to answer was my admiration for all that the woman before me had accomplished, her position at the hospital, and her status within the Sparrow world. I supposed my lack of response boiled down to one common denominator: respect. I had it in spades for Renita Dixon. I knew her history and how she'd become part of the Sparrow world and the devotion she had to Sterling Sparrow and his undertakings. Her life, like so many others, had been touched by the atrocities of Allister Sparrow and Rubio McFadden. She'd lost a sister to a world she never knew existed.

With her determination and Sparrow's financial help, she worked her ass off to get to a place where she could also help people. Now, I was her patient.

Renita's eyebrows arched and her eyes widened.

It was a look I knew well. I'd received it over the years from both my grandmother and mother, and more recently from Lorna. That expression was a secret weapon that women possessed. Maybe they shared it with one another, but honestly, it baffled the entire male population. It was that ability to speak volumes without moving their lips.

"I could lie to you," I replied a bit sheepishly.

"You could, but you won't."

She was right. I answered as honestly as I could, knowing I would be back on 2 the first chance I had. "I'll try to rest."

Dr. Dixon shook her head, her lips drawing together. "Listen, I never hesitate to help when anyone from Sparrow calls. I would much rather deal with issues that aren't in my specialty." She was a cardiologist by specialty. "For example, your arm will be fine. There will be a scar, but it should heal fine. The bandage will need to be changed twice a day and along with updating some shots, take all the antibiotics until gone. The fact remains that the EKG shows a small area of damage to your heart. Once the heart muscle is damaged, it stays that way."

"So you're saying it doesn't matter if I rest or not?"

"She's saying to rest."

Renita and I both turned to Mason, my self-appointed bodyguard, the man standing near the windows with his arms crossed over his chest and a scowl on his lips.

"I'm saying," she went on, "if you were my son, I'd ground you to where you are right now."

"How will sitting at a computer cause more damage?" I asked.

"How is your headache?" Renita asked.

"As far as headaches go, it's a fine one."

Mason shook his head as Renita took on the scowl.

"Take breaks," she said. Turning to Mason, she added, "Encourage breaks. No long stints at the computer or even watching any kind of screen."

Before I could answer, the door to the apartment opened.

Standing with her hand on the doorknob, Lorna stilled, her green gaze going around the room.

"Fuck," Mason muttered. "I forgot about your hair."

Lorna's gaze narrowed as she ignored her brother and concentrated on Dr. Dixon. "Why are you here?"

When the doctor didn't respond, Lorna voiced her question less directly. "What is going on?"

Uncrossing his arms, Mason let out a sigh as he walked toward Lorna. Reaching for the ends of her hair, he flipped one side before laying a kiss on the top of her head. "I guess if you could welcome me back with a new face, I can call you sis with whatever hairstyle you want."

As she gazed up at him, I saw what I've known for as long as I've known my wife. Lorna's capacity to love unconditionally didn't make her an island unto herself. It made her a fountain where everyone around her drank, whether we knew it or not. Even a man who had worked the dark web as Kader softened in her presence.

Slowly, her smile faded as she turned back to me, still lying upon our sofa. "Should I be frightened?"

Renita shook her head. "Grateful is a better sentiment."

Lorna came to me, sitting her fine ass on the cushion at my side.

Though I tried to hide my pain behind my complete admiration for my wife, my face contorted and a small wince escaped. Her hands immediately came to my bandaged arm and then to my chest, now covered with a clean gray t-shirt. She moved her hands over me, no doubt feeling the bandages beneath. According to the x-rays, I had two cracked ribs, none fully broken, and an ultrasound determined damaged cartilage in between.

"Oh my God, Reid, what happened?" Her frightened stare circled the room before returning to me as her body began to tremble at my side.

The clicking of the handle had us turning toward the door. Lifting his hand, Mason waved. "Keep him here until morning, sis.

Dr. Dixon wants him to rest, and I'd babysit his candy-ass, but I'm pretty sure you have this covered."

Lorna nodded as she tried to make sense of what was happening. "Mace," she called before he disappeared.

Craning his neck, he looked back.

"Thank you for bringing him back to me."

Mason shrugged. "It's not exactly like that. Let him fill in the blanks." Shutting the door behind him, Mason left the three of us alone.

Swallowing, Lorna turned back to me, her green eyes glistening. "Will you? Fill in the blanks?"

Closing my eyes, I nodded. When I opened them, Dr. Dixon had moved near the breakfast bar and was talking about my care.

"Lorna, I have written instructions. Reid will need his bandages on his arm changed every twelve hours. The ones on his ribs are there for support. He should avoid getting them wet, and they can come off in a few days. His ribs will still be tender. I have some pain medicine." She lifted a pill bottle and shook it. "He's already said he won't take it, and I'm not pushing. Just know it's here and should help with sleep. He must take all of the antibiotics. With the combination of the IV antibiotics and oral, there's a chance they'll make him nauseous."

She nodded. "Okay. I'll do whatever I need to do." Her beautiful emerald stare came back to me. "What happened?"

I reached for her hand, slowly entwining our fingers as hers still trembled. "I'm here with you. That's what happened."

She looked at Renita. As she did, I nodded. Maybe it was the coward's way out. Maybe it was that I never wanted to cause my wife pain or sorrow. No matter, I didn't want to be the one who said the words.

"Lorna, Reid was shot today."

"What?" Her entire body startled with the news.

"I'm here."

"How? Where?"

Renita came closer and sat in a nearby chair. "He was wearing a vest which no doubt saved his life. One shot hit his arm, grazed it. That's why he needs the antibiotics. The other shot hit him in the chest..."

Lorna continued to nod as Renita went through what had happened as well as the effects the shooting had on my body, including my heart. "...we'll need to continually check his heart for arrhythmia. The damage that occurred could result in an array of arrhythmias from slow to fast or irregular."

"What does that mean for long term?"

"It means we'll monitor him. Irregular heartbeats are not uncommon. Most people have no problem and many go undetected. Some require medication, others surgery. Right now, Reid is healthy and a very lucky man. We'll keep an eye on things. Let me know if" —she looked at me— "you notice being more tired or any other unusual symptoms."

"What about now?" Lorna asked.

"Now, your husband is beside you. That's all that matters."

I saw the tears as Lorna stood and embraced Renita. "Thank you."

"I'll call tomorrow."

Lorna nodded as she walked her to the door. As she began to open it, she said, "Oh, I can't get you to the garage."

"I can."

My neck stiffened at the voice. It wasn't that I didn't want to talk to him or see him. It was that in the nine plus years we've lived here, Sparrow rarely made visits to this floor. I think it was more symbolic than anything. This glass castle in the sky was his dream. When he brought Mason, Patrick, and me here for the first time, the construction of these floors was mostly complete. He asked for suggestions or, in Sparrow style, opened the door for our suggestions. I'm not sure he *asks*. Sparrow made a point that this floor was meant to be ours. Even with the power he wields, he hasn't deviated from that promise. Though I waited, Sparrow didn't appear. Instead, he was out in the common area.

Lorna looked in on me. "Will you be all right for a minute?"

"What does he want?" I asked as I tried unsuccessfully to sit up.

She feigned a smile. "I'll find out. Reid, listen to Dr. Dixon and rest. I'll be right back."

With that, the door closed, leaving me stranded with a million conversations going through my mind. The foremost one was the circumstance of my injury. I still wasn't sure how to tell Lorna about Gordon Maples. Nevertheless, I sure as hell didn't want it coming from Sparrow.

LORNA

Sparrow nodded to Renita as he turned, escorting her to the elevator. He moved with all the power of his position —a king secure in his realm, and yet as he and the doctor spoke, I sensed there was more. The responsibility Sparrow had willingly accepted weighed heavily upon his broad shoulders. After thanking the doctor for her help, he stepped into the elevator, hit G for the parking garage, and stepped back out before the doors closed.

His dark stare met mine. The air around us crackled with an uneasy combination of tension and anticipation as I continued eye contact, wondering what he would say. It wasn't that I was intimidated any longer by the man who ran the underground of Chicago. Through the years, our friendship had come too far. However, it rarely included the two of us alone. We joked and laughed while within our larger group. We spoke directly about matters of insignificance. This encounter was different. It was out of character—a noteworthy disparity when facing a man who was always in character.

Sparrow ran his large palm down his face. The movement

highlighted the exhaustion showing in the lines near his dark eyes. His suit coat was gone as was his tie. His Adam's apple bobbed above his shirt, now unbuttoned at the collar.

"Lorna, I..." Sparrow began before stopping and starting again. "You should know..."

The uncertainty emanating from one of the most certain and confident men I knew left me unsettled. Shifting my feet, I yearned to help in some small way. "Would you like to see Reid?" I asked, gesturing toward our apartment door. "You're welcome to come inside."

"No. I saw him. I thought I should see you."

I wrapped my arms around my midsection. "Okay. Why?"

Sparrow's wide chest inflated and deflated. "I didn't make an effort—well, I did. I made an effort not to see you when...before." He shook his head. "I was blinded by what I considered my failure to keep one of my men safe. I either didn't think about how the loss of Mason affected anyone but me, or if I'm honest, I didn't care." Turning a bit, he lifted his hand to behind his neck, his bicep flexing in his rolled-up sleeve. "This time...I thought maybe...this time I should tell you what I didn't say then."

Heaviness filled my chest with too many emotions. Hugging myself tighter, I said, "*Then* was a lifetime ago. This outcome is different."

"Today could have been another lifetime, and I want you to know something."

The small hairs on the back of my neck bristled as we stood amongst the stupid furniture that no one ever used. "Okay."

"You were brought here by Mason. You stayed here because of Reid. That was then...before. And I will fucking kill either of them if they put us through this again—today was bad enough—but if that day ever comes, I want you to know your future is in your own hands. Finances should never be a concern, but if you want to stay here, in your home, here with your family, that decision is not contingent upon either your brother or your husband. This is your home, Lorna. There are no qualifiers on that statement. You may opt to take the first fucking plane out of here and that's your prerogative." He took a deep breath. "The possibility of that decision came to me today, and I decided it was important that you never need wonder where you fit in all of this."

With each blink, another tear joined those now flowing down my cheeks. "I don't want to consider that day."

"No one does. Even so, today when I first got word that Reid was down, my second thought was you, followed by what an ass I'd been when it was Mason."

I shook my head. "Like we've said, that was a long time ago."

The tips of his lips moved upward. "Even so, I've been told I'm still capable of displaying that characteristic today."

My cheeks rose. "No comment from me." I looked toward our apartment door. "Are you sure you don't want to come in?"

"I'm sure. I'll let you two have some time alone."

"Thank you." My gratitude was genuine, not only for the invitation and admission of my place within this Sparrow world, but more so for the effort Sterling Sparrow had just made. In the reality of our pecking order, the king of the jungle didn't owe me anything, and yet he'd made an effort, given me his word, and solidified my position with his promise.

Sparrow nodded.

Turning, I took a step toward the apartment as Sparrow pushed the button beside the elevator. Quickly, I turned back. "What was your first thought?"

"What?"

"You said when you got word that Reid had been shot, your second thought was about me and how things went when Mason...What was your first thought?"

"That I'd fucking burn Englewood to the ground because payback is a bitch."

"Englewood?"

"Yes."

The mention of the neighborhood made my stomach twist. "Why Englewood?"

"That was where it happened."

"Oh, I guess I didn't know that. Why was Reid in Englewood?" *Why wasn't he on 2 where he usually stayed?*

Sparrow reached for the elevator door, holding it open and keeping the elevator in place. "That's a discussion that needs to be between you and your husband." He stepped inside. "Tell him he better not enter 2 until Renita gives him clearance or else."

A grin bloomed over my lips. "I'll tell him."

Instead of turning away, I watched the elevator doors closing, inch by inch, obscuring Sterling Sparrow. It was clear that the mission he'd set out to accomplish was complete as he lifted his chin and inhaled. Stress still showed upon him—the clenching of his jaw, the tightening of his neck, and even in the stiffness of his stance. Perhaps it was because of what happened with Reid or the kidnapping or maybe about his future child. With a man like Sterling Sparrow, rarely did he share those thoughts or worries.

When night came and Sparrow finally closed his eyes, I doubted it was without contemplating the burdens of his reign. Yet the vastness of the Sparrow world was his doing. And I knew that he would continue doing whatever it took to maintain that status without complaint while occasionally allowing someone like me to catch a glimpse into the man under the king's crown.

Once the elevator was fully closed, I made my way back to our apartment door as questions and thoughts swirled through my mind. Why would Reid be in Englewood? Did this have anything to do with our kidnapping?

I hoped that whatever took him to that part of the city was because of Sparrow business. I paused with my hand on the doorknob—if it was Sparrow business, the king himself wouldn't have answered the way he did.

His answer meant one thing. Reid was there because of something other than Sparrow.

Was he there for me?

Turning the doorknob, I stepped inside our apartment. Reid's eyes were open wide.

"Well, shit, what did Sparrow say?"

LORNA

I tried to read my husband's expression as his question
hung in the air.

"Sparrow said that if you enter 2 without Dr. Dixon's
permission, you're in trouble."

Seeing the anguish in his grimaced expression, I decided more
questions could wait. "Let me help you." I hurried over to him as he
tried to sit up. After placing more pillows behind him, I reached for
his large hand. "I want to know what happened, but even without
details, I know that I almost lost you." The tears came back.

My husband had been shot.

"You promised me you'd come home."

Letting go of my hand, Reid palmed my cheeks and pulled me
closer until our lips touched. Though I was worried my proximity
would cause him more pain, his hold was unrelenting as our kiss
deepened. In his grasp, warmth returned to my skin, and my body
relaxed. When I finally pulled back, I stared into his eyes, our noses
almost touching.

"I'm here." His deep, comforting tenor settled over me,
reassuring me that my fears hadn't fully materialized. Yes, there was

more that I wanted to understand. The concept of not telling me or any of the Sparrow women what went on would not suffice today. Something akin to anger bubbled within me. "But you almost weren't. I don't want to lose you."

"I never want to leave you, Lorna, know that. Never doubt it."

"Then tell me what happened."

"What Renita said...there were two shots. One hit my arm" — he lifted his right arm— "and the other my chest."

"I know that part. Tell me where you were and why you were there. Tell me who shot at you and why." When he didn't respond, I stood. Balling my fist, I brought it to my hip. "No, Reid. This isn't one of those times when you don't need to or can't tell me. I demand to know why you were in Englewood."

He grimaced as he took a deep breath. "How did you know that was where we were?"

"Sparrow let it slip, but he wouldn't tell me anything else."

Reid shook his head. "I don't know how much to tell you."

"All of the truth." When he only stared my direction, I added, "I can handle it, damn it. I can. Don't treat me like Mason does. I'm not twelve."

At the jab, my husband visibly flinched. "I fucking know you're not twelve. You were ten."

"What?"

"Mason and I went to Englewood to visit someone from your mother's past...someone from your past."

My stomach twisted as I tried to connect the dots.

Englewood.

My past.

My mother's past.

Ten years old.

I made a connection, but how could he? There was no way any of those dots should even be on my husband's radar. "What are you talking about?"

"Come here," he beckoned. As I neared, Reid reached for my

hand. "Last night, do you remember what you said after you colored your hair?"

I didn't. It was a bit of a fog, one I assumed I'd created with the sleeping pills. Although, I did recall our conversation this morning. "Something about you fucking a brunette?"

Reid sighed. "Sweetheart, last night you were upset and saying things that didn't make complete sense. You talked about not looking like *her* and saying you weren't *her*. Then you used the name Anna."

Letting go of his hand, I stepped away. "I don't recall that. You know that I took sleeping pills. I was probably delusional; besides, I don't even know an Anna."

Tilting his head, Reid stared for a minute, his dark, penetrating gaze searching beyond my surface, beyond my new darker hair. A chill scurried over my arms and legs as silently he stripped away my rebuttal.

"Reid, it must have been the sleeping pills."

"You did know an Anna, Lorna. You worked with her."

I shook my head and walked toward the kitchen. "Oh yeah." My dismissive tone reflected my desire to end this conversation. "That was a long time ago and even so, I haven't thought of her, well...since I left that fleabag hotel."

My stomach twisted as memories returned, ones I'd cast aside when Mason moved me to this tower.

Inhaling, my husband's wide chest inflated as his expression grimaced. "I'm not Laurel. I don't understand how memories work or how they can be recalled. Last night, after you were asleep, I asked Mason about Anna."

Spinning in place, I slapped my hands on the countertop of the breakfast bar and looked into the living room. "If you have questions about me, ask *me*. Again, I'm not made of glass. And I'll answer. There's nothing to recall. She was a bitch of a manager."

"You said you remembered smells and being told you were pretty like your mother."

Simply hearing his words caused my already-twisted stomach to drop and my skin to feel tight. "No, you're wrong."

"I know what I heard."

"Maybe you were dreaming, or you're delusional. Or maybe I was. I'm still fighting memories or the drug that's blocking them. Those thoughts and confusion are caused from recent events, not twenty-five years ago."

With concerted effort, my husband moved his feet from the sofa and slowly stood.

"Stop, you need to rest."

I crossed my arms over my chest as he slowly came my way.

"Last night, you said that Nancy told you rape only involves intercourse."

This wasn't a conversation I wanted to have or thoughts I wanted to entertain. My mouth felt unusually dry. Spinning toward the sink, I reached for a glass from the cupboard above and after turning on the faucet, filled the glass, listening to the water instead of the man coming nearer. As I drank, my ears filled with the pounding of my pulse thundering in my ears.

As I put the empty glass on the counter, Reid's words penetrated my thoughts, coming in fragments or syllables.

Reaching for my shoulders, he spun me until I was facing him. "Lorna, are you listening to me?"

Even though I nodded, my truthful answer was no. I wasn't listening. I was watching his full lips, knowing their movement as they spoke my name, imagining their taste when we kissed, or their power of persuasion when that kiss deepened. Leaning toward him, I stood taller on my tiptoes and brought my lips to his. When I backed away, I feigned a smile. "Let's not talk about this. You should rest."

"Lorna, you lived in Englewood when you were young."

My head shook as I rubbed my suddenly cooled hands together. "I lived in a lot of places when I was young."

"His name was Gordon Maples."

The shaking of my head increased in speed. "He wasn't significant. I don't want to talk about him."

"Gordon Maples didn't deny my accusation."

"Stop." I stepped farther into the kitchen. "I should make us dinner."

Reid's strong hands were again grasping my shoulders. "Lorna, you were a child. You didn't do anything wrong."

"No. No." My pitch rose above his deep tenor. "Stop talking about it. We can't discuss it."

Oh God, I remembered his yellow teeth and dirty hands.

The stench of him.

Reaching for the collar of my top, I pulled it up, stretching it over my lips and nose as my shoulders rolled forward, and I looked down at the floor.

Our floor wasn't like his. Our home was clean. There were no stacks of empty beer cans, no stains on the carpet, and no piles of dirty laundry.

With veiled eyes, I peered up at my husband. "Please, Reid."

"Talk to me, Lorna. God, I want to help you."

The room blurred as I sniffled, pushing my blouse down from my face. "This isn't helping me. I haven't thought about..." Would saying the words aloud bring the darkness back?

"He hurt you."

"He hurt everyone including Mason and Nancy."

Reid's arms surrounded me, securing my arms to my sides as he pulled me against his hard chest. Tucking my head under his chin, he enveloped me—captured me. As my eyes closed, I was surrounded by his warmth, the rhythm of his breathing, and the lingering scent of his cologne. His baritone voice and steady cadence vibrated his chest as he spoke. "Lorna, I'm not trying to upset you. Fuck, I'd do anything to take it all away."

Keeping my eyes closed against his clean shirt, scenes I'd tucked away played like a highlights film, small snippets of recollections. Shaking my head, I pushed the memories away and looked up. "I'm fine. It wasn't what you think." I peered upward. "It wasn't rape." I shrugged. "He called it a game."

"Grown men don't play those kinds of games with little girls."

I leaned into my husband's embrace. "I don't want to talk about it."

His large hand gently rubbed my back. "If you ever do, I'm here. If you never want to, I'm still here."

The weight of what happened so long ago fell over me like a weighted blanket. I spoke my words muffled by Reid's chest. "I didn't want to play, but he would say that if I didn't, he'd play with Missy."

"Fucker," Reid mumbled.

The guilt gnawed at my stomach. "He didn't force me."

Reid pinched my chin between his thumb and forefinger, lifting it until our eyes met. "Using your little sister as leverage was forcing you."

My mind knew Reid was right. As a grown adult, I could see the interaction differently than I did as a child. "You're right."

"He can't hurt anyone ever again."

"What did you do?"

"Lorna, he admitted to hurting you. I would wager you weren't the only one he ever hurt or played games with. Men like him don't deserve the luxury of breathing."

I took a step back. "He's dead?"

Reid nodded.

"Oh my God. Is that why you were shot? Did he shoot you?"

"When I told Mason what you'd said last night, he was as determined as I to talk to Maples face-to-face. No, Maples didn't shoot me. Mason and I had backup Sparrows. We were prepared. Mason insisted on the vests."

My trembling hand went to my husband's chest. "I'm so glad."

"His daughter Zella was there when we got there."

I scrunched my nose. "She was older than Anna. Why would

she be there? When I worked at the motel, she was married to some guy."

"I believe she was living with Maples. They have a child together."

My head was again spinning as it shook. "No, he's her father, her biological father."

"He bragged about the kid being his and being a boy."

Inhaling, I took a step back and leaned against the kitchen counter, unsure if I wanted to hear more. "Just tell me how you were shot."

"When we arrived, Mason sent Zella and the baby away on a fake mission. But before she left, Maples told her to take her baby to someone. We later figured out it was a code. When she left the house, she didn't go on the mission but instead went across the street. After Maples was dead, we called for cleanup and stepped out onto the porch. A man named Stephens came out of his house across the street with a shotgun."

My head was shaking. "What happened to him?"

Reid's head tilted. He didn't need to answer. I saw his response in his eyes. I pushed myself away from the counter. "This is wrong. I don't want people dead because of me. It wasn't..." I remembered Maples's stench, the phantom odor causing my nose to wrinkle, and his voice as he tugged on my hair.

I reached for my hair, pulling a curl forward, barely seeing the new chestnut shade. "This is entirely my fault. I shouldn't have said anything." I looked over at Reid. "I didn't mean to and now you were shot and two people are dead because of me."

"No, Lorna, Maples is dead because he was scum." Reid again reached for my hand. "Men like him never stop. He remembered you, Lorna, and he fathered his daughter's child."

A chill ran through me. "That's not the first one."

"What?"

I swallowed the bile bubbling in my throat. "I remember one time, in the middle of the night, I saw him with Anna. I didn't understand what was happening—what they were doing—but now I do. It was before we left his house. Anna was only twelve. Her oldest child is her father's. She married to get away from him."

"She told you that?"

"Not in so many words. I think it was why she still hated me when I worked at the motel. She was jealous because I got away."

"He was a sick man." Reid's Adam's apple bobbed. "Why would anyone go back to him?"

"You mean Zella?"

"I mean, Zella and your mother."

"Nancy went back to him?"

My husband palmed my cheeks. "You've been struggling with not remembering and not knowing. Do you want to know more? Or would it be better not to tell you what happened and what we learned?"

Inhaling, I inclined my face, relishing his touch. "Don't tell me how he died. I don't want to know what you did."

Reid nodded and offered me his hand. "Let's go sit down and I'll tell you what we learned."

REID

As Lorna and I walked back to the living room, I hit a button, bringing our fireplace to life. While the autumn weather was bringing a chill to Chicago, our apartment was warm. The fire I'd just started wasn't for heat but because I knew my wife and her affinity for warmth, color, and light. The orange and yellow flames sparked as we sat upon the sofa. Ignoring my sore ribs, I wrapped my arm around Lorna's shoulders and pulled her to my side as we both stared into the flames.

"Are you sure you want to know?"

Lorna nodded. "I think that maybe my flashes of a dark-haired man brought back things I'd forgotten or packed away about Maples." Turning, her green stare met my own. "I want you to know that I never purposely hid that from you. I had" —she shrugged— "I guess, hidden it from myself."

"Now that you remember, were there others who hurt you?"

Lifting her chin, I watched as the flames from across the room reflected in her eyes. "Reid Murray, it isn't your job to right every wrong in my life."

"It might not be my job. It is my passion—you are. If I could go back in time and change the circumstances you and Mason dealt with at too young of an age, I would."

"I wouldn't."

"How can you say that?"

Lorna sighed, turning back to the fire and leaning against me. "I was talking with Madeline earlier today. If anyone has reason to wish for a do-over in their life, it would be her, and today she said that she wouldn't change a thing because that road led to where she is today. I feel the same." She turned as a smile curled her lips. "In the last month, I was kidnapped and today you were shot, but we're here right now. That's what matters, not the past."

"You're fucking amazing."

Sighing, Lorna turned back to the fire. "To answer your question, I don't think there were—others. I really don't. After we moved from Mr. Maples's house, we lived in that one-room apartment I've mentioned." She stilled for a moment. "I think I talk about it because it was the first place that seemed like a home after our grandmother died. And then after Missy disappeared, Mason and I were pretty inseparable. Even as a preteen, he was always overprotective. I was of him too. After losing Missy, we didn't want to lose each other."

"So, Nancy never had men visit?"

"There were men now and then who would show up at our door at any given time, but for the most part Nancy kept them away." Lorna shrugged her shoulders. "Sometimes she'd stay away for days or even a week. I don't know if she went to hotels, made house calls, or what. At the time, Mace and I would go on as if she were there."

"Why?"

"There was always a fear of being taken away."

"She didn't deserve to have you."

"Maybe not," Lorna said, "but if we were taken by DCFS, Mason and I were afraid we'd be separated."

My wife tensed under my embrace. "What is it?"

"That was what she told me." Lorna sat forward. "Yeah, that's why I couldn't tell anyone about Mr. Maples. If I did, the people would take me away."

My jaw clenched as I considered the injustice of placing that responsibility on a child. "Lorna, it wasn't your responsibility to keep that secret any more than it was your and Mason's responsibility to take care of yourselves."

"As I got older, I realized my mother's disappearances were probably related to substance intake. There were times she'd come back and act like she'd been there that morning when in reality it had been a week. It was like time disappeared to her."

I took a deep breath. "Like I said, Gordon Maples admitted to having seen your mother in the last five years."

"I don't understand why she'd go back to him."

"Maybe she ran out of options. I doubt we'll ever know," I admitted, hating that we had so many unanswered questions.

Lorna sighed. "I also don't understand how she ended up with me in Montana."

"We don't know that yet. However, we may have one source of information."

"Zella?"

I nodded. "Mason set her and the kid up at a halfway house; essentially, he currently has her on house arrest."

"She can't leave?"

"Not alive."

Lorna sucked in a breath.

"Sweetheart, Zella played a role in my shooting. The only reason she's not dead now is because we plan to question her."

"I shouldn't feel bad. She was never nice to any of us."

"Right now," I said, "Zella and the kid are being guarded by trusted Sparrows. Honestly, I don't recall what happened at the scene after I was shot. Mason said he plans to question her." My cheeks rose. "Your brother has a knack for getting answers."

Lorna shook her head. "I don't want to know those details either."

As memories returned of previous inquisitions, I was certain I didn't want to tell my wife what her brother was capable of doing. "Let's just say he's persuasive."

"Zella never liked our mother." Lorna wrapped her arms around her midsection. "I can't see them cohabitating unless it involved drugs." Her nose wrinkled. "We should look to see if she has needle marks. I didn't see any, did you?"

"I didn't look that closely, but no." I took a deep breath. "There's something else we learned."

"What?" my wife asked as she turned back to me.

"Maples mentioned that at one time your mother received payments from a Mexican named Garcia."

"A Mexican?"

"His description, not mine."

"Why would anyone..." Her body stiffened. "Oh, wait. Remember my dream? It seems more and more that it was real. If it was, Nancy told me that she sold Missy." Her words came faster and faster. "Missy looked different than me and Mason. Her skin and hair were darker. I never noticed until we went to school and people made comments. Grandma would say that God made everyone unique." Lorna stood. "This is all making sense. Missy was half-Latina, and I recall Nancy saying she sold her to her birth father."

I nodded. "It does seem to connect dots."

My wife spun in place, the palms of her hands slapping her jean-clad thighs. "Reid, don't you get it? We have a name. What did you say, *Garcia*?"

"Do you have any idea how common that name is?"

"But it's a name." Plopping back down beside me, Lorna reached for my hand. "Please tell me you'll work on this. Reid Murray, you can do anything when it comes to information. Find Missy Garcia."

Tears filled her eyes, and for the first time in weeks, they weren't of despair or fear but of hope. I refused to be the one to dampen this new positive emotion.

"Melissa?" I asked, realizing I'd never questioned that before.

"No, her name on her birth certificate was Missy, not short for Melissa. She was...maybe *is* eleven months younger than me. I'll give you her birth date. Tell me you'll look."

I leaned over and kissed the top of her head. "Yes, sweetheart, I'll look."

A knock came to the door.

"Let's not mention this yet to whoever is out there," I suggested.

Lorna nodded as she walked to the door. When she opened it, Araneae and Laurel stood at the threshold with trays of food in their hands.

"I hope we're not interrupting. I tried to text," Araneae said.

"Oh," Laurel said, talking to Lorna, "your hair is cute."

Lorna stepped back, allowing the ladies to enter, and shrugged. "In hindsight, it was a rash decision. It's short and brown, but thank you."

"I always wanted purple," Araneae said.

The ladies laughed.

"I was limited on my choices," Lorna said, gesturing the other ladies inside our apartment. "You two didn't need to bring this food down. I could have come up or made us something here."

"You have to try these," Laurel replied. "They're really good. The vegetable one is my favorite."

After placing the trays on the dining room table, Araneae and Laurel both turned their eyes on me. Araneae lifted her hand. "And I admit...the food was our excuse. We wanted to see Reid."

I pushed off, using the sofa's arm to stand.

"No," Laurel said, "stay seated. You're supposed to be resting. We just wanted to see for ourselves that you're all right."

"As all right as I can be."

Laurel came close and lifted her arms, but stopped inches away. "Wait, can I hug you? I don't want to hurt you."

From across the room, I saw my wife's smile. "I think I can take a hug."

"Oh, then make it two," Araneae said as she also wrapped me in a quick embrace. When they stepped back, Araneae's tone turned stern. "Sterling said that you're supposed to rest, and if he finds out otherwise, well, he said a lot of things, but I'll paraphrase: he'll be mad."

Her warning made me grin. "How many times do you think worrying about Sparrow's anger stopped me from doing what I do?"

She smiled. "Probably zero, although earlier today would have been a good time to start."

"I deserve that."

Araneae laid her hand on my arm. "Seriously, Reid, please give him a little time. Having anyone hurt affects him. Let him feel like he's in control, at least for tonight."

In reality, Sparrow was in control, more than just tonight. However, when it came to those of us in this tower, we took liberties—liberties that came with friendship.

I nodded. "Tonight."

"Oh, before I forget," Araneae said, "you may already know this, but before all hell broke loose, I messaged you."

"I didn't..." It was the first time I realized I didn't have my phone. I looked at Lorna. "Text Mason and see if he has my phone." I turned back to Araneae. "What happened?"

"There was some kind of attempt at breaching our security at the institute this afternoon. Patrick has Sparrows investigating. I figured you'd want to know."

My thoughts raced. The security there was top-notch, much like the security at Mason and Laurel's ranch. Maybe that wasn't what she meant. "Physically breach?"

"No, it was all encrypted. Patrick called it malware. If left to do what it was supposed to do, it had the potential to work its way into not only our security but also protected files."

"Including mine," Laurel added. "I have all my research backed up, and I definitely don't want it getting into the wrong hands. It's taken me basically this long to get back to where I was on my research at the university."

A million questions floated through my head. I wanted to get back to 2 and see what programs were being run. What information they had about the malware and how they think it was installed into the institute's secure system.

"No," Lorna said, shaking her head at me. "I know you, Reid Murray. I see the wheels turning, and don't for a second think I can't tell what you're thinking. You just promised Araneae you wouldn't leave this apartment tonight."

"And tonight ends at tomorrow's breakfast," Araneae said.

"Breakfast? It seems unfair to change the definition of time without warning," I said with a smile.

"I'll keep him here if I have to tie him to the bed," Lorna said.

Laurel and Araneae laughed. "No more information."

After the two ladies left, I slowly made my way to the dining room table. Lorna looked up from her phone screen. "Mason said he doesn't have your phone. He'll check with the other Sparrows on the scene." Her head tilted, making the ends of her new shorter hairstyle curl near her chin. "Missy?"

Though my thoughts were on my missing phone, I wouldn't dash any hopes budding within Lorna's thoughts and radiating through her shining gaze. "I will start looking when I can."

Lorna took a step closer and lifted her arms to my shoulders. "I love you."

"Sweetheart, I can't promise we'll find her. Don't get your hopes up."

Lorna's smile returned. "They already are. Before I was kidnapped, we knew in our hearts she was dead. Over the years, I've had horrible thoughts of how she died and what she went through. Now, it's taken two horrific events to give me hope." Her lips brushed mine. "Madeline was right. Dark times don't last forever. Eventually dawn comes."

I tugged her body against mine, flattening her breasts as they pushed against my bruised chest. "If I hadn't been shot today, I'd say forget dinner, and I'd take you to our bedroom just to keep that smile on your lips."

"If you hadn't been shot, I'd let you."

Intertwining my fingers in her hair near the nape of her neck, I pulled it back, bringing her chin upward and taking in her grin. "I think I'd rather be the one tying the knots."

Her head tilted. "What knots?"

"You told Araneae and Laurel you'd keep me here even if you had to tie me to the bed. If you are the one bound, I wouldn't leave."

"Keep that in mind for when you're feeling better." After another kiss, she stepped back and lifted a dome off of one of the plates. As she did, fantastic aromas floated through the air, yet my thoughts returned to the missing phone.

"What do you think?" Lorna asked.

I looked at what she'd revealed. "What are those?" I inhaled. "They smell great."

"Mini-pies. I could try to tell you the Russian name, but I promise I'd butcher it."

REID

"What are you doing?" Patrick asked as I entered 2.

"Coming to work."

"I told Sparrow we should change the scanner to keep you on the apartment level."

The steel door closed behind me as I walked with less effort than the night before. That didn't mean I wasn't sore as hell—I was. The bindings Dr. Dixon had placed on my chest helped my ribs, and at the same time, made breathing a bitch.

Who restricts your breathing and then emphasizes the need for deep breaths?

The most important change from yesterday was my arm. Whatever the doctor did worked. I now had full range of motion, and my fingers were more than ready to start typing away on my keyboards.

"Then you'd miss my smiling face."

Patrick interlocked his fingers, placed them behind his head, and leaned back against his chair. "Word was that the queen said you wouldn't be here until later."

"I told the queen tomorrow. This is tomorrow."

Patrick shook his head. "She said she specified after breakfast. It's four in the morning."

The overall sense of darkness that came with the kidnappings had lessened with my recent survival. There's nothing like living through a shot to the chest to change a man's perspective. That didn't mean all was right with the world. We needed answers, and I was ready to find them.

As my lips curled, I went to the coffee machine, added a pod, placed a mug beneath the spout, and pushed the button. "I promised Araneae I'd wait until after breakfast."

"And."

"And...I ate a leftover mini-pie before leaving the apartment."

Patrick scoffed. "Seems like a reasonable loophole to me. Are you sure you're up to working?" He relaxed his arms and sat taller. "Because I could sure as hell use your input."

Even with my bruised chest, his admission gave me a sense of worth, belonging, and importance. We all had our jobs, and there was comfort in knowing where each of us fit.

I'd been determined to be on the outside of this glass castle and face Maples. Even with the injuries I'd sustained, I wouldn't trade what we'd done, but now I was back where I belonged. Back to where I knew I made the biggest difference. It was time to connect the clues we'd been given. "Tell me what you have."

"First, your phone."

Setting my freshly brewed cup of coffee on the desk, I shook my head. "I'm pissed. I've never lost my phone—ever. I figure it must have happened at Maples's house."

"It did and given that you were shot and without a pulse, I think you deserve a pass." Patrick tapped a few keys. "Besides, I found it."

A map of the greater Chicago area came up on the overhead screen. The signal was coming from southwest of the city. "That's not Englewood."

"No, but close." He zoomed in and turned the image from a map to real-time satellite. The greenish hue was the night vision, giving the city an eerie feel.

"Where is that?"

"It's the halfway house where the capos took Zella Keller, Maples's daughter, and" —Patrick's expression appeared as if he'd taken a big bite of a tart lemon— "son-slash-grandson."

Yeah, that tidbit was more than a little disgusting. "She has my phone?"

"I've confirmed with the capos that they don't have it. That leaves Zella at that location unless the kid is a technical wizard." He didn't even pause. "The capos took her phone from her when they seized her from Stephens's house. They let her gather a few things and my guess is that she found yours. She kept it hidden. Once we figured all of that out, I instructed the Sparrows at the halfway house not to let on that they know she has it."

"At least she couldn't activate it."

"You were right," Patrick responded with a grin. "All of our phones are impossible to access without our retina scan. So basically, it was useless until I realized she had it. Once I did, I remotely wiped all the information within and began a program that reports everything she tries to do in real time."

I sat at my desk and took a slow, deep breath. Patrick may believe I deserve a pass, but I would disagree. Losing a phone is a rookie mistake. I wasn't a rookie in this world. "So she can't access the internet or contact anyone. What is she doing?"

"Oh, she's been trying all of the above," Patrick said. "I've given her just enough rope to hopefully set us on a trail."

"I thought the saying was enough rope to hang herself."

Patrick shrugged. "That too."

"Whom would she call? Or whom did she try to contact?"

"Well, it's not the authorities. She's called this number" —a string of numbers appeared on the screen— "six times and tried to send a few text messages. The calls didn't connect, and the texts were intercepted."

"Where does that area code go?"

"Would you believe Indiana?"

"What did she say?"

"Here it is," Patrick said after a few more clicks of his keyboard.

"I NEED YOUR HELP. I THINK THEY KILLED DAD. THEY HAVE ME AND GORDY. YOU SAID TO ONLY CALL IF IMPORTANT. I DON'T WANT THEM TO KILL ME, AND I NEED TO GET GORDY TO A SAFE PLACE. CAN YOU TRACE THIS? I DON'T KNOW EXACTLY WHERE I AM."

"She's received an error message each time. Each message has been basically the same. Pretty soon the phone will die without a charge." Patrick tilted his head toward my desk area. "I have you set up with a new phone. I was able to remotely switch all the storage on your phone and your cloud to this new one. Right now, your old phone is nothing more than our connection to Maples's daughter."

I took a drink of my coffee and considered Zella's situation. As the warm liquid coated my tongue and throat, I mulled over the idea that we now had her kidnapped, as Lorna and Araneae had been. "If Lorna or Araneae would have had access to a phone, or thought they did, whom would they have called?"

"One of us."

"Right. If the average person were taken and given access to a phone, whom would he or she contact?"

"If they believe they know someone who is capable of helping, they'd contact that person or persons. If not, I'd assume the police."

Patrick's train of thought was mirroring my own. "Now, Zella Keller is being held in an unknown place and she isn't trying to contact the police or an emergency number. Instead, she's trying to contact—"

"Someone she thinks will help," Patrick interrupted.

"Who is that?"

"I can't identify who, but I do have a where."

We both looked up again at the overhead screen.

"Shit," I said, "is that DC?"

"It is."

"Who in the hell would Zella Keller know with a number linked to Indiana now located in DC?"

"That's where I could use your help. I have the location of the device narrowed down to a city block, but that includes high-rise office and residential buildings."

Putting my nearly empty cup on the desk, I sat forward and brought my computer to life.

As we both worked, I ran multiple searches. One was of the telephone number in question. Soon I was getting the last three months of data. The phone was a burner. Of course it was. However, it had been used with some regularity from around the country.

"Fuck," I said. "That number was in Montana three weeks ago to a month."

"No shit," Patrick said. "I think we should cross-reference dates and locations. Ten bucks says this is Jettison."

"How in the hell would Zella Keller know Jettison?"

"I'm not sure, but if she does, it's a connection that I didn't see coming."

As I compiled the data for the program to accomplish what Patrick mentioned, he spoke. "Speaking of connections, last night, we had some success at Dino's Liquor."

"Some?"

"The Sparrows that accompanied Romero made the owner an interesting offer."

I took a drink of my coffee. "Let me guess, help us or lose your business."

"Something like that. And since the owner lost his nighttime cashier earlier in the day, the capos made a rather convincing argument. The problem is that the store's security is ridiculously old. There's a literal tape, and it's been recorded over so many times, the quality is shit. That said, I've confirmed the presence of the black truck and a dark-haired man. He was the only one present."

"Do we still believe that too is Jettison?"

"Other than the fact he's officially dead, I do. And the good news is that as we speak, Dino's Liquor Store is getting new security cameras."

"And you're sure the owner won't inform the delivery person?"

"I'm not sure, but if the deliveries stop, we'll know he did it, and then things won't work out well for him or his business." Patrick stood and stretched his arms over his head. "The circumstantial evidence connecting Andrew Jettison to the kidnappings, arms sales, and somehow Maples and Zella is stacking up."

"It makes no fucking sense, but I agree."

Patrick took a deep breath. "Is Lorna having any memories of the kidnapping?"

Numbers and codes were running in sequences upon my screens. I turned to Patrick. "It seems as though she fully remembers talking to Nancy Pierce."

"Then there has to be more."

"Laurel's the expert on this," I said, admitting my deficiency on the subject.

"I get your and Sparrow's apprehension," Patrick said, "but I think it's past time we encourage memories from Araneae and Lorna. I realize this hasn't been easy, but I think that between the two of them they may be able to piece more together."

I let out a long sigh. "I don't know what's best for Lorna. She's dealing with a lot."

Patrick's blue eyes turned my way. "She's strong. Hell, she wouldn't have put up with all of us for this long if she wasn't."

There was no denying my wife's resilience, but how much was too much, even for someone like her?

What had she said...something about the dark not lasting and dawn coming?

If there were windows on this floor, we'd see that sun rising in the next few hours. I took a breath. "Lorna's pretty certain that the recent resurrection of childhood memories came about because of whatever she suffered in that bunker. She's also mentioned a dark-haired man."

"We could show them pictures, like a lineup. I'll put together pictures including Jettison from six years ago and ones more recent. I'll also add some fillers. We'll question the women separately."

The thought of causing Lorna more distress ate away at me while at the same time I wanted to discover more concrete evidence. "Why would Jettison have Nancy Pierce and take Araneae and Lorna? Why would he want Laurel?"

"We're assuming it has to do with her research."

"What if it doesn't?" I sat taller. "Think about it. Whoever took them has *a* formula. We know the Order has *a* formula. What other reason was there to take Laurel, Lorna, and Araneae?"

"Sparrow?" Patrick answered.

"Laurel offered to be a target."

Patrick shook his head. "Mason told us. No one supports that."

"Even if it is connected to Sparrow, how in the hell does Nancy Pierce fit this equation?" I asked.

"I agree that seems like an outlier."

"The only connection is Zella and Maples. He said that he'd seen Nancy and that she'd been in Englewood."

We turned as the steel door opened, and in walked Mason with a tangle of freshly wakened hair. When his early-morning green stare met mine, he shook his head and lifted his phone. After typing a text message, he said, "I figured this was where you were."

"Shit, did Lorna wake you?"

"Since your phone is AWOL, yeah."

"I should have left a note. I figured she'd stay asleep."

"It wasn't only her who woke me," Mason said, making his own trip to the coffee machine. "I got a message from Top."

LORNA

$\mathcal{M}$ason's text message telling me that Reid was on 2 was exactly what I needed to lull me back to sleep. One would think after all of these years I would know my husband was safe. While that had always been a constant worry, today I realized it was more than a concern—it was a reality. Waking to his empty side of the bed filled me with more apprehension than I was willing to deal with alone.

I'd told Reid that even when we were young, Mason and I were protective of one another. I think it was and still is more than simply protecting; it was that sense that no matter what, we could depend on one another. Knowing that Reid's phone wasn't available and accessing 2 was beyond my ability, texting my brother, even before five in the morning, was my next thought.

A smile came to my lips as I read my brother's text message one more time.

. . .

"VISUAL CONFIRMATION, SIS. HE'S ON 2. GO BACK TO SLEEP KNOWING ARANEAE WILL CHEW HIM A NEW ONE LATER TODAY."

I replied.

"HE DESERVES IT. THANK YOU. SORRY I WOKE YOU."

Mason:

"I WAS GOING TO GET UP EVENTUALLY. GET SOME MORE SLEEP."

My alarm was set for less than an hour from now, yet a little more sleep sounded too good to do without. Cuddling under the covers, I scooted to Reid's cool side of the bed, laid my head on his pillow, and inhaled his scent. There were too many specifics to name, yet with my eyes closed, I knew the aroma was him. It was a combination of clean and fresh bodywash, the kind they advertised with clothes on an outdoor clothesline, and the spicy scent of his cologne. His aroma was never overpowering, but there.

The morning melody from my phone woke me as if I'd only seconds before fallen asleep. Yet the clock told me it had been almost an hour, an hour of bliss with no thoughts or dreams. As I made the journey into consciousness, I noticed the light streaming from beneath our bathroom door.

Throwing back the covers, I wrapped my robe from a nearby chair around me and with bare feet, padded across our bedroom. With a slight push of the door, I had the perfect view of the man inside. I could concentrate on the bandages around his torso, the ones Dr. Dixon told him not to get wet, or the wound on his arm, the one he was now dressing with fresh gauze. Instead, I did as I'd asked him to do for me weeks ago and looked past his injuries and saw him.

The *him* I saw was every inch of the man I loved, my Prince Charming, my knight, and my husband.

Apparently, Reid hadn't heard me with his concentration on the gauze and other dressings.

If I mentally took away those bandages, my husband was standing in front of the vanity as I was beneath my robe, nude. For a moment, I marveled at his muscles, the way they flexed in his arms, legs, and his tight ass. I even marveled at his resting penis. My gaze lingered a bit too long, my mind and body recalling his capabilities in that particular area of his expertise.

I wasn't certain what my specialty was, but I knew that I lacked artistic ability in the sense of drawings, paintings, or sculpture. And still as I slid my bottom lip beneath my teeth and stared, I imagined how a talented artist would draw this man, the one who I'd been given back from the jaws of death. No doubt, that talented individual would concentrate on each feature much as Michelangelo did when he created David.

"Fuck," Reid mumbled as the clip he'd been about to place on the exterior bandage fell with a clank to the bathroom floor.

As I opened the door farther, my husband's dark eyes met mine as he was about to crouch down to rescue the lone clip. "I didn't mean to wake you."

"You didn't. Let me," I said as I brushed my lips over his, immediately noticing the fresh mint taste masking his one or two cups of coffee I was certain he'd already consumed. I knelt to retrieve the clip. It was as I looked upward that my breath hitched and my core woke with a twist.

"Lorna."

A grin came to my lips as I stared upward. The cock that moments ago had been at rest grew before me with little provocation on my part. I retrieved the clip and placed it on the counter. Still on my knees, I ran my hands over his muscular thighs, reveling in the strength they were capable of yielding while relishing that he was still here with me. "I almost lost you."

"You didn't," he replied, his voice now thick with the possible concoction of desire and anticipation. That mixture swirled in an intoxicating fog around us.

Peering up, I noticed the way his wide chest moved with each breath. With one hand, he grasped the edge of the vanity while the other remained at his side. The air around us snapped and crackled with electricity.

In that moment, I had an idea how Reid had felt when he brought me home from Montana. There was nothing I wanted more than to run my tongue over his velvety skin, to lick the gleam from the tip of his thickening rod, and take him as far as I possibly could between my lips until he came undone at my doing. However, the bandages I'd looked beyond were nonetheless present. He had been injured.

According to Dr. Dixon, his heart had stopped.

I looked up until Reid's dark gaze met mine. "I don't want to hurt you."

"Fuck, Lorna."

Licking my lips, I waited for an indication from him, encouraging my intended path or dissuading me. I was ready for either, and as we stayed as we were with me kneeling before him and his intense gaze on me, I realized I wasn't to receive either.

The decision to proceed or stop was mine and mine alone.

Sticking out my tongue, I ran it all the way from the dewy tip to his curly dark hair. My hands moved around him, and my fingers grasped his ass. Again, I licked, his cock twitching. Over and over, I simply licked, slow and steady, as beneath the wet warmth of my tongue, his cock grew until it jutted toward me, the skin stretched and lined with veins.

"Tell me to stop if this is bad," I said, again looking up with my veiled gaze.

"Shit, Lorna, bad isn't even close."

"I don't want to hurt you."

"You're fucking killing me."

I sucked in a breath. "What?"

Reid reached down and with his thumb and forefinger pinched my chin before lifting it upward. "Sweetheart, I love you, but if you move any slower, I'm going to come all over this floor."

It was the encouragement I wanted, the knowledge that this Greek god of a man was mine for the taking.

With a deep breath, I opened my mouth, sheathing my teeth with my lips and took him deep. At the same time, I wrapped my fingers around his base and worked my mouth and hands in unison.

Deep, guttural curses and moans resonated through the bathroom, bouncing off the colorful tile while I too added sounds and wanton whimpers to the chorus. Though Reid still hadn't touched me, my nipples were as hard as diamonds, and my core was painfully twisted and thoroughly drenched.

My knees scooted and I fidgeted with unspoken need as I pulled him closer, his cock teasing the back of my throat. With my other hand, I rolled his tightened balls as I bobbed my head faster, my lips running up and down his length.

The muscles in his thighs and ass tightened as finally his hand came to the back of my head.

"Shit, sweetheart..."

I didn't stop or slow as I added my tongue to the mix until his hips began to piston against me. If our sounds and noises were a performance of the Chicago Symphony Orchestra, we'd reached the crescendo. Reid's muffled roar came in time as his body shuddered and warm liquid filled my mouth.

The familiar salty taste was welcome as I swallowed what he had to give me.

It was as I looked up that my husband's expression took me by surprise. Instead of satisfaction, there were lines of concern near his eyes, his nostrils flared, and there was an uneven tenseness to his lips.

"Are you okay?" I asked as I stood, licking my lips.

Reid's large hands came to my cheeks. "Are you?"

I searched his gaze for understanding, but I was lost. "I don't know what you mean. You're the one who was hurt. You came. Was something wrong?"

The brown surrounding his dilated pupils swirled with specks of golden emotions I couldn't identify as his unwavering stare searched my own. "Never wrong, Lorna. You're fucking perfect."

I laid my hand gently over his chest. "Is it your heart?"

His grasp of my cheeks tightened as he held my gaze to his. "It's my heart. You own every fucking piece of it, and right now I am terrified to hurt or upset you."

I tried to shake my head, yet his solid grasp gave little room. "Reid, you're not hurting me. I've healed." It was true. My injuries from a few weeks ago were either on the mend or mended. Yet I could see there was something he wasn't saying. "Tell me what you're thinking."

"I fucking did, Lorna. I think you're the most amazing woman in this godforsaken world, and I love you more than life itself."

I reached for his shoulders. "I love you too, so why does this feel weird?"

He gestured toward the floor. "That was what he made you do, wasn't it?"

He.

Mr. Maples.

My breath caught in my chest as my eyes opened wider. "Yes, if you must know. Yes, it was."

Reid head shook. "I don't want to remind you—"

"You hadn't until a second ago." I lifted myself to my tiptoes until our lips met. I didn't stop until mine were parted and our tongues danced to a new slower melody. A soft moan escaped my lips as Reid's fingers twisted in my hair and my body melded to his.

When we pulled away, I smiled. "You aren't him. You never have been. That" —I gestured toward the floor— "wasn't because you told me to do it or demanded that I do. Fuck, Reid, I like being close with you. I like your cock throbbing in my mouth. Maybe I'm no better than Nancy. Maybe that makes me some kind of whor—"

Reid's lips met mine, silencing the conclusion of my next word.

"It makes you an amazing lover," he said when our kiss ended. "I love being close to you too." His full lips turned upward. "I like tasting me on your lips and vice versa. What we do together doesn't make you anyone or anything except mine and me yours. I'm sorry I reminded you of the past. This is new territory for me. I never suspected you had been hurt, and now I'm worried. I don't want to fuck it up."

I shook my head. "Then rule number one, don't bring him up during..." I changed my mind. "...Ever. Besides, the last I heard, he's dead. Those memories can die too. What he made me do wasn't this."

"But you said..."

"Technically, but it's not the same. You were right, Reid. What he—he and I did—was wrong and the blame lies with him alone. I didn't want to play his damn game. We—you and I—are different. With you, what I just did was me showing you how much I love you, being intimate and open. I want that. Hell, Reid, I crave it. I want more, not less. That's what we have."

"I believe what we have is called love." Reid wrapped his arm around my waist and held me against him.

"Yes, we have *love*. That isn't what it was with him." I took a deep breath. "Back then, I felt dirty and wrong. Right now, I feel" —I tilted my head— "loved and wanton."

"So," Reid said with a grin, "telling you to suck me is off the table?"

I reached up and laid my palm over his cheek. "Stop overthinking." It was what my husband did, what he excelled at doing. I shouldn't have been surprised that he was doing it now. "I have no problem with you telling me what you want as long as you're okay with me doing the same."

"What do you want, Mrs. Murray?"

Though other options were on the tip of my tongue, I answered, "Sixty more years of this."

Reid scoffed. "I'm not exactly confident in my physical ability to do this when I'm ninety."

"As long as we're ninety together, I don't care if we are just holding one another."

The bandage he'd been placing when I first walked into the bathroom was no longer in place, the gauze had fallen to the floor and the thick black stitches looked like barbed wire upon his skin. I ran my finger over the threads. "Does it hurt?"

"No."

Leaning over, I gently kissed his wound. When our eyes met, I smiled. "Let me help with that bandage."

By the time I had his arm again cleaned, covered in antibiotic gel, gauze, and the ace bandage, I looked at the clock. "Shit, it's after six. I need to shower and get upstairs. I'm letting my breakfast cooking lag."

Reid tugged on the tie of my robe, loosening the knot, and grinned as the soft material fell open, exposing all of me, including my treacherous still-hardened nipples. "Or we could skip breakfast upstairs" —he leaned down and sucked one nipple, pulling back with a pop— "and work on that wanton feeling you mentioned."

Though my empty core, heavy breasts, and tight nipples liked his suggestion, I wasn't sure Reid was ready for more, not physically, and if I wanted sixty more years, I was willing to wait a day or two to have him inside me. And then I remembered something. Pushing his face away as he neared my other breast, ready for a second assault, I grinned. "Nice try."

"What?" he asked innocently.

"You're trying to avoid Araneae because you went to 2 before breakfast."

"I ate a mini-pie."

"And I'm sure that will get you off the hook."

Allowing my robe to flutter to the tile, I walked to the shower and turned on the water, but not before a large hand made a playful slap at my ass. "What was that for?"

"Because I can't keep my hands off of you."

REID

"You don't really want to be a part of this," Mason said.

"I want to hear what she has to say." Leaning my head against the leather seat, I sighed. The bumps along the roads were enough to make me consider pain medication. Romero was at the wheel while Mason and I rode in the back seat of the SUV on our way to the halfway house. Beyond the windows, dreary landscapes and scenes of south Chicago competed with an overcast sky for the title of most depressing.

"I'm trying to remain impartial, but it's fucking difficult." Mason turned to the window and then back. "Have you ever wished to have power over someone? I'm talking about someone with whom you were theoretically powerless."

"I'm sure I have. I mean, doesn't that thought occur to most kids?" I considered his question for a moment. "There was this kid in elementary school—I don't even remember his name. He used to say things about me not having a father." I shook my head. "I remember wishing each day on my way to school that he wouldn't be present. His desk would be empty. I'm not sure I took it further in my mind, such as why he was missing. I wasn't wishing death. I was wishing for a reprieve."

"I fucking carried it further in my imagination. I was an eleven-year-old skinny, hungry kid at the mercy of Gordon Maples and his bitchy daughters. The two girls would do shit and tell their dad it was one of us just to get us in trouble. Even then, I took it further in my head, but I was powerless to carry it through. Back then, I didn't know what I was capable of doing. Now I do.

"For the last twenty-four hours, that skinny kid has been reveling in the fact that he's in the driver's seat. Zella left Maples's house before I introduced myself to her old man. She has no clue that I'm Mason Pierce. Fucking Maples knew before you gutted him. Now, I'm waiting for *that* look, the one where Zella realizes she's fucked."

I had no urge to ask Mason what he had planned. My brother-in-law was a complicated man who could quite easily be misdiagnosed with dissociative identity disorder. If I recalled correctly, I believed I'd even heard Laurel joke that she'd mentally diagnosed him with DID before Mason broke free of his Kader facade.

When I think about the man beside me, the one who loved and admired his wife or the one who cared for his sister throughout their lives, it was difficult to imagine he was also Kader—a well-oiled killing machine. Yet even now, when situations called for Kader, the dark web's assassin for hire, there was reassurance in knowing that he was close at hand.

The issue that I wondered about right now was how Kader, a rather stoic and goal-focused individual, would behave when fed by Mason's childhood traumas. I'd been the one to gut Maples. Mason had been the one to kill him quickly with a slit of the femoral artery. In that move, Mason was cool and detached as a killer should be.

What would this next encounter entail?

"What about the kid?" I asked.

"I looked up Zella's other kids. They're both girls. One is twenty-five, married, and living in Michigan. The other is twenty and single, living in Kentucky. There's no sign that either has had any contact with their mother in the last year."

"Does the older one have kids?"

"A boy a month younger than Zella's."

"Fucked-up family. Zella's kid would be that kid's uncle."

Mason shook his head. "I talked to Dr. Dixon. She recommends involving DCFS to determine if that household is a safe and viable fit. The way I see it, living with his sister can't be worse than living with Zella and Maples."

DCFS was Department of Children and Family Services, a governmental agency we didn't need involved in our cleanup. "DCFS brings another layer of inquisition."

"I've thought about that too," Mason said. "Wrapping the kid in clean blankets and abandoning him at a firehouse has also occurred to me."

That would involve more than governmental investigations, the news media would be all over that shit. I shook my head. "You know what Allister would have done?"

Mason nodded. "That market is still out there. The Sparrows have connections to adoption attorneys. It seems to me that someone willing to put down fifty to a hundred grand on a kid sounds like a reliable parent who at least has the financial means to take care of it."

"Him, not it," I corrected. "And Sparrow wouldn't approve."

"You're wrong. This isn't sex trade we're talking about. It's illegal adoptions, and they happen every day. They also happen without all the digging and inquiry that would happen at the firehouse or if he gets delivered to one of his sisters. The right attorney draws up the paperwork and bam—it's done and legal, at least on the surface."

"You make it sound like the best option," I admitted.

"Because in many ways it is."

The SUV exited the interstate and came to a halt at a stop sign.
I looked at my new phone. The halfway house was less than two
miles away. With traffic, we'd be there within ten minutes. I
continued to consider Mason's stance on the subject of adoptions.

"What if we find the Garcia whom Maples mentioned and he
did what you're talking about with Zella's kid? He bought Missy."

Mason inhaled. "I've thought about that more than I want.
First, I fucking hate that Nancy or anyone else has gotten Lorna's
hopes up that Missy is alive."

"Second?" I asked.

"The same principles apply. It was awful that we lost Missy
when we did. Nancy is a cunt if she sold her own kid. That's neither
here nor there. She's always been a cunt. At least Zella isn't making
that decision; she'll have no choice. One point for her. Then again,
if this Garcia had the money and the financial wherewithal to
continue making payments, maybe Missy lucked out. I always
thought she ended up like" —he took a breath— "the others. Fuck
no, I don't approve of Nancy selling her own daughter, but maybe,
just maybe, it was the best option and Missy made it out."

"Lorna wants me to search."

Mason turned toward the window. "Of course she does."

"What do you want?" I asked.

"I've got everything I want, all of it."

His answer surprised me, most significantly because it didn't
address the subject of my question. "You're saying you don't care if
we find your sister if she's out there to be found?"

"No, I'm saying it won't affect *now*. I have everything I want
even though I don't deserve any of it."

"That's not true."

Mason's stare narrowed. "Over the last twenty-four hours, I've
fucking been considering heinous acts, things no decent man would
even think of, and yet they've been playing on a fucking loop in my
head. I could say I read about them or I saw them in some sick
movie, but that's not true and hell, Reid, I'm not lying to you. I'm a

sick fuck. I'm not sure if life made me this way or if I always have been. Maybe Nancy's selfish money-grabbing act to satisfy her addictions gave Missy an out Lorna and I never had. If that's the case, she probably has a decent life. Why would she want to find Lorna and me and remember the shit beginning she had?"

My gaze narrowed as I stared at my brother-in-law. "Do you think Laurel or Lorna look at you and think you're—to use your own words—a sick fuck?"

"They don't really know me."

I scoffed. "Bullshit. You're wrong, Mason. They know you. I know you. Sparrow and Patrick, we all know you."

"Yeah, well the three of you aren't exactly upstanding citizens. The women wear blinders. They see what they want to see." He shook his head. "It was the way Laurel saw me, seeing something other than pure evil, that had me so fucking off-kilter when we met again."

"Maybe they see what we don't show the rest of the world."

Mason took a deep breath. "I have a torture session in my near future. This isn't the best time to convince me of my internal goodness."

"I'm not talking about today," I said. "I'm talking about Missy. You're right, Lorna has her hopes up. If we can't find your other sister, then Lorna will have me, you, and everyone else to convince her that she has enough in her life. But if you're suggesting that if Missy is out there, she'd be better off *not* knowing her brother and sister, the people who looked after her for the first nine years of her life, who still love her, and who want to see her, my response is you're wrong."

"Lorna's rose-colored glasses have worn off on you."

Romero weaved us through narrow streets. When I looked out the window, a light mist had begun to fall. The buildings were no longer residential but more industrial. "Halfway *house?*" I asked, emphasizing the last word.

"Not exactly," Mason answered. "I didn't trust Zella to stay quiet, or the kid. Most of these warehouses around here have been sitting empty for the last few years. We have access to one that is conveniently near a few that are still functioning. These particular ones are currently rented by a private company that collects and refurbishes used corrugated boxes."

"Why?"

"The process is inexpensive and they can resell cheaper than new." That wasn't my question, yet he continued speaking. "With online sales increasing, they're fucking making a mint with shipping companies. And on the plus side, their machinery is loud. Their cleaning process uses chemicals that stink. The company isn't huge, but they have just enough employees that an extra car or two doesn't warrant investigation."

"You've used this place before."

Mason nodded. "I know from experience that Zella—or anyone who is being questioned—can scream their head off and no one will hear."

My nostrils flared as I exhaled, willing myself not to give too much thought to Mason's questioning process and screaming subjects. "Impressive thought process regarding location."

"Logical," he corrected.

It was logical.

"Have you spoken to the capos who are watching Zella?" I asked.

"I just received another text. It seems *Mommie Dearest* is now demanding smack."

Another name for heroin.

"Fuck," I said, staring out to empty parking lots, boarded-up windows, and giant empty buildings. "Her argument for mother of the year is eroding by the minute."

The SUV entered a chain-link-fenced area, the tires bouncing on the dilapidated parking lot pitted with potholes and cracks. We passed five or six cars lined up near a loading dock. Romero continued driving around until we reached the other side of the building. This side appeared more abandoned. As he slowed, he hit a button. A large garage door opened before us. He drove us inside.

The only light inside was the white illumination from our headlights, glowing into a dark cavern. The only exception was the presence of other vehicles.

"This place gives me the creeps," I confessed.

Mason smiled. "You haven't seen anything yet."

REID

*R*omero held a light and his handgun, ready to react as he led Mason and me through the darkness. Particles of dust stirred and floated in the stale air within the tunnel of light. Over Mason's shoulder was the strap of a duffel bag he'd removed from the back of the SUV. His gun wasn't in his hand, but I knew from experience that it could be in a millisecond. My hand itched to once again free my gun from its holster as every little noise had me on full-alert.

The cold, damp chill penetrated my clothes, making me wish I'd worn a coat. With each step, my nose scrunched as I took in a multitude of offensive odors. Every now and then a stronger odor, one I couldn't place, would tease my gag reflex.

When Romero lifted his sleeve to his nose, I asked, "The corrugated-box company?"

Mason nodded. "Keeps transient people away." He kicked a plastic bag lying in our path. "Most of them."

Slowly, my vision adjusted to the shadows beyond the flashlight's beam. Debris littered the concrete floor, including leaves that had made their way inside along with rodent droppings, trash, and the occasional carcasses that crunched under our boots.

When we finally reached the far end of the cavernous empty shell, Romero opened a large metal door. The hinges creaked, echoing in the emptiness, as he pushed it open.

At one time, the area we were entering appeared to have been the office area for the warehouse. The center of the large room was empty, yet when the light hit the floor, tracks for the type of dividers used to separate desks and work spaces were visible. Around the perimeter were multiple doors. Without hesitation, Romero took us to a door that led to a stairway. My ribs hurt and the metal steps creaked under our weight as we climbed two stories. The higher we went, the more intense the odor from below became. Mason reached for Romero's arm and turned to me.

"Reid, after you've heard enough, come back out here. You can either wait here or Romero will take you back to the car."

I wanted to remind my brother-in-law that I'd been the one to gut Maples. I'd served beside him for two tours in the desert and made my occasional appearance when needed on the streets of Chicago. I wasn't exactly a newbie to this world. While I considered reminding him of those things, as my arm throbbed and my chest ached with each step, I simply nodded.

When Romero reached for the next door handle, a loud, squealing noise reverberated through the stairwell. The high-pitched sound reminded me of the noise of a power saw cutting through a hard surface.

We all stilled as Mason lifted one finger.

Nearly a minute later, the awful noise ended, reverberations echoing off the cold cement-block walls.

"That was from the machines next door. They come in thirty-minute intervals," Mason said. "A series of five—"

The squealing began again.

When it ended, he added, "There will be three more and then a nearly twenty-five-minute pause."

After the fifth loud squeal, Romero opened the door to a hallway.

The three of us stood taller as Romero placed his gun back in his holster and the Sparrow standing guard outside a door stood up from the chair where he'd been seated.

"Ryan," Romero said, addressing the Sparrow.

I wouldn't have been able to place him on the street, but I knew of him. At nearly six feet two, James Ryan was nondescript—weathered skin, dirty-blond hair, and brown eyes. Those characteristics made him a perfect infiltrator into any situation. He neither stood out nor was memorable. Yet he had a reputation for getting information. It seemed that now he was a babysitter. Thankfully, our Sparrows were versatile.

The odor was still present. I wasn't sure if I was growing accustomed or if it had faded.

"Sir," Ryan said. He turned to us. "Mr. Murray. Mr. Pierce."

"How are our guests?" Mason asked.

"Fucking loud. She's something else and the kid..." He shook his head.

Mason nodded. "We have someone coming for the kid. She should be here soon."

"Tell her to bring diapers. That bitch in there only brought two, and we've had them here for over twenty-four hours. Sam had one in his car from his kid. I would have gone out for more, but we didn't think diaper shopping was a good way to stay under the radar."

Mason's head was shaking. "How old is it?"

"*He's* fifteen months," Ryan said. "I'm no expert, but I'd say there's some speech delay."

Ryan's assessment made me grin. It was true that as Sparrows we followed our own rules, many that took liberties with the law, but we weren't monsters. A good number of our men and women had husbands, wives, and children of their own. "How old is your kid, Ryan?" I asked.

"Turned two last week, Mr. Murray."

"Boy?" I asked.

"Little girl," he said with beaming pride. "My wife says that girls tend to hit milestones before boys, but still, that kid in there, he needs someone to care for him."

Mason's green stare met mine as if to reiterate that the illegal adoption road would be the best option. Mason turned to Ryan. "That's the plan. Besides, his mother will soon be unavailable for the job."

"If you ask me," Ryan said, "she already is."

Romero took his phone from his pocket and read the screen. "Sirs, pickup for the kid is here. The team just entered the garage."

I spoke low to Mason. "Where are they taking him?"

"Nowhere permanent yet, just away from here."

Ryan opened the door to the office, allowing the three of us to enter. A second guard was inside the room. If my guess was right, this was the Sam who came through with a diaper. Mason laid the duffel bag near the wall and approached Sam.

A large man with a clean-shaven head, Sam's skin tone was a few shades darker than mine. Like Ryan, he was wearing a suit, tie, and shiny leather shoes. He'd probably heard us out in the hallway because as we entered, he was already standing with his hands in front of him.

"Mr. Murray. Mr. Pierce. Mr. Romero."

While Mason addressed him, I peered around the empty room. Once again, it was an open room with doors around the perimeter. The size of this one reminded me of the size of the Sinful Threads office in downtown Chicago. The cries of a young child could now be heard through a closed door.

"Anyone else in there?" Mason asked.

"No, Mr. Pierce," Sam answered, "just the two of them."

"Get the kid," Mason said. "Marsha is on her way up to take him."

"Marsha?" He grinned. That was all he said as he nodded and unlocked the door.

With each inch the door opened, the child's cries grew louder as the disgusting stench of human waste overtook the already foul air. I sucked in a breath, trying to stifle my flinch, the one that could have been caused by either the noise or the stench or the combination.

"Oh hell no," a female voice screamed from within. "I told you before, don't touch my boy. Stop. If you want to take him, get the other guy, the white one." It didn't sound as though Sam replied when she yelled louder. "You can't take Gordy. He's my kid. Let go of him."

As the sound of footsteps grew closer, the crying softened.

Sam reappeared, holding the dirty and agitated toddler to his shoulder as he turned and closed the door, muting Zella's complaints. The child's small body trembled with each of his quivering breaths. With his little arms spread out over Sam's wide chest, he seemed to be soothed by the attention. Sam would need his suit dry cleaned, but undoubtedly, the kid was more content to simply be picked up.

"Could she not get to him?" I asked as Zella continued her rant from behind the closed door.

The man's fingers splayed, his large hand gently cradling the back of the boy's head. Against the man's suit, the boy's face appeared smudged with dirt and his nose ran—gushed—the snot and saliva pooling on the expensive material.

"She could," Sam answered, his large body swaying as he spoke. "She just wouldn't. She hasn't for at least the last twelve hours. She said she needed H and without it, she couldn't take care of him."

"She refused to care for her own child," Mason asked, "because *her* demands were unmet?"

While I simultaneously asked, "Did he cry the whole time?"

Sam nodded to Mason and turned to me. His expression softened. "No, sir. Ryan and me, we've been taking turns holding the boy. I don't give a fuck about that piece-of-shit druggie in there, but this boy, he doesn't deserve to suffer any more than he has." Sam's cheeks rose as he looked down at the more content child.

"Sam," Ryan called from the doorway.

We all turned as two brunette women entered. I knew the taller one immediately. "Jana," I greeted, surprised to see her. "You're here for the kid?"

"Mr. Murray, Mr. Pierce." She smiled as she reached for the young boy, taking him from Sam. "Thank you, Sam." She looked up at the big man. "Anyone ever tell you that you're a big softy?"

"Not anyone who wanted to live," he said with a gleam in his dark eyes.

Jana scoffed as she situated the boy on her shoulder. As she moved, a string of what I hoped was drool seemed attached to Sam's jacket. I'd been right; his suit would need to be dry cleaned.

"Marsha called me," Jana offered as she smiled down at the boy, still dirty, but much more content. "This won't be the first little one my husband and I've helped." Her voice changed, growing an octave higher. "Hi, little guy."

"Gordy is his name," Marsha said as she made notes on her phone. Marsha looked up at us with a business-like stare. "Mr. Murray. Mr. Pierce. I told Mr. Kelly I had plans this weekend. I said I'd change my plans, but when I suggested Jana, Mr. Kelly said it would be all right to let her help."

Neither Mason nor I gave a fuck; however, it was customary for Marsha or anyone else to explain when plans changed.

With his dirty and matted blond hair, Gordy rested his head upon Jana's shoulder. His long lashes fluttered as his body moved with a deep sigh and his dirty thumb went into his mouth.

"I'm going to get him a bath, some clean clothes, and a good meal," Jana said. "We have space and a portable crib where he can sleep. We're happy to help. Just let me know when you're ready to pick him up."

"Thank you, Jana." Mason escorted the two women out into the hallway. For a moment, I wondered about allowing them to walk alone through this big building. That thought lasted only a moment. I'd never met Marsha before, and at about Lorna's height with long brown hair pulled back in a ponytail, she didn't look the part, but her reputation preceded her. From what I'd heard, she could give Mason a run for his money on interrogation. She had her stint in the military along with a shitty excuse for an ex-husband for both her training and resourcefulness.

What was left of that ex-husband was now slush at the bottom of an acid barrel, and Marsha was a loyal Sparrow. The only reason Marsha wasn't questioning Zella was because Mason insisted on handling her personally. Only the future would tell if Zella was better off with Mason. My money was on the third option—either way she was fucked.

I looked over at Sam. "I expected Marsha to be..." I searched for the right word.

He lifted his chin. "If you're going to say taller, I agree, Mr. Murray. But I wouldn't say tougher. Damn, that woman is as tough as they come. I've seen her paint one or two houses and come back for more on the same night."

Mason returned and looked at the closed door.

If Zella was still yelling, her volume had decreased.

"She isn't pounding on the door," he commented.

"No, sir," Sam said. "She's chained to the register. We got tired of her attitude."

Mason nodded. "Thank you, Sam. I'll need a cleanup crew here tomorrow morning."

His eyes widened. "Not sooner."

"No need to rush," Mason said with a grin. "You and Ryan patrol the ground level. I don't want any curious onlookers." He looked to Romero. "Romero will keep guard up here."

"Yes, sir," Sam said before leaving and closing the door to the outer hallway.

"Romero," Mason said as he went to pick up the duffel bag,

"take the post in the hallway and connect to the closed-circuit security. Ryan and Sam can't patrol the entire building, and I don't want to be interrupted." He turned to me. "You're free to leave at any time."

"I guess that depends on what I find out about my wife."

LORNA

"I don't know why I'm nervous about this," I said as I sat forward in the kitchen chair, placing my hands on the table. Across the table were Laurel and Patrick.

"There are no right or wrong answers," Laurel said with a reassuring smile.

Taking a breath, I savored the familiarity of being in the large penthouse kitchen. I knew every inch of this room, the contents of every drawer and every cupboard. This glass tower was my house, and since the day, nearly a decade earlier, when Sterling Sparrow told me that he wanted me to stay, it's been my home.

I'd lived within this glass palace in the sky longer than any other place. It was funny to consider Araneae's theory—that to the rest of the world, these floors didn't exist. And yet within them, I'd found everything I ever wanted and more than I ever dreamt. It wasn't the luxury of the furnishings, the clothes in my closet, or the jewelry I had in my jewelry box. What I'd found here was more valuable.

I had the love of my husband and friends. In those people, I'd found my family, one that extended beyond my brother and husband to everyone present.

Gathering my thoughts, I peered toward the large windows.

The early afternoon sun streamed through the panes, bringing shine to everything in its path. The sunshine was a welcome change from this morning's rain and wind. That was Chicago in a nutshell. The weather could change on a dime. Heck, this time of year, in another hour, we could have large flakes of snow fluttering past our windows. For now, the clouds had lessened with peeks of blue sky and intermittent streams of sunlight.

"Before we begin," Patrick said, "can you tell us what you've remembered?"

I inhaled as I looked down at my hands, my fingers interwoven on the top of the granite table. "My mom."

"You remember seeing her?" Laurel asked.

"I do. Remember when I told you about my dream?"

"You now are sure that it wasn't a dream?"

"I think it was real." I closed my eyes and tried to bring back the scene. "It was raining." I remembered something else. "I was cold. I'd taken off my clothes." A cold shiver came over me. "Ants. I remember the ants. They woke me. After I brushed away the ants, I saw this woman. I didn't know who she was at first. It was dark and beginning to rain. I went to her, to help her. She was so thin." A lump came to my throat. "Her voice was scratchy." I looked up to Patrick's blue eyes. "You know how someone sounds who has been a smoker? That was her voice. And her skin was thin. I thought she looked hungry. I told her I could help her."

"In the wilderness?" Laurel asked.

The tips of my lips moved upward in a sad attempt at a grin. "I couldn't. I couldn't even remember the last time I'd eaten, but I wanted to help her. I guess to give her hope."

Patrick flashed a real smile. "Lorna, for over nine years you've been feeding us. I would never doubt that was your intention."

I shrugged one shoulder. "I know what I do isn't much. I'm not you," I said, looking at Laurel. "What I do here" —I gestured around the kitchen— "is just my...contribution."

Patrick nodded my direction. "Don't sell yourself short. Taking care of this ragamuffin crew is something substantial. Did she accept your help?"

The room around me disappeared as I tried to recall that night. The rain began falling harder, large raindrops plopping upon the hard ground. Thunder rolled in the distance, its rumble came closer as its volume grew, and streaks of lightning zigzagged across the sky.

I looked down. Instead of the shiny tile floor beneath my shoes, I saw the rising water around my bare feet and the way the earth dampened and morphed from solid to a rising stream. "I was worried about the rain."

"The rain?" Laurel asked. "Why?"

"It was coming down so hard that the ground couldn't absorb it. Within a short period of time, it was as if we were in a shallow stream. The woman was sitting by a rock. I went to her."

"Did you know who she was?" Laurel asked.

I shook my head. "No. She looked familiar but old and ragged. And then she laughed. It was a witch's laugh—a caricature of a witch, such as they would show in a cartoon."

"What happened next?" Patrick asked.

"I asked her who she was." Before they could respond, I added, "I asked if she was me." I forced a grin. "I know that sounds crazy, but I was afraid I was seeing myself."

Laurel's head shook. "Nothing sounds crazy. Remember, no right or wrong answers? Did she talk to you?"

"She said she was nobody."

"Why would she say she was nobody?" Laurel asked.

My lips pursed as I recalled the conversation under the deluge of rain. "I-I'm not sure."

"What happened next?" It seemed to be Patrick's go-to question.

I brought my suddenly chilled hands to my lap, wringing one and then the other. "The woman started talking. As she did, her voice grew weaker, fading into the sounds of the storm. Maybe she knew she didn't have much time. She told me that I knew her, and she apologized for being a bad mother, saying she knew now how we'd felt." I looked up. "That's a lie. Our grandmother, her mother, was a saint. There's no way she knew what it was like to grow up as her kid."

"Let's concentrate on what was said and what you recall," Laurel said calmly.

Nodding, I again closed my eyes. In my mind, I was back in the cold rain with thunder and lightning. "Nancy said if she could do it over again, she would." I took a deep breath, recalling the way her green eyes stared up at me through the rain and growing storm as the large drops saturated her hair and clothes. "She said she told them. No, she said they forced her to tell."

"Who is *them*?" Patrick asked.

"I don't know. She said they forced her, and I should know." I paused, trying to recall exactly what she had said.

"Lorna," Patrick said, "did she use the plural them, not singular him or her?"

I didn't speak for a minute as I recalled. Swallowing, I sat taller. "Yes, she definitely said them."

"Go on," Laurel said.

"And that's when she confessed that Missy didn't go missing. Nancy said she sold her to her birth father. She said that they know so I should too."

Both Patrick and Laurel's expressions revealed uncertainty.

"And then?" Patrick prodded.

"She fell asleep." I opened my eyes and looked across the table. "She died."

"What did you do?"

Tears came to my eyes as my chin dropped to my chest. "It doesn't matter."

"It might, Lorna," Laurel said.

"I sat beside her and tried to keep her warm."

A warm hand covered mine. When I opened my eyes, it was my sister-in-law now in the chair beside me with her hand covering mine.

"Kind of pathetic, right?" I asked.

"The opposite," she replied. "Lorna, you're a loving person. That isn't a fault."

"Maybe she felt that before she died."

"You can choose to believe she did," Patrick said.

"What do you recall next?" Laurel asked.

"Waking up and seeing Reid."

"Let's talk about before," Patrick prompted. "What do you recall before?"

"It's so odd. I don't actually remember being at the ranch, yet I know the ranch. I've been there before. I have had a few visions— or maybe flashes, like you said."

"Can you describe them?"

"White walls. And then there's a man with dark black hair."

Patrick smiled from across the table. "We have some pictures."

I nodded.

"We are trying to not lead you. We went through this earlier this morning with Araneae."

"Did she remember?" I asked, genuinely curious.

Laurel smiled. "Let's concentrate on you."

"Okay. I guess that makes sense. I mean, Araneae probably knew more. She's smarter, she's somebody." I forced a grin.

Laurel's voice was as soft as silk. "Why is she smarter?"

"Look at her. She helped create Sinful Threads, and now she's done so much with the Sparrow Institute."

"Right," Patrick said. "I don't see a correlation with those examples and intelligence, perhaps opportunity."

"But look at me." I opened my eyes wide. "I'm not complaining, but I have a high school diploma and I cook and clean."

"Have we ever," Patrick began, "made you feel like your contribution to this household was insignificant? Because, Lorna, if we did, if any one of us ever did, I want to apologize."

Heat filled my cheeks. "That's not it. I shouldn't have said anything."

Laurel's hand again covered mine. "Araneae had some memories. We want to see how they match up with yours. This isn't a test."

I took a deep breath. "Okay."

"Lorna," Patrick said, "some of these photographs are of the bunker that the Sparrows found near your shoes, and others are decoys."

My gaze met his. "Decoys?"

"Think of it as a lineup. The perpetrator may or may not be in the lineup, but if he or she was the only person, what choices would you have?"

"Okay," I said, wishing Reid was with me. "Let me see."

Patrick opened a folder and placed five pictures before me. Each one was 8 x 10, black and white. I took in each one. There were two that elicited a physical response. My skin cooled and the small hairs stood to attention. One was of a cell, or what appeared to be a cell. I didn't see bars or a cage, yet seeing it reminded me of a cell. There was a bunk bed, toilet, and sink. The other picture that made me bristle was of a similar concrete-block room. This one looked like an interrogation room.

I wasn't even certain what was in the other three photos. My eyes were glued to the two.

"Those," I said, pointing to each of them.

REID

*A*s the deafening screech ended and its echoes faded, Mason reached for the door handle, pushing the door within with me a step behind as we both entered the room. Taking the baby away did little to alleviate the stench of human waste. It didn't take long to locate the source. The word *bastards* was scrawled across the wall, written in three-foot letters, using shit as the medium of choice.

In that millisecond, I knew all I needed to know about Zella Keller.

None of it was good.

Any sympathy I might have had for this woman regarding her relationship with her father evaporated. I'd already determined she was an awful mother and a mean, vindictive child, and she was at least partially responsible for my shooting; the new information upon the wall did nothing to elevate my overall opinion.

Zella barely moved as we entered. As she lay upon the floor in a semi-fetal position, I scanned what I could see. Her bleached hair, darker at the roots, was greasy and matted. The long t-shirt and torn soft pants she'd been wearing yesterday were still her attire.

Her feet were now bare, the soles filthy. Slowly, she lifted her head and stared in our direction. Perspiration covered her face, her pupils were nonexistent despite the dimness of the room, and her hands trembled. "Did you get me smack?"

I would have expected her first question to be about her son. I'd be wrong.

Slowly, Zella stood, making it to her knees before she was fully erect. Around her ankle was a shackle, the kind seen in movies, attached to a thick chain. With each of her movements, the solid links clanked against the floor. Zella grunted as she tugged on the slack. Crossing her arms over her chest, she leaned against the shit-painted wall.

"I-I need it," she muttered. Her cold gray eyes looked from Mason to me. "I can blow you, both of you if you want."

Crossing my arms over my chest, my lips formed a straight line as my stomach reeled. Without doing a full inventory of my entire life, I was most certain that I'd never received a less appealing offer.

"Zella," Mason said, pulling up a metal chair from the far wall and placing it just outside the circumference of the chain's reach. He spun the chair around and straddling the back, he sat. "I need answers."

Her head shook violently from side to side.

He reached into the chest pocket of his shirt and pulled out a small ziplock bag filled with off-white powder, catching her immediate attention. The chain pulled taut as she lurched forward. Mason and the smack in his hand were just outside her reach.

Her gaze stayed fixed on the bag until he put it back in the pocket of his shirt. "I-I'll tell you anything." It was as she looked up that a bit of recognition seemed to register. Tilting her head, she looked from Mason to me and back. "You. I know you."

"I didn't get a chance to introduce—" Mason began.

She interrupted. "The two of you killed Daddy." Her gaze darted between us before she asked Mason, "The darky your bodyguard?"

Mason craned his neck toward me, his grin showing until he turned back to her. "No, Zella. Mr. Murray is my associate."

She kept her attention on Mason. "You killed my dad. I saw what you did. Darrell should have killed both of you." When we didn't speak, her volume rose. "Why'd you do it?"

"Why do you think?"

"I don't know. He was a good man." The chain clanked as she paced back and forth, pulling on her hair as she shook. "You lied to him. You said he won money. He never lied."

Her display continued for a few minutes, recalling the happenings of the day before, sprinkled with accolades for a man who didn't deserve them. Through it all, she worked herself into a frenzy, kicking the chain and pulling at her hair. Finally, Mason stood. "Zella, I'm Mason Pierce. Do you remember me?"

Her eyes opened wide. "You're dead. I read about it. Your mom said you died." Her body quaked. "Am I dead?" She looked at me. "I saw you shot." She began to scream. "I'm dead."

"No, Zella." Mason spoke calmly. "You're alive at this moment and so am I." Mason sat back in the chair, still straddling the back. "What can you tell me about Nancy?"

"She's a crackhead piece of shit who would do anything for a hit."

There was a saying about a pot and a kettle that was on the tip of my tongue.

"When did you see her last?" Mason asked.

Zella's head again shook from side to side. "No. I can't talk about that."

Mason looked at me and lifted his chin toward the duffel bag. Following his lead, I went to it and picked it up. Mason stood and took the bag, placing it on the seat of the chair.

"What is that? What do you have? I don't like kink, but I'll do it. No whips. I don't like whips. Is that what you have?" Zella's questions continued as Mason removed items from the bag.

The first item was a rope, thick and strong, made of a tough blend that was less likely to result in marks. Next was a ball gag. I continued to watch as various instruments were revealed, including but not limited to dental extraction pliers, wire cutters, knives, and scalpels. By the time he had everything laid upon a felt sheet, Zella's questions had ended. Or at least, she'd stopped vocalizing them.

Her complaints changed to whimpers as together we secured her to a different metal chair, her legs attached to the legs, her hands attached to the arms. The undersides of her arms were littered with needle marks. Her mouth opened wide to accommodate the ball as he secured the gag behind her head.

"I told you that I need answers," Mason said once she was in place. "First, I want to remind you of who I am."

I stood back and watched as a combination of Mason Pierce and Kader went to work. Initially, he sliced the front of her top, revealing her sagging tits and post pregnancy stomach. It wasn't so much fat as stretched non-elastic skin on her too-thin frame. Next, he cut the pants. I'd be lying if I didn't admit I was relieved she was wearing underwear. Her thin legs were covered in small bruises and scabs, indicative of heroin use.

With her skin now exposed, Mason picked up the scalpel. It sliced her skin with the ease of a butter knife going through warm butter. No incision was anything more than superficial as crimson dripped from various wounds over her arms, torso, and legs.

As he worked, he reminded Zella about their childhood. The stories he told turned my stomach even more than Zella's offer of sexual pleasures. Though Mason spoke without emotion, I couldn't help but picture a young and helpless Mason and Lorna.

My heart ached with the pain that he wasn't vocalizing. As I watched, my mind was on Lorna, wanting to get back to her, wanting to hold her and do whatever I could to make up for the shit I'd never known she'd experienced.

Finally, Mason removed the gag.

Zella spit and coughed as she moved her jaw back and forth. "You son of a bitch."

"Technically, you're right." Mason brought the scalpel to her cheek. "If I didn't want to hear your answers, I'd cut out your tongue." He smiled in an alarming way. In that moment, I understood the comments Patrick and Sparrow had made about Kader and agreed wholeheartedly that we were fucking lucky that he was on our side. "Do you have any idea how much a human tongue bleeds?"

Zella's lips came together in a humorous show of defiance.

"Primarily," Mason began, walking around her chair, "the tongue receives its blood supply from a branch of the carotid artery." He skimmed the blade over her neck. "You know, this one." He moved the scalpel and placed his fingers on her neck. "Right now, I feel your pulse. It's hammering like a drum. If I gave you the smack you want, it would slow."

The mention of the heroin changed her focus. "What do you want to know?"

"When did you see Nancy?"

"When she lived in Dad's basement."

"She lived in the basement?" I asked.

Her gray eyes came to me. "She was his pet."

I had never thought I'd feel anything but abhorrence for Nancy Pierce, but there was something in Zella's tone that put a crack in that assumption. I made a mental note to have the basement searched.

Mason ran the scalpel across Zella's neck, not penetrating the skin. "You said *was* his pet. What happened?"

"You know how it is with bitches? They run away."

"Is that what happened? Maples was housing and feeding her, probably supplying her with dope. Why would she leave?"

"Maybe she was in heat." She laughed at her own joke. "Maybe she got tired of his dick in her ass."

This time Mason pushed the scalpel deep into her thigh. Her scream filled the air.

"Answer the fucking question."

Zella shook her head. "I can't. I ain't supposed to say."

"Then tell me what you know about her receiving money."

"The bitch spent it or lost it. Daddy said she had a sugar daddy paying her, but when that ran out and no one would pay for her smelly cunt anymore, she ended up on his doorstep."

"What was the sugar daddy paying her for?" I asked.

Zella sneered my direction. "Not her loose cunt. She said the money would just show up twice a year until it didn't."

"Show up where?" I asked.

"Figure it out. I don't know, maybe under her pillow like the fucking tooth fairy."

I exhaled. "What was she being paid for?"

"I'll tell you if you give me the snow." She narrowed her gaze. "How do I know it's real?"

Mason brought the baggie from his pocket, licked his finger and placed it in the bag. Bringing it out, he took his finger to her lips. Without direction, she opened her mouth and stuck out her tongue.

He laughed, pulling his finger away. "It's real and it's good."

Zella's breathing quickened. "The Mexican girl. I don't know who paid for her, but that cunt sold her." She looked up at Mason. "She never gave two shits about any of you."

It wasn't much more than we already knew, but it was confirmation.

"Where did Nancy go?" I asked.

"Like I said, I can't say."

"Why?" Mason said, walking in front of her. "What will happen? Will someone kill your daddy, take your kid, and then kill you?"

Her cheeks paled with the realization that was all happening. "You're going to kill me anyway, you piece of shit," she spoke defiantly. "Why the fuck would I tell you anything?"

"You're right. You're going to die. It can either happen with this smack in your system, or I will continue this little carving session, add a few of my favorites like cutting off a finger or toe and pulling a few of your rotten teeth. Then, I'll give you just enough heroin to keep you awake as we leave and the rats finish the job."

Her eyes widened. "What about Gordy?"

"That's the first time you've asked about him," I said. "Do you care?"

"Yeah, I care. You killed his daddy. If you kill me, who'll take care of him?"

"Where is Nancy?" Mason asked as he made a long slit over her thigh.

"Daddy sold her."

"To who?"

"I don't know their names."

Mason made another cut in the other thigh as the screech from the nearby facility returned.

"Make it stop," Zella screamed.

"What did they look like?" Mason asked, speaking above the screech.

REID

*T*urning off the hot spray of water, I inhaled, hoping the residual offending odors from the warehouse had disappeared down the drain, along with the copious amount of soap and shampoo that I'd used. My ribs ached, but not as much as even earlier in the day. Prior to the shower, I'd removed the bandages the doctor had placed. Reaching for a towel, I wrapped it around my waist, noticing above the enduring ringing in my ears from the loud screech at the warehouse that the nearby shower had also stopped.

By the time Romero drove Mason and I back to the tower, the sun had set. Neither of us went to our apartments or wives. Instead, we went straight to 2 to rid ourselves of any reminders of the day and deed we'd just completed.

As water droplets beaded upon my skin, I walked barefoot through the shower room and into the room with the large vanity. While this amenity was as luxurious as every other part of the tower, this expensive rendition of a locker room lacked the color and personality of the bathrooms in Lorna's and my apartment.

The tile varied in shades of tan. A white marble vanity contained four sinks with a long mirror that reached from one end to the other and a row of lights overhead. Three additional rooms were accessible from where I stood: besides the door leading to the central room of our command center and the hallway to the showers where I'd just been, there was another room divided into stalls and a second room for dressing.

This may have been constructed with a locker-room feel, but other than the vanity, all the facilities were private. There was only one person I wanted with me in my shower, and it wasn't any of the men I considered my family and brothers-in-arms.

The purpose of this bathroom and dressing room was exactly why Mason and I were using it now. There was no need to show our wives the ugliness that our jobs sometimes required.

I slowed as I neared the vanity, seeing Mason standing before the large mirror. With a towel around his waist, his long hair dripped down his shoulders and back, flowing over his colorful canvas of tattoos.

His eyes met mine in the mirror and for a moment, I had the sensation of a child caught looking at something he wasn't supposed to see. Never before had I seen so much of my brother-in-law's artwork exposed.

There were thousands of subjects we could discuss, including the last few hours of Zella Keller's life and the information she'd shared, yet at that moment I was mesmerized by what I'd only been given small glimpses of over the last few years.

Mason's head shook. "Before Laurel, I would probably have to kill you right now."

"I know you're capable," I said with a grin, stepping up to the vanity. "What made you choose those designs?"

He shrugged his wide shoulders. "I didn't know."

Turning toward him, I pursued the subject. "Army medallion and Airborne Special Forces?"

Mason's hands gripped the edge of the vanity, the muscles under the colors strained. His green stare met mine in our reflection. "You just spent hours watching me torture a woman and you want to discuss my tats?" He looked at my reflection. "Damn. You're still feeling that bruise, aren't you?"

I ran my hand over my chest. Fresh from the shower, the center of my chest appeared a shade of purple, darker than my skin. "Hurts like a mother."

"You took off the bandages."

"Showering seemed more crucial." I turned to Mason. "Today's field trip wasn't far off from what I expected."

"Then you're a sick motherfucker too."

There was always that possibility. One didn't stay in a place of power in the Chicago underground without a tendency toward the extreme. I didn't shy away from pushing the limits of the law, or blowing through those limits as we did today, as long as I could justify the means. Today's exercise did that—twice. What occurred with Zella was both retaliation for Lorna and Mason's childhood traumas and a search for information to help us find Jettison and his blonde partner.

I reached for the deodorant. "Where did you learn to do what you did today? They didn't teach us that in basic."

"I had a different basic, one that made me useful to the Order."

"Before you remembered who you were, did you recall serving in the army? Why would you have chosen those tattoos?"

Mason exhaled. "I didn't remember a fucking thing. I was told shit. The focus was on the present and future, never the past. I was part of a special unit. Only those with previous military experience were part of the Order."

"Marines or navy were also possibilities."

"You forgot fucking merchant marines and coast guard." Mason tossed a different plastic deodorant container into a sink. "I wasn't taught as much as I was encouraged to explore," he said, answering my earlier question. "I watched and learned. It's simple. There are certain ways to coerce cooperation. Humans have pretty basic survival instincts. You're smart. You know the five stages of grief.

Today Zella knew on some level—even in her strung-out mind—
that she was going to die."

I nodded. "Denial is the first stage."

Mason grinned. "Right. And then anger. It doesn't matter if the
person was Zella or a four-star general. You can count on anger and
fighting back, at least verbally and the bigger they are, the more
they like to bluster. Next?"

"I'd guess your favorite stage, bargaining."

"It's the most useful. Give the person just enough possibility to
let them think they have the ability to bargain for their life. It's the
moment when a sheik will offer his daughters and wife. A world
leader will offer launch codes. Even a piece of shit like Zella will
offer something. Everyone has something to offer."

"I'm guessing you had better offers over the years than Zella's
offer of a blow job?"

Mason cringed. "There's no fucking way I'd want her lips
anywhere near me."

I thought back to a day ago. "Maples didn't bargain."

"He gave us some info," Mason said as he ran a comb through
his shoulder-length hair. "We let him die too fast. Now, I wish we'd
learned more about the payments from the Mexican. Today, I
wanted information on Nancy. I was taught or learned over time to
maintain this stage as long as necessary.

"Pain is a powerful incentive. Pull teeth or remove toenails. The
pain lasts longer than the earlier use of the scalpel. However,
without the earlier show, the person in question will fail to believe
your capabilities. Let's face it, it takes a sick motherfucker to cut
off a finger or toe with wire cutters."

I recalled the scene. Without the high-pitched squeal above
Zella's pleas, the crunch of the bone was audible. "Do you think she
was telling the truth about not knowing more about the money
Nancy received?"

"Yeah, I do. Maples had said Nancy received money until
eighteen. I think he meant until Missy was eighteen. I'm assuming

it was like child support but backward. This dude paid so that he could maintain custody." Mason's eyes again met mine in the mirror as I applied antibiotic gel to the stitches in my arm. "You said you looked for Nancy after you thought I died and when you and Lorna married?"

"I did. It was as if she disappeared. There has been nothing since about a year after Lorna's high school graduation..." I made the connection. "Shit, that would be around the right time of Missy's eighteenth birthday."

"I was thinking the same thing. We need to go back and see what we can find. How was she getting payments? Where were they coming from?"

"My first thought would be offshore, hidden through a tangled mess of shell companies and LLCs." I worked to wrap my bicep with clean gauze.

"Why?" Mason asked. "Some man was paying a strung-out whore. What information would she share as long as she was getting her payments?"

"Would you want to be caught in an IRS audit paying a strung-out whore a yearly stipend?"

"Zella said twice a year," Mason replied as he handed me a clip from the first-aid kit to secure the ace bandage.

"Same question," I said, "now it's every six months. Do you have a business or a wife or political ambitions? That shit is frowned upon."

"It's our first lead," Mason said. "We need to see what we can find."

"Time is not on our side, but skill is. Those payments started nearly twenty-five years ago."

"And ended roughly sixteen years ago."

"Technology has improved," I said, considering the changes since we'd taken over Sparrow. "Back then, the go-to was the Cayman Islands. Let's hope this guy didn't think outside the box."

We fell silent for a moment as we both headed into the dressing room to a small bay of something better than lockers and less than closets. Each one of us kept extra clothes here for occasions such as this. Everything we wore to the warehouse today would be incinerated. As I opened my closet area, I turned to Mason. "If I'd been thinking straighter, I'd have worn different boots. I fucking liked those boots."

"Killing 101, be sure to dress accordingly."

"Well, my usual victims are assassinated via the computers in the other room. No need to burn my clothes." As I dressed, I thought about what we'd yielded. "Do we know more than we had from the traffic cams and security footage? Zella described a tall dark-haired man and a smaller woman with blonde hair who always wore gloves."

"I'd call it more of a confirmation of a connection between the kidnapping of the women, the firearms supply, and Nancy." Mason was now fully dressed in a long-sleeve shirt, jeans, and his usual cowboy boots. I hadn't noticed he'd worn different ones earlier today. Crossing his arms over his chest, he leaned against the wall. "My gut says the Order."

"What did Top's message say the other night? Fuck, with all that's happened, I don't remember."

"Nothing to remember. He said to contact him and that he has information for us. He specified that he wanted you, Lieutenant Colonel Murray's son, to attend."

"Why the fuck haven't we contacted him?"

"I did. He wants to meet in person. So far, he hasn't responded with a date, time, or location."

In my mind, I went through the information Zella finally shared. Her dad had been given ten thousand in cash for Nancy Pierce. It wasn't a fucking large sum of money even to someone like Maples. "Why would Maples give up Nancy?"

"Money."

"It wasn't much."

"Or it was more than Zella knew. It doesn't matter, he did it.

Zella sounded like she was happy to be rid of her. I'm sure it was the fucking *Brady Bunch* with the three of them."

"Zella said it was before little Gordy was born. Do you think they'd kept Nancy in that bunker for the last year and a half?"

Mason shook his head. "The only thing I give a fuck about when it comes to Nancy Pierce is learning her damn connection."

Once I stepped into the canvas loafers I had on hand, and we began to walk out of the bathroom together, I said, "The blonde woman sure as fuck sounds like Stephanie Moore or Morehead."

"It can't be. Top said she was found in the office of the ranch. The heat alone from the fire should have killed her. That office was constructed like a fucking safe. She should have cooked in there like a turkey on Thanksgiving."

"What if she didn't?"

"Then who did they find in that office?"

We both stopped at the sight of Sparrow and Patrick near our computers in the command center. "Look at the footage from Dino's Liquor," Patrick said.

LORNA

I sat forward as the door to our apartment opened inward. The soft blanket covering me fell to my waist. As Reid entered, I sleepily checked the clock on the mantel. Its hands, visible from the warm glow of flames coming from the fireplace below, told me it was after midnight. It wasn't unusual during times of high stress for the Sparrows that Reid would work into the night; however, since I'd come home from Montana, it hadn't happened.

Not until now.

"Lorna," my husband said as he came toward me, sitting on the edge of the sofa at my side. "Why aren't you in bed?"

"I tried to wait up for you."

Reid brushed a few stray strands of hair away from my face as his warm hand cupped my cheek. In the seconds that followed, a silence fell over us, one that I sensed held captive information he wasn't certain he could share. His touch lingered, his stare intensified. Beyond his silhouette, the orange and red flames crackled in their artificial resemblance of a real blaze.

The flames were real. The logs weren't. The combustion started with the touch of a button, one that would begin and maintain with a puff of gas and a spark. Even without the actual burning of logs, heat radiated from the contained fire. It wasn't the only source. The faux blaze paled in comparison to what I was witnessing in my husband's eyes.

Inclining my head to his palm, I asked, "What happened?"

His Adam's apple bobbed as he swallowed his answer. Finally, he responded, "I fucking love you."

My hand came to his, sandwiching it between my palm and my cheek. "I know that, Reid. I never doubted it. Even when I was in that bunker, I knew I was loved beyond measure. My fear was that I'd failed to let you know that the feeling was mutual."

Our hands dropped as our fingers intertwined and his expression changed. Whatever had been on his mind was superseded by his concern for me. "You remember being in the bunker?"

Swallowing, I nodded. "Not all of it but parts—more than I had."

"That's good?" he asked apprehensively. "Or isn't it?"

"I think it's good. I want to know what happened."

"How did you remember? What made you recall?"

"I agreed to an experiment with Patrick and Laurel."

Reid took a deep breath. "I should have been there with you."

My head shook. "I know you think I'm made of glass, but I'm not."

The tips of his lips curled upward. "Sweetheart, if you're made of glass, it's bullet-proof. I know you're not fragile. It's not a question of your capability. I want to be with you, not because you need me to be there, but because I want to be there if only to applaud your continued strength."

"It's not that I don't need you, Reid. Don't ever think that, but more importantly, I want you." A memory from long ago returned. "I remember my grandma saying that when I find *that* person, I should decide if I need him because I want him or I want him because I need him."

"Is there a right answer, according to the wisdom of your grandmother?"

I nodded. "A."

Reid's eyes narrowed. "Need because you want."

"That's what she said. What she didn't say was that she didn't believe her own daughter lived under that principle. Our mother wanted men because she needed what they could and would give her. Whether that was money, sex, drugs, alcohol, or a roof over her head. She needed them to supply her needs."

"Oh, sweetheart, I want to supply your needs."

"You do that, but more importantly, you've shown me that I'm capable, and while I know I'm capable, I most importantly want you."

I wiggled to sit up and as I did, my hands skirted over Reid's torso. My eyes opened wide. "Your bandages are gone."

"I took them off."

"Was it time? Did you see Dr. Dixon?"

"I decided it was time."

My thoughts filled with the good doctor's response to this, yet at the moment, there were other unspoken concerns swirling in the air around us. Together, we moved so that we were both facing the fire. Reid's arm encircled my shoulder as I leaned against his side and curled my legs on the sofa to my side.

"Tell me what you remember," he said.

"I recall the conversation with Nancy vividly." I turned to Reid as my smile grew. "Laurel isn't sure, but she thinks it could be the venom from the ant bites that interfered with the drug that I was given. That's why I could recall the scene with Nancy." I stretched out one of my legs over Reid's lap. Wearing a nightshirt, my legs were bare. The multitude of bites had begun to heal. They no longer itched or were angry and pus filled. Instead, my legs were peppered with smooth red dots. "My mind knew it was impossible to rationalize a conversation with someone I hadn't seen in almost twenty years. I told myself it was a dream, not a memory."

Reid's attention went to my leg. His large hand gently grasped my ankle, slowly running his touch up my leg and moving upward until he reached the hem of the nightshirt. Before he could go higher, I stopped him. "You're not ready to do what that will lead to, and I want to tell you what I remember."

His lips came to my forehead. "I'm always ready to fuck my wife."

Tilting my chin upward, our lips met in a soft kiss of comfort and understanding. Passion, such as the fire burning across the room, waited like a burning ember, present yet biding its time as we faced the current issues at hand.

"But I can wait," he said. "Go on."

"I don't recall being on the ranch. It's odd. I can picture us on Sparrow's plane headed there, but then my next recollection is in the cell." Reid's eyes opened wide. "Patrick said you saw the pictures of the bunker."

"I did."

"I remember that room. I remember lights and a loud alarm-like sound. I can't remember being in there with Araneae, but she now remembers being in there with me." I shook my head. "It's hard to explain. Think of that timeline much like a recorded television show. Somehow, I'm rewinding and watching the end before the beginning."

"Do you remember any people besides your mother?" Reid asked.

"The dark-haired man. He was tall and..." I had practiced this part over and over in my head. It wasn't that I couldn't say it. My concern was more for the man listening and holding me at this moment.

"And?"

"I think he tried to attack me. I think he was going to rape me. I remember fighting with all my might. I kicked. He hit me. I remember he pulled down my pants." I turned to see my husband's stoic expression. Sitting taller, I moved to my knees on the sofa, so my nose met Reid's. "I'm all right, Reid. I remember fighting. He unbuckled a belt. As I screamed, he said something like if I kept fighting, he'd take me another way."

Reid's eyes closed as he exhaled.

"I don't want you to think that sex is now off the table," I said matter-of-factly. "Reid Murray, I remember fighting for my life, my dignity, and for you. Don't waste your thoughts on him; concentrate on me."

My husband's dark eyes glistened in the light of the flames as his body stiffened. "I'm going to watch that son of a bitch take his last breath."

"That isn't necessary."

"Oh, it's fucking necessary." Reid exhaled as his hands came to my waist, holding me in place. "And before he dies, I'm going to let him know that it was my beautiful and strong wife who kicked his ass, fighting someone twice her size."

"No bloody body parts at my feet," I said with a grin.

Reid's expression changed. It was only a microsecond, but I saw it.

"What happened today?"

"We got some information."

"From?"

"Zella," he answered, his responses coming out flat, matter-of-fact, with no emotion.

"Is she alive to get more information from?"

"No." When I didn't respond, Reid asked, "Do you want more information?"

"Were you alone?"

"No."

"Mason helped?"

"Credit where credit is due. I was merely the assistant."

I didn't want to think about the details of what had happened or what they did. "Did you learn anything helpful?"

"We have every reason to believe that the man you recall—from

DNA, we believe his name is Andrew Jettison—played a role in acquiring your mother from Maples."

Andrew Jettison.

Andrew Jettison.

I repeated the name in my head. There was something familiar about that name.

"Lorna, are you all right?"

I nodded. "Yeah. I think I've heard that name."

"Andrew Jettison?"

I hurriedly scrambled from the sofa and began pacing. My senses were on full-alert as I pushed myself to recall. My bare feet and legs warmed as I stepped closer to the fireplace. I wiggled my toes in the softness of the area rug. Around us, the fire hummed as the lingering scent of freshly ground coffee remained in the air from earlier in the night. Beyond the large windows, a fine mist had begun to fall.

"That must be his full name." I stopped and looked at Reid. "She called him Jet."

Reid stood and came to me. "Who called him Jet?"

"The woman." My pulse increased with the excitement of my mental discovery. It was as if I were Nancy Drew from the children's mysteries, and I'd found a valuable clue. Or at least, I believed it was valuable. I opened my eyes wide as I stared up at my husband. "I fought him, but now I remember thinking I couldn't fight any longer. He was there, right there" —I gestured with my hand, moving it between our chests— "I don't know if I spoke aloud, but I was apologizing to you."

"To me?"

I nodded. "I was sorry I hadn't fought harder, and then she called his name. I fought, but it was her who stopped him from raping me. And then" —my circulation sped even faster— "after they left me alone, the awful noise and flashing light started. I don't know how long it lasted. When I woke, I was on the ground with the ants." My husband continued his stare as I moved around our living room. "Don't you see, Reid? This is good."

"It is?"

"Yes, I'm remembering. And when I spoke with Laurel and Patrick, I'd forgotten the woman. Now, I remember. If I keep working on this...Oh" —I smiled in the glow of the fire— "I'm remembering."

"I wonder if Araneae recalls a woman," Reid said.

My gaze went to the mantel clock. It was now after one in the morning. "It's too late to ask her tonight."

"Talk to Laurel first," Reid suggested. "There was concern that the two of you would feed off of one another and perhaps share incorrect memories."

My head was moving from side to side. "This isn't incorrect, Reid. I know it in my bones. The man's name was Jet."

"Can you recall what the woman looked like?"

As if the wind changed, my metaphoric sail lost tension, defeating my earlier elation. "No, I can't picture her, but I know she was a woman."

My husband reached for my hand. "Sweetheart, bring back that beautiful smile. You're remembering and you may remember more. Even what you just said helps."

"I want to help," I said honestly.

He lifted my hand to his lips, lightly kissing my knuckles. "Mrs. Murray, you're the best help. Now, if I could get you to join me in the bedroom, we both need some sleep. It's late."

REID

Waking before the sun, my body told me to go back to sleep; my mind, however, was already a cyclone of thoughts. I could tell myself if I got out of bed now, I'd nap later, but even I wouldn't believe that. Once I woke, I was awake.

Before lifting the covers, I turned to the sleeping woman at my side. Although she was now the one saying that sex could wait and that I needed to heal, we drifted off to sleep together with nothing separating us. Skin to skin, her soft curves molded against my toned muscles, her body radiated heat at my side, and her gentle mint-scented breath teased my skin.

Did all couples enjoy the familiarity that Lorna and I shared?

I wasn't one to ask others questions about such matters. And yet I hoped they did. From the first time Lorna and I were intimate, we had a connection I'd never imagined. My comfort around her and hers around me seemed so natural and over the years has only intensified.

Placing my elbow on my pillow, I lifted my head to my hand and stared through the darkness of our bedroom at my wife. Even in sleep, she radiated not only her external beauty but her internal heart. Lorna loved without pause, cared for everyone, and gave of herself without question.

The thoughts and feelings circulating through me at the sight of her naked beside me ran the gamut from acceptable in polite company all the way to downright erotic. For only a moment, my thoughts drifted back in time.

Our first meeting.

The day I proposed.

The day we married.

For some reason, in my extremely limited knowledge of love and marriage—because I'd never thought it was a route I'd take—when those milestones occurred, when we held hands and were pronounced man and wife, I believed we'd reached the pinnacle of our journey.

We were two people with completely different backgrounds who found themselves in the same world. We'd successfully met, fallen in love, and made it official before God and man.

What more could there possibly be?

I teased a brunette curl, springing it between my thumb and forefinger before pushing another stray curl away from Lorna's stunning face and peaceful expression. As my sight adjusted to the lack of light, I took in her features. It was amusing how I could see her every day and never tire of anything about her. Her long lashes fluttered, her pert nose pointed subtly upward, and her lips parted slightly with each breath.

My mind went to what the world thought of love. The older I became, the more my reading interests strayed away from fiction, focusing more in the reality of nonfiction. Biographies, as well as scientific, political, and mathematical research held my attention. Yet over the years, I'd picked up a few of Lorna's romance novels. Many of them ended with the saying of vows and the committing of two souls to one another, as if that was the end.

Looking back with the hindsight of almost a decade, I realized how incredibly wrong I'd been and how misleadingly superficial those storylines were.

The day Lorna and I committed our lives to one another wasn't the destination. It was only the first leg of our journey, one that I hoped would last for at least another fifty to sixty years. The love and pride I felt that day as she walked down the makeshift aisle holding tightly to Patrick's arm was greater than any emotion I'd ever known. It had felt as though my chest would burst with adoration, and now my same chest ached with the hunger for more.

While the overabundance of emotion currently within me could easily be attributed to our recent traumas—the reality that I could have lost her in Montana or she could have lost me in Englewood—I believed the cause was more substantial and less superficial than that.

I knew from experience that the overwhelming love I was experiencing tonight paled in comparison to what I'd feel tomorrow or in another ten years. Perhaps it was what the officiant meant when he'd said to love and cherish from this day forward.

The love he described wasn't static. It wasn't an emotion that could be placed in a box to open now and then when it was convenient or practical. No, what he'd meant was that true love was dynamic—a living, breathing entity. It needed to be nurtured. And when it was, it satisfied while simultaneously created a hunger for more of that other person.

Our other half.

Watching Lorna was no longer enough. I needed more. Softly, I ran my fingertips over her warm curves. Even in slumber, her parted lips came together, curling into a grin. As I circled each nipple and moved my touch lower over her flat stomach, Lorna squirmed against the soft sheets and rewarded my effort with soft mews that threatened to reroute my circulation.

That love we shared on our wedding day wasn't meant to be the greatest we ever knew. Instead, it was a seed that we planted together, tended, and allowed to grow.

Exhaling, I laid my head back on the pillow and stared up at the ceiling.

Images of Maples and Zella infiltrated my purer thoughts.

Lorna deserved a good man in her life. My participation in recent events, as well as a long litany of previous crimes, precluded my ability to qualify for such a descriptor. I wasn't good. I couldn't even claim a desire to change my ways.

As I recalled the recent deaths, I didn't feel satisfied. The blood I'd tasted hadn't quenched my thirst for justice and retaliation; it whetted my appetite. I wanted more.

My list grew.

Andrew Jettison, a.k.a Jet, was at the top.

Stephanie Moore/Morehead or whoever the blonde woman was came in second.

A new thought occurred to me.

Anna Maples.

Where was she now?

How had she added to my wife's distress?

I stilled as Lorna's petite hand came to my chest and she lifted her head. "Are you going to leave me?"

"Never."

The tips of her lips curled upward as she rested her chin on my shoulder. "Good. I meant, are you headed to 2?"

"Soon. I was momentarily distracted by the fucking gorgeous woman in my bed."

Lorna's hand slipped lower until her fingers surrounded my now-hardening dick.

Exhaling, I closed my eyes, stretching my neck as I lifted my chin toward the ceiling. "Fuck, Lorna."

Her hand moved up and down as she lifted herself. Short brown hair veiled her profile as she gently peppered my chest with kisses. Flipping back her hair, she turned, her seductive gaze meeting mine. "You're the one who took off the bandages. How do you feel?"

"Like I could fuck you and then run a marathon." That wasn't entirely honest. I'd probably need to choose one or the other. At this moment, there was no question which one would win.

The emerald of Lorna's gaze sparkled with the perfect combination of desire and naughty thoughts. This was the moment where the emotions I'd recognized earlier tilted away from the purity of wedded love to the erotic musings of one man and one woman.

"What if we take it slow?" she asked.

Rolling toward Lorna, I held myself over her. Her pert tits stared up at me, her nipples reddening as they grew harder by the second. "Mrs. Murray, I will go slow, but I want you to know I've come to a realization."

Smiling, her shorter hair fanned out around her beautiful face like a dirty halo. It was perfect for the thoughts I was entertaining. "What realization would that be, Mr. Murray?"

Bending my neck, I seized one of her nipples, sucking it taut. Her whimper reverberated through our bedroom as I did the same to the second. "You, Lorna Murray, married a bad man."

Lorna shook her head against the pillow. "I married the best man."

"No, sweetheart, because at this moment, I want to do very bad things to you."

REID

*L*orna's breaths deepened as my lips connected near her collarbone and worked south, kiss by kiss, and nip by nip, until I made my way to her core. One lick told me that my wife was already wet and ready for me.

"Reid," she called out my name as I spread her legs and buried my face in her slick, warm cunt. One arm over her hips kept her in place as her body writhed at my onslaught of ministrations. As her hands searched for something to grasp, her fingers came to the top of my head. The more I tasted of her sweet essence, the harder my dick became. I could drink from her fountain as her moans of ecstasy floated through the air for hours and never grow tired.

Every now and then, I'd tease her clit with my tongue or teeth. The latter caused her to gasp and her legs to push toward me, creating a vise I had no desire to escape.

"Reid, shit, I'm going to come."

"Let go, Lorna. Enjoy it. I promise it won't be the last time." As my tongue continued, I added two fingers and my thumb pressed against her tight hole. It was as my thumb pushed through the resistance that her body stiffened, her cunt quivered, and satisfied noises filled the air.

When Lorna opened her eyes, I was there, our noses touching. "Tell me, sweetheart, how slow do you want it?"

Her lips met mine as her tongue sought entrance, sharing her sweet taste. When she pulled back, she said, "I don't want to hurt you."

I sat back. "Roll over, Lorna, show me your ass."

For only a millisecond, she hesitated.

I was a smart man. My knowledge wasn't a quality I gave much consideration, but this move I was about to make, I'd considered. I knew exactly what I was doing.

Running my hand over her ass, I hummed. "Your ass is perfect. My cock is so fucking hard."

Lorna's forehead fell to the pillows as I spread her legs and worked my way in between on my knees. Wrapping an arm around her waist, I worked her clit with one hand as I pumped her cunt with two and then three fingers.

The expectancy was more than I could take. Spreading her folds, I lined up the head of my dick with her entrance. For a moment, I waited.

A soft whine came from my wife as she wiggled with anticipation.

Without further hesitation, I plunged balls deep inside her warm, wet pussy. Lorna's gasp filled the air as my fingers gripped her hips, holding us both in place.

I tried to do as she said and move slowly though my instinct was to do the opposite.

I didn't know if my chest no longer hurt or if it was that my cock felt too good to think of anything else. I refused to give it more thought. My concern was the sensual woman who not only took everything I could give but pushed back, giving of herself and wanting more.

Slowly and deliberately, I pistoned my hips, moving in and out.

This position allowed me to plunge as deep as possible. The friction was off the charts, setting every nerve in my entire body on alert. It was as if there was a time bomb within me, ticking away. Detonation was imminent.

The wanton desire within me continued to build until moving slowly was no longer a possibility. Perspiration beaded on my forehead as my speed increased. The way Lorna's body contracted around mine was like a silken glove two sizes too small. My balls tightened as the sounds of our union filled the room until beneath me, Lorna cried out. Her fucking cunt squeezed me in a series of contractions as she came undone for a second time.

With my cock slick with her come, I pulled out, finding my next destination.

"Reid?" she asked, her neck craning as our eyes met.

"I'll make it good."

Lorna nodded before sucking in a breath as the head of my dick pressed against her tight hole. Her fingers gripped the pillows as I pushed through the first barrier. I ran my hand down her back, beginning at her neck, feeling each vertebra down her spine. "I don't need to tell you to relax. You can do this."

I knew my wife, inside and out. As moments passed, I sensed her conscious effort to grant me entrance to her most-guarded opening. Such as a series of connections, each link loosened until the lock was freed. From the top of her head to the tips of her toes, her muscles relaxed.

"That's it."

Reaching around, I found her clit, rubbing circles as I whispered praise and adoration in her ear. With the sound of my voice combined with my attention to her bundle of nerves, Lorna's breathing slowed and her knees began to bounce. Deeper still, I moved. "Almost there."

Lorna nodded against the pillows as I found my way home. "That's my good girl. Your ass is so damn tight." I reached forward, stroking her neck and cheek. "Talk to me, Lorna."

"Fuck me, Reid."

Closing my eyes, I did as she commanded.

Every move felt too good, too tight.

"Touch yourself, Lorna."

Beneath me, she repositioned to do as I said.

Soon our bedroom filled with sounds, primal noises that had passed the lips of men and women for centuries. Words mixed with utterances, some making sense while others simply cried out with wanton desire. These were sounds shared by two people who found the utmost pleasure when joined as one.

"God, Reid, shit, I'm going to come again."

Her timing couldn't have been more perfect. The rush came from deep within me as I held tight to her hips and we both came undone. Lorna's body quaked as my cock pulsated and I filled her with my seed. My knees gave out seconds after Lorna's as we fell to the bed.

Summoning all my strength, I pulled out and climbed from our bed. In less than a minute, I cleaned myself and returned with a warm, damp washcloth, ready to tend to the woman I loved more than anything.

After I was done, Lorna rolled over to her back and reached for my hand. Her head tilted to one side. "I love you."

"I love you."

"I'm surprised after what I told you about Jet—"

I brought my finger to her lips. "Don't say his name or Maples. Sweetheart, I took you, your wet, warm cunt and your tight ass for one reason."

She grinned. "Because they're yours."

"No, Lorna, because they're yours and you let me. For not the first time, you shared yourself, all of you, with me. It's the fucking best gift you could give and I'll accept that gift every time, and I promise to care for it, to treasure it, and to love you not because of it but always.

"I'm not living with the ghosts of those deviants in our bed with my wife and neither will you. One is dead. The other one will die sooner rather than later." I touched Lorna's forehead. "When you think about a dick inside you, think of mine. Only mine."

Her emerald eyes glistened as she nodded.

"Lorna, there might be some women who would have had a problem with what we just did."

Lorna shrugged.

"Be honest with me, did you have a problem? Are you one of those women?"

"No, because as I've said a million times, Reid Rendell Murray, I trust you."

"I can make love gently, but that wasn't my plan tonight."

"It wasn't?"

"No, I'm not treating you like glass, Lorna. You've shown me time and time again you're not going to break. I guess, I wanted to show you that I know that about you. I know you're the strongest woman in the world, and I don't need to treat you with kid gloves."

"Thank you."

"You and me, sweetheart, we're going to move forward from all of this. When we're making love, there will be no thoughts of anyone else. You can be certain that you're the only one on my mind."

She grinned. "You make it hard to think of anyone else."

"No, Lorna" —I winked— "you were the one who made me hard."

Her smile grew before fading as she brought her hand to my chest. "Are you sure you're all right?"

"I'm not made of glass either."

"I guess that makes us an unbreakable team."

"I guess it does." I brushed my lips over hers. "You have a few more hours before your alarm. If you think you can sleep."

Lorna stifled a yawn. "I had at least three earthshaking orgasms in the last hour. I'm positive I can sleep."

Standing, I lifted the blankets over her and planted another kiss on the top of her head.

"You're going to 2," she said, more as a statement than a question.

"If you're all right with that."

"I'm afraid if you stay here, I won't get any more sleep."

"You're right. I'd be too tempted to help you with number four."

A soft pink hue filled her cheeks. "That wouldn't be so bad." She sighed. "Go, Reid. Do what you do. But before you leave, you need to know something."

"What is that?"

"You're wrong about something you said. You're not the bad guy. You, Mason, Sparrow, and Patrick, are the good guys. I don't need to know by what means you accomplish your goals because I know you and all of them. You are the good ones. I married the best." She craned her neck upward and kissed me. "I love you."

"I love you, too, Lorna."

Her eyes closed as she settled under the covers.

As I dressed and headed to 2, my wife's praise rang in my head. I wasn't certain I deserved it, but I wouldn't deny it was a comforting lyric to have playing in the background.

LORNA

*A*ll five of us ladies turned toward the archway of the kitchen at the sound of footsteps upon the tile. The discussion the four men had been having stilled as they turned the corner, passed the grand staircase, and entered the kitchen. Simultaneously, the discussion the other four ladies and I had been having also quieted.

Our conversation hadn't been anything consequential. After all we'd been through, including the memories Araneae and I were having, insignificant fit the bill as we worked together to create a breakfast fit for nine. Once, after Madeline and Ruby moved in to the tower, Reid asked me how I felt about no longer being in charge of the penthouse kitchen. I'd smiled and told him I still was. Officially, it was Araneae's home, and while she could toast and butter English muffins with the best of us, cooking wasn't her forte nor did she want it to be. She was content to let me lead.

And if I were completely honest, breakfast and its preparation was my favorite meal of day. The sun rose and grew brighter outside the large windows as each of our inhabitants started their day alongside the others. No matter what had transpired the day before, the week before, or even privately in our own apartments, each morning was a new start.

My green gaze met the dark brown one I adored as a smile curled my lips and my mind slipped back to some time before the sun rose. Simply recalling Reid's and my time together made my nipples tighten and my core twist. It wasn't that Reid had left me wanting; that couldn't be further from the truth. After he'd left me, my completely satiated body had melted blissfully into our bed under the warm cover of blankets, and I'd drifted peacefully into a hard-earned, sex-induced slumber.

Even upon waking, as my alarm rang its morning song, my mind was on my husband. Yes, I thought about his unmatched ability to bring me to orgasm, but I also thought about his words. More than once, Mason had said that Reid was quiet. I wouldn't say my husband was boisterous in any way. His words were weighed and measured.

That quality made each and every one of them all the more sincere and heartfelt.

As if knowing my thoughts, Reid came closer and brushed a chaste kiss to the top of my head. "Did you get some sleep?" he whispered with a smirk.

Warmth filled my cheeks as I reached for the cup of coffee I'd just poured for him and handed it his direction. If we were alone, I could respond with an appropriate retort, one that would match the pink blooming on my cheeks. Instead, I replied, "Yes. Thanks for asking."

"Breakfast smells wonderful," Patrick said more loudly as he went to Madeline and kissed the top of her hair. "How are you feeling?"

She shook her head.

"We made her sit down," Araneae offered. "I'm no expert, but I think you should stay in Chicago, Patrick."

"Mom won't say what's going on," Ruby added, "but she's quieter than normal. Who would believe that I'd think my mom was too quiet."

Patrick's blue eyes opened wide as he stared at his wife. "Contractions?"

Madeline shrugged. "I think."

The entire room stilled. If this were a television show, this would be the moment where one person would narrate, telling the audience the thoughts of each person. Instead, we all remained quiet as we waited for more.

Madeline lifted her hand as if to minimize our concern as Ruby walked over to her mother.

"They're not strong or close together," Madeline reassured us. "The doctor said to wait until they are regular." She sucked in a breath as she sat taller.

"Mom?" Ruby asked, her one-word question laced with concern.

"I'm all right, honey."

Patrick's hand went to Madeline's midsection. "Are you having one? Is it normal for you to feel so hard?"

Ruby's hand joined her dad's.

The rest of us stood quietly by as Madeline reassured her husband and daughter that it was normal and she'd call if things progressed. Ruby also promised to not leave her mother's side.

As they stood there, the three of them, emotion bubbled within me. For any other family, to be together and having their second child in eighteen years may seem surreal. For the Kellys it was no less than a miracle.

It was as I opened the oven to remove an egg casserole we'd made earlier that I noticed Sparrow across the room. Leaning against a counter, wearing his suit for Michigan Avenue with his feet crossed at the ankle and a mug of coffee in his hands, his dark eyes narrowed and his jaw clenched as he silently observed Patrick and Madeline.

I nudged Araneae, standing nearby cutting fruit. Her soft brown eyes met mine. I tilted my head toward Sparrow. "If you ask me," I whispered, "your man is realizing that childbirth will be something he won't be able to control."

We both turned to him, completely unnoticed. Sparrow was too lost in his thoughts to see us.

Araneae laid down the knife, smiled at me, and walked toward her husband. From my vantage, I couldn't hear what she whispered or what Sparrow replied in response. My only clue was body language, a rare visual glimpse of what the two of them shared in private. As they spoke and she smiled, his muscles relaxed until he had his hands at her waist, holding her close.

Even in our large kitchen filled with family, it appeared as though the queen had just soothed the king. She'd recently entered her third trimester, and despite our ordeal, everything was on schedule.

Slowly, the murmurs around the room grew louder as Laurel, Ruby, and I moved the food to the large granite table, and the men refilled their mugs with fresh coffee. In no time, we were all seated, discussing everything from the cooling autumn weather to local and national news. Throughout it all, Patrick watched his wife as if she could disappear before his eyes.

Mason mentioned that he may be headed to Washington DC for a meeting and let it slip that my husband could be accompanying him.

My lips came together as I lowered my fork to the side of my plate. "I thought your job was here on 2?"

Sparrow's stare bypassed me and went to Mason. "I'm going on that expedition. Don't even consider going without me."

Araneae's gaze met mine.

"I don't know if that should make me feel better or worse," I said.

"Better," Sparrow replied. "No one gets shot when I'm there."

We all turned to Reid who smiled and lifted both hands. "One day we'll move on to other news."

Sparrow's gaze narrowed. "Don't hold your breath. Today isn't that day." He shook his head. "I have some important meetings this morning; I can't leave before noon."

It was as Madeline stood that I realized she hadn't eaten.

"Mom, are you sure you're okay?" Ruby asked.

Madeline's complexion had paled. "I think I should head to our apartment and rest."

Patrick's chair scooted across the floor as he hurriedly stood. As he reached for Madeline, she gripped the back of a chair. Her face contorted, her fingers blanched, and she bore down, bending her knees.

I momentarily turned to the sink, thinking I'd heard something.

When I turned back, her green eyes glistened.

"I'm sorry."

"Madeline, it's—"

"Oh my gosh," she interrupted, looking toward the floor, "my water just broke."

The next few minutes sped by at warp speed. All our chairs screeched over the tile. Sparrow pulled out his phone and barked orders as Patrick instructed Ruby to hurry to their apartment for the bag Madeline had packed.

"Garrett is in the garage," Sparrow said, "ready to take me to the office. Go now, he'll get you to the Women's Hospital." He turned to Araneae. "This is why I wanted a delivery room set up here."

As she shook her head, I stood. "I'll call your doctor, Madeline," I volunteered, thankful that I'd added all the numbers to my phone earlier.

Sparrow and Mason exchanged looks.

"Don't worry," my brother said, "I'm calling now. She'll be fully guarded. No one is getting near her or Patrick."

"Or me. I want to be there," Ruby said.

Madeline reached out to her grown daughter and turned to Patrick who nodded his approval at Mason.

"Don't worry about a thing," Mason said. "Reid will have the place monitored electronically, and I'll have it crawling with Sparrows." He grinned at Reid. "Our meeting in DC will need to be postponed."

REID

As everyone dispersed, Lorna reached for my hand. "Let me know if you hear anything."

"You too. I imagine Ruby calling or texting you or Araneae before Patrick calls one of us."

"But won't you know?" She tilted her head, her green eyes questioning. "How far can you infiltrate the hospital's computer system?"

"My focus will be on security. Patrick already has it worked out where Madeline will be in a secure and private wing. This won't be the first baby delivered to a family who requests the utmost privacy." When Lorna didn't respond, I added, "Money has its privileges."

Leaving the kitchen as it was, Lorna rode down the elevator with me, stopping at the apartments. As the doors opened, she lifted herself on her tiptoes and brushed my lips with hers. "Get to work. I'm going to talk to Ruby."

Before she was out of reach, I seized her hand. "We haven't talked about this in a while."

Lorna's eyes opened, the emerald clouded with confusion. "What?"

"There has been a lot of baby talk around here, and I was thinking that it might be nice to be where Patrick and Madeline are." I wasn't convinced what prompted my statement. It could be the baby who was about to arrive or perhaps it was the toddler yesterday. Nevertheless, the idea of a child had been recurring in my thoughts.

Lorna's lips curled. "I think it would be better to be where they will be after Madeline pushes out an eight-pound baby boy."

I squeezed my wife's hand. "I'm open to talking about it again."

"I'm open to sex as much as you or I want because talking won't give us a baby."

My thoughts went back to this morning. "Neither will coming in your ass."

Pink filled her cheeks. With a twinkle in her eyes, Lorna looked around the common area beyond the elevator, no doubt verifying that we were alone. Her tone lowered. "No, Mr. Murray, it won't." Her smile dimmed and her breasts moved with her respiration. "We can have this conversation another time, maybe when Madeline and Patrick aren't about to be parents again or you aren't out for revenge. You know that I haven't taken birth control in over seven months. Maybe we should face the possibility that having a child might not be in our future, but" —she forced a smile— "I can make a kick-ass surrogate aunt to this little boy and Sparrow and Araneae's baby."

Though the doctor said we were prematurely concerned, we'd had a few preliminary tests run. There was no detectable issue stopping Lorna from getting pregnant, and my swimmers were given the doctor's seal of approval. So far, we simply hadn't conceived.

My chest twisted with my wishing I hadn't mentioned a child, at least not right now. "Sweetheart, I'm sorry."

"Don't be," Lorna said. "Let's not talk about it now."

I nodded as she released my hand and walked toward Patrick and Madeline's apartment door.

Before Lorna reached the barrier, it opened inward, and Ruby rushed out, rolling a travel suitcase behind her. "Hold the elevator," she shouted.

Following the suitcase were both of her parents. Madeline's fingers blanched as her grip of Patrick's hand tightened. Her expression was contorted as she blew short puffs of air.

"Ruby, please keep us posted," Lorna said. "Text me or your aunt."

Excitement sparkled in Ruby's blue eyes while her lips tightened with worry. "The last time Mom did this she was my age."

Lorna turned to Madeline. "Every eighteen years."

Madeline shook her head, her expression softening. "I'm afraid I will be too old in another eighteen years." Her hand went to her midsection as her eyes went to Patrick. "I can't believe this is real, that we're doing this together."

I stepped from the elevator. "Go, because I don't think you want one of us delivering your son."

Patrick slapped my shoulder. "Thank you. I'll keep you updated. Let me know how the security is going."

"I sure will."

As the elevator doors began to shut, Patrick reached out and stopped them. "Reid, I began searching for that money trail we discussed this morning. You'll see some programs running on my computers on 2."

"Everything else can wait, Patrick. Go, Reid Kelly is ready to meet his mom and dad."

Patrick smiled as the doors shut.

"Do you know the name they chose?"

"No. They've both been very tight-lipped about it."

"I'm sorry if we never have a little Reid."

Wrapping my arm around Lorna's waist, I pulled her close. "I don't need a little Reid. As a matter of fact, I don't think I'd want to name a son after me." My mind went to Little Gordy and the way Gordon Maples boasted about having a son. "I think it would be good to give a boy or a girl their own identity."

For the moment, we were stuck on our floor, waiting for the elevator to return.

There were stairs for safety purposes, but the stairwell was monitored, physically blocked by faux decor—much like the elevator in the penthouse was hidden behind a pocket door—and attached to a very loud alarm. If Sparrow could have constructed the tower without stairs, he would have done it. The fact that they're well-hidden and protected was completely due to his need to keep the tower safe.

Going to the elevator, I scanned my palm again, telling it to return once Madeline, Ruby, and Patrick were in the garage and hopefully in Garrett's car under protection.

"I need to get back upstairs and clean the kitchen," Lorna said.

"I'll be on 2. And with the baby coming, no one will be leaving town."

"I like that."

When the doors opened again, the elevator was empty. Lorna and I entered. "I guess I'll go up before I go down." I hit the button for the penthouse.

Lorna took a step forward and leaned into me. "You know, all the steamy romance novels and movies have a hot sex scene in an elevator."

Without thinking, my gaze went up to the trim between the walls and ceiling before I wrapped my arm around her and pulled her to me. "Do all of those scenes include voyeurs?"

She gasped, stepping back. "There are cameras, aren't there?"

"Yes, sweetheart. And while there'd be a good chance I'd see the footage first, there's an equally good chance of it being either Patrick or your brother."

As the doors opened to the hallway in the penthouse, she replied, "Never mind."

"Anything I should know?" Sparrow asked as he held the door open, allowing Lorna to step out.

She shook her head. "Absolutely not."

Sparrow grinned as he entered and the doors closed. "Garage."

"I guess my new role is elevator operator." I hit both the 2 and G buttons. "Who's driving you to Michigan Avenue?"

"Christian was closest. He'll drive me to the office and wait until Garrett is back from the hospital."

Again, the elevator stopped. Holding the doors ajar, I asked, "Are you confident in the team of Sparrows Mason is installing at the hospital?"

Sparrow nodded. "Watch the security and infiltrate the patient information. Check to make sure no one else is in the system. There's no reason for us to assume that Jettison or his partner would be after Patrick or Madeline. Everything points to Laurel."

Thousands of questions I'd asked myself earlier came to mind. However, as Sparrow stood in his Michigan Avenue attire, I knew now wasn't the time to discuss them with him. I'd do my own research. As the elevator closed behind me, I scanned my palm on the sensor.

The steel door slid open.

LORNA

*a*s I stepped onto the marble floor of the penthouse hallway, I heard noises coming from the direction of their home office. For many years—until Araneae arrived—the room had been Sparrow's office and his alone. Walking toward the slightly open door, I smiled, recalling my surprise at Sparrow's willingness to share this space with his then acquisition or girlfriend or whatever title he'd bestowed upon her.

I pushed the door open, seeing Araneae standing near her desk where there used to be a sofa. Her desk didn't match her husband's. Sparrow's was a large wooden one with ornate carvings. Truly, his desk was the one piece of furniture that didn't fit in this room or the entire tower. Araneae's desk was sleek, made of glass in an 'L' shape, and hosted multiple screens. Her back was to me as she scrolled something that looked like lists and lists of numbers. From where I stood, I couldn't see the particulars.

Rapping my knuckles on the doorjamb, I waited.

Araneae turned toward me and smiled. "I'm sorry."

"Why are you sorry?"

"I got a call from Louisa and have been caught up in these

reports. I'm afraid I left the kitchen as it was. I can help you clean up in a—"

I shook my head. "I don't mind. I want to stay busy. My thoughts are on Madeline."

Araneae let out a long breath as she leaned back in her leather chair. "If I'm honest, I think I welcomed the distraction of these reports. At least Madeline knows what to expect. I've read books and watched videos." She shook her head. "I don't recommend the videos." She laid her hand on her very visible baby bump. "The thing is, I think it's a bit too late for me to back out."

"I'd agree. It's too late for that. Didn't Madeline have a cesarean section with Ruby?"

Araneae nodded. "She did, but the doctor said she could deliver this boy naturally since it's been so long."

"Can you imagine having children eighteen years apart?"

Araneae's hand was still on her midsection. "Right now, I'm having trouble imagining having one child."

"What about your friend Louisa? She has two children, right?"

"She does, a girl and a boy. Louisa says that no matter what the birth is like, holding the baby makes it all worth it."

"Sounds like good advice," I said. "Are you going upstairs anytime soon?" I was asking about the second floor of the penthouse. "I was going to clean up there today. I want to stay busy and since I saw Sparrow leave, I figured this was a good time."

"I should say that I'll do it."

"And then what would I do? Besides, those numbers look boring to me." I gestured toward her computer.

"Oh, they're really not. The Sinful Threads holiday merchandise that was previewed in New York is a hit. We have orders from distributors all over the country. The numbers are ridiculous. That's what Louisa called about. If we plan to meet these orders, we'll need to ramp up production. She thinks we should consider limiting sales."

"Isn't it better to sell more?" I asked.

"Not really. We learned early with Sinful Threads that the exclusivity of our merchandise allowed us to create a higher quality product, charge more, and make higher profits. If the market is flooded with a product, it becomes less desired." She laughed. "I think about brand-name purses and outlet malls."

"Like you shopped at an outlet?"

Her brown eyes widened. "I most certainly did. Kennedy did."

"Araneae Sparrow doesn't."

"No, and Araneae Sparrow doesn't shop anywhere very often."

That was true. We all had personal shoppers who knew our likes and dislikes, our sizes, and our styles. Walking aimlessly around a store or shopping center was one of the freedoms we'd relinquished as wives of top men in the Sparrow outfit.

I'd had more freedom in the past. That ended about the same time Araneae came to the tower. Now the idea of walking through an open-air market gives me the chills. I think the men's warnings along with the recent attempts on our safety have helped to ensure our willingness to stay put in the tower and let others do some of those activities for us.

"Okay," I said with a wave. "Enjoy your numbers and let me know if you hear from Ruby. I'll be around."

As I turned to go, Araneae stood. "Lorna, I remember more."

I wrapped my arms around my midsection, recalling the man named Jet. "Do you remember a woman?"

Araneae nodded. "And a man she called Jet."

I nodded. "I remember him, but I can only recall hearing her. Did she ever say her name?"

"No, but I remember she was very stark and seemed in charge."

I tried to recall. "I explained it to Reid like my memories are a recorded television show and I am watching it from the end to the beginning. I remember the time before I was found, and slowly I'm recalling ones further back but not being taken or even being at the ranch."

"The security video from the ranch shows we were unconscious when we were taken." Araneae reached out and put her hand on my arm. "Lorna, I remember almost all of it." Her soft brown eyes turned glassy with unshed tears. "I can never thank you enough for the way you took care of me. I don't know if I would have survived if you hadn't been there."

Swallowing, I laid my other hand on hers and grinned. "I don't remember that. I'm sure I did what anyone else would have done."

Araneae shook her head. "No. I remember the woman questioning me, and she asked me about you and Laurel." A tear slid down her cheek. "She was a bitch."

"The woman? Did she hurt you?"

"Yes, her." Araneae took a step away and paced between the two desks. "No, not like that. She said things about both of you, trying to make me choose one."

Something clicked. "Choose one of us." My eyes opened wide. "I think she asked me to do the same. I remember now. It was you or Laurel."

"Yes, for me it was you or Laurel too."

"She had blonde hair."

Araneae nodded. "I couldn't do it. I wanted to tell you because you were so good, and God, Lorna, I love you. You were here in this tower when I got here, and from the very beginning, you made me feel welcome." She shook her head. "Even so, I couldn't choose one. I wouldn't."

I reached for her shoulders and smiled. "I didn't either. I wouldn't. I remember that now, too. She was upset, but I couldn't." I let go and hummed. "One of her hands seemed different."

"I remember she wore gloves."

"I'm still not remembering it all."

"The things she said." Araneae took a deep breath. "They made me think about what you do around here, and I'm sorry I'm not more appreciative or helpful."

"I'm not." I inhaled. "We all have our roles and that's what makes this family of misfits work. I love Sinful Threads products, but I don't want to run a company. I couldn't begin to do what Laurel does, and even Madeline is finding her way here and at the institute. Without one of us, it wouldn't be the same."

"Lorna, you are so fucking important to this" —she gestured around— "all of it. The men have their roles too, but I realized in that room with a table and chairs that you are our glue."

It was my turn to tear up. "I love you too, by the way."

"Please know that everything you do is appreciated." Araneae grinned. "I guess you're the female Patrick."

"I am?"

"You're the one who notices everything, who asks questions, and who takes the time to care." She wrung her hands. "The woman made it sound like you didn't matter. She was wrong."

I had a vision of standing in this same office nearly a decade earlier having a similar heartfelt conversation with Araneae's husband. I looked my friend in the eye. "We are all somebodies."

"Yes."

As I began to leave, both of our phones buzzed. I pulled mine from my back pocket and looked at the screen. "It's Ruby."

Araneae looked up from her screen the same time I looked up from the message.

"They have Madeline settled," she said. "And she's five centimeters dilated."

"Sounds like we're going to have a baby today."

We both hugged before I made my way to the kitchen.

Our conversation played in my mind, sprinkled with memories of Sparrow's and my conversation years ago.

We are all individually a somebody.

And we were all as a family having a baby.

Whether I ever gave birth or not, I was content in knowing I'd have my role in Madeline's son's life as well as in Araneae's child's.

The kitchen was exactly as we'd left it. The food and dishes were on the table. Even the oven was still on. And as I busied myself, I couldn't have been more content to stay working.

About an hour later, the food was all put away, dishes were in the dishwasher, and the surfaces sparkled with the sunshine streaming through the large windows. As I was climbing the stairs to the second floor of the penthouse with a million small tasks on my mind, my phone buzzed again. This time it was a call.

My screen read *Reid*.

"Have you heard from Ruby?" he asked in lieu of a greeting.

"Araneae and I received a text from her about an hour ago. Madeline is dilated—"

"Get Araneae and Laurel, I'm on my way up."

I heard the concern in his voice. "Tell me what's going on."

"I'd rather—"

"You're scaring me."

"Ruby is missing."

REID

An hour earlier

For the first time in quite a while, as I entered 2, I was alone. Earlier this morning, all four of us had been present, not unusual in the middle of the night-slash-early morning. Now, the entire floor was still except for the hum of the computers. My steps echoed in the vastness and the scent of coffee lingered in the air. As the steel door closed behind me and I traveled deeper into our command center, a peace settled over me. This floor was my sanctuary. That wasn't meant to diminish the apartment I shared with Lorna. The two were separate. Upon entering each one, my expectations differed. These desks, keyboards, and monitors were who I was and what I did. The weight bench, the coffee pot, and the other amenities were all familiar extensions.

I supposed in many ways this floor of the tower was cathartic for me. Within its realm, I lose all track of time as I delve deeper into my work. While it all focused in some way on some aspect of the Sparrow outfit, it was where I could contribute the greatest.

As I hit the button for another cup of coffee, I had a realization.

I was back.

That wasn't a statement that referenced my physical presence. Instead, it was a statement that implied my mental focus. Since Lorna was taken, 1 had been scattered on too many fronts. The need to seek revenge fueled an inability to see what I usually saw, to do what I usually did.

Maybe it was the deaths of Maples and Zella that gave me a taste of retaliation. Perhaps it was being shot that brought a new appreciation for each day. Or more likely, it was the one woman in the world who could look at me and know my inner thoughts. It was the strength and resolve she'd proclaimed and demonstrated that made me stronger.

Carrying my fresh cup of coffee, I made a quick stop at Patrick's workstation. He'd begun his search of Nancy Pierce's financial transactions prior to her disappearance. I could have started the work on it, but when it came to following the money, Patrick was our resident expert. Of course, his focus changed as soon as Madeline's water broke, as it should.

I brought his screen to life. It was filled with the compiling data. Along with Nancy's name, we knew her Social Security number. Of course, that would only work if these transactions were done in a legal manner. If they weren't legal, our answers wouldn't be as straightforward.

Taking the coffee, I made my way to my workstation and brought my screens to life, including the one overhead that had continuous feeds from around the city. I pulled up our new feed from Dino's Liquor store. The last interesting piece from there was a late-night visitor the owner had in the back alley. It wasn't Jettison and the only exchange appeared to be a liquor deal. The man appeared to buy two kegs of beer. It was Patrick who noticed that the kegs didn't have taps. That meant either the purchaser had taps of his own, which would be the case with a tavern or bar, or there was something besides beer in those containers.

Mason had Sparrows following up on the license plate. Once the purchaser was found, he'd receive a visit from a few of our men—a follow-up of sorts.

There was nothing unusual I could see as I scanned the different locations throughout the city. Traffic was normal for a Wednesday and the time of day. Businesses were opening. Pedestrians were walking the sidewalks. Even with the autumn chill, the parks were filling with people. Basically, it was a typical day in Chicago and the surrounding neighborhoods.

A few hits of my keyboard and I found myself rotating the cameras and views of the parking lots and parking garage at the Women's Hospital. It didn't take long to find the car Garrett drove. All of our cars had trackers. It would be a bad day if some punk ever tried to steal one—bad day for the punk.

The inside of the hospital was under constant surveillance. The system was closed-circuit, meaning it didn't broadcast and was used in-house. Knowing that Madeline and Araneae would both give birth and that the Women's Hospital was the best labor-and-delivery hospital in the greater Chicago area and also had a great NICU, we'd made the effort to infiltrate their system in advance.

Because Ruby needed care upon birth, Madeline was adamant about the NICU unit.

With everything happening, it had been a few weeks since I'd run a scan. It would assure me that we were able to still see and hear. It would also confirm what Sparrow had suggested in the elevator—determine that no one else was infiltrating the system, that we were alone in our methods.

My phone vibrated in my pocket with a text message from Patrick. It was brief—a room number and a note that they were settled in the room. I could assume that Mason was given the same information to station the Sparrows as needed.

The Sparrows wouldn't gain access to the private wing; however, they could monitor the exits and entrances from the outside. There were three such entries. One went to the access hallway, the main entrance to the wing on the fourth floor. The elevators to reach the correct floor were scattered throughout the hospital. A second went straight into the neonatal wing, and a third was the stairwell facilitating the emergency exit.

There weren't cameras in the hospital rooms, for obvious reasons. I could only see the hallway outside of their room as men and women in scrubs went in and out of the door, letting the door close in their wake. While I couldn't see within, I did tap into the nurses' station and gained access to the vitals and other monitors coming from each room. There were only five rooms in this exclusive wing. Two were currently in use.

Subdividing one of my screens, I kept watch right outside their room door as well as the three entrances, including the waiting room and elevator bay near the main entrance. There were two men in that waiting room, not near one another. One was older, much older, the second was a Sparrow. I was ninety-five percent certain.

I sent Mason a text message:

"SEND ME PROFILES ON ALL THE SPARROWS IN THE HOSPITAL."

My phone vibrated almost immediately.

"WILL DO. GIVE ME FIVE."

The dark hair caught my attention, probably because most of the medical staff wore coverings over their hair. It was Ruby, stepping out of the room and walking down the hallway.

"Where are you going?" I asked aloud despite the fact she was miles away at the hospital.

Soon she was out of range of the camera I'd been using. I switched to another in time to see her enter a doorway. My mind scrambled with possibilities. I was certain there was a bathroom attached to the delivery-and-care room, so it had to be something else. I continued watching, certain there wasn't another exit to the room she'd entered. I opened another screen and pulled up the trackers we had in all of the ladies' shoes and purses.

Most of the signals came from this tower, which wasn't surprising. Three came from the hospital room, which would be Madeline's shoes and purse and Ruby's purse. I could also track their phones. Before I did, the other tracker came from this mysterious room, coming from Ruby's shoes.

It took roughly three minutes—it was two minutes and forty-seven seconds—before she reemerged with two large cups with covers in her hands. I let out the breath I'd been holding as she walked the beverages back down to the room with her parents.

As I went back to Patrick's desk, I thought of something we hadn't discussed. The people who kidnapped Araneae and Lorna took their shoes and used them as bait to lure us to the bunkers. In other words, the kidnappers knew about the trackers. Either they had knowledge of our plans or were able to pick up on the transmitting signal.

It made me think of an alternative. Despite the perceived value in each of our wives' wedding rings, neither lady had them removed. I made a note to talk to Mason about incorporating a transmitter in the bands as a backup plan. It would be best if the signals were also less detectable.

"Fuck," I muttered as I began to scan Patrick's screen.

We were coming up empty on any recent bank accounts in Nancy's real name with her real Social Security number. There was record of one account at a popular bank not far from where her parents lived. I clicked a few keys looking to go farther back in the history of the account. Since it had been closed for so long, I had to jump through a series of hoops and microfiche. Whoever thought it was a good means of information storage should be ashamed.

The hair on the back of my neck stood to attention at the deposits. They weren't large and occurred monthly. Around the time of Missy's disappearance, the amount was reduced by a third.

"She was getting payments for her children," I said. "How much of that money went to the kids, Nancy?" I knew she couldn't hear or answer me, but damn, I wished she could.

I double-checked the dates Mason and Lorna had given me. It appeared as though Nancy was getting money even when her mother was caring for her children. The payments ended altogether after Lorna's seventeenth birthday.

This wasn't what we'd been looking for. It didn't have a mystery connection or raise eyebrows. This was simply welfare.

The other program still running was looking for another connection when my phone rang. It was Mason.

"Did you send me the profiles?"

"Can you see Ruby?"

"What?" I jumped up from Patrick's chair and hurried to my own. The hallway outside the room was clear. "No, I can't see into the room."

"She isn't in the room. Patrick just called. She stepped away and hasn't returned."

"Shit." I pulled up her trackers. "Fuck, Mason. She's not in the hospital."

LORNA

"*R*uby is missing."

"What do you mean by *missing?*" I asked, trying to comprehend. "She's at the hospital with Patrick and Madeline."

Images of the beautiful teenager came to mind. I wasn't simply imagining her outward beauty. There was so much more to Ruby than that. There was her wisdom and grace beyond her years, the things in life that she'd witnessed, and the still sweet and even innocent nature of her heart. My head began shaking. "No, you're wrong."

"Lorna." His tone was neither jovial nor questioning. It was direct and not open to debate. "Get Araneae and Laurel, and I'll fill you all in on what I know."

"Tell me Ruby's going to be okay."

"I fucking hope so."

Taking a deep breath, I gripped my phone tighter as I hurried down the penthouse steps and turned down the hallway to the Sparrows' home office. Pushing the door inward, I didn't slow. The door bounced off the wall behind, its bang announcing my entrance.

Araneae turned away from her computer, her eyes wide. "What?" she asked.

My head shook.

"I need to go," she said into her phone seconds before she disconnected the call.

"I'm with Araneae," I spoke to Reid. "I haven't seen Laurel since breakfast."

"What's happening?" Araneae asked.

"Meet me on the apartment level," my husband said through the phone. "Laurel isn't here in her new space on 2, so she's probably in her apartment."

I nodded my response as the call disconnected. Looking up, I met Araneae's intense light-brown stare.

"Is it Madeline? The baby? Oh, please not the baby."

My head shook. "It's Ruby. We'll know more when we get downstairs."

"Ruby? What happened to Ruby?"

Together we hurriedly made our way to the elevator. Araneae opened the pocket door as I scanned my palm on the sensor. In no time, the doors opened.

"Lorna, tell me what you know."

My head shook as my pulse raced and my stomach twisted. "I only know that Reid said she's missing." I felt tears threatening the backs of my eyes. "He says she's not at the hospital."

"No, that doesn't make sense."

"I know."

Stepping into the elevator, we were whisked to the floor below.

As soon as the doors opened on A, the apartment level, Araneae and I headed to Laurel and Mason's apartment. Using my fist, I banged on the wood door.

Why didn't we have doorbells?

I'd never questioned that before.

It didn't take long before Laurel was standing before us. Her hair was pulled back in a ponytail and besides wearing casual, soft 'lockdown' clothes, her feet were covered in only socks. At nearly the same time as her door opened, Reid stepped off the elevator.

"What happened?" I asked, turning to him.

"Where is she?" Araneae questioned.

"What's happening?" Laurel asked as we all waited for Reid's responses.

"From the information I've received and been able to ascertain, Ruby isn't at the hospital."

The three of us stared, dumbfounded. "No," I finally said when no one else spoke. "Find her."

"We're working on it. Patrick wanted everyone to know."

"Does Madeline?" Araneae asked.

"What about her trackers?" Laurel asked. "She has them the same as the rest of us, right?"

"I'm not sure what he's told Madeline," Reid responded. He turned to Laurel. "Yes, and the trackers in her shoes and phone are on the move outside the hospital."

"Her purse?" I asked.

"Still in Madeline's hospital room."

"Why would she leave without her purse?" I asked, looking at Araneae. We'd both been taken without our purses. That thought alone nearly buckled my knees. I reached up to my cheek, the one that had mostly healed thanks in part to the plastic surgery, as a vision of Jet, anger in his eyes as his hand repeatedly hit me, flashed before my eyes.

Was she taken by the same people?

I wrapped my arms around myself, sucking in a breath and silently saying a prayer that Ruby was safe.

"Lorna?" Araneae asked.

I shook my head, afraid if I spoke my concerns, they'd come out between sobs.

She reached for me. "You're remembering, aren't you?"

Nodding was all I could do as I swallowed.

"Fuck," Reid said. "Lorna, are you all right?"

"Yes" —my voice cracked— "I am now. Find Ruby and make sure she doesn't have memories like mine."

"I need to get back to 2, but I thought" —Reid ran his hand over the top of his head— "I just thought it would be better for you three to hear the news in person."

"Reid," Araneae said, "Ruby is young, but not that young. Think where we all were at her age."

"She's been protected, sheltered."

"She isn't dumb," I said, my voice growing stronger with determination. "She didn't just walk away from the hospital. Find her. She has been sheltered but not from living a danger-filled life. The girl grew up in the care of a Russian bratva. She lives here now. She understands safety. Do you have footage of her leaving the hospital?"

"Not yet. I need to get back to 2."

"We'll do whatever you need," Laurel said.

Reid nodded. "Ruby's phone and her shoes are signaling that they're moving at a high rate of speed. Mason and other Sparrows are following."

Laurel wrapped her arms around her midsection as she moved her head back and forth. "No, it's a trap."

Reid looked right at Laurel and stood taller. "Why would you say that?"

"It's like the shoes at the bunker."

Reid shook his head. "Your husband won't fall for a trap."

"He might to save Ruby or one of us." Laurel straightened her neck. "I love my husband and I know enough about his past and present to know he's more than capable of anything he sets his mind to. I also know that since he remembered Mason, he has triggers that Kader didn't have. In all that six feet seven of muscle, tattoos, and scars beats a heart of pure gold. Kader was successful because for years Mason lived without that heart. When it returned, it beats with one purpose."

Again, I felt tears threaten the backs of my eyes as I listened to my sister-in-law. "Protect."

Laurel nodded. "Reid, please, do what you can. I want Ruby back, and at the same time, I can't lose my husband again."

Reid nodded as his Adam's apple bobbed. "I'll do everything within my power, Laurel. I promise." He sucked in a breath and addressed all three of us. "I know this goes without saying" —he moved his gaze from one of us to the other— "but lockdown is in full swing."

He turned to head back to the elevator. As he did, I watched the way his shoulders sagged before straightening. The change in posture wasn't obvious and maybe the other women didn't see it. They didn't know my husband the way I did. The weight of this incident was sitting heavily on him. I could only imagine the way the other men were reacting.

Was it out of the question to think they might risk themselves to save her?

The answer was a resounding no.

"Reid," Laurel called out, "Ruby is smart."

Araneae and I nodded as he stepped into the elevator and turning, nodded our direction.

Once the elevator doors closed, Araneae slapped the sides of her thighs, the way she did when she was exasperated. "I want to do something." She paced in a circle in the common area. "I'm sick of being trapped and protected like a precious jewel hidden away in a fucking velvet-lined box."

I understood her emotion. It was impossible not to feel the same way. It was one thing to be trapped in this glass castle and be productive. It was another to feel totally helpless. Nevertheless, the influx of memories from our kidnapping gnawed at me. I didn't want to have Ruby experience anything close to what we had, and if I were honest, part of me feared being taken again.

"We couldn't leave if we wanted to," Laurel said. Looking to Araneae, she added, "You're the one who told me years ago that what keeps you here when everything inside of you wants to leave and wants to defy Sterling is...Sterling."

Araneae sighed as she plopped down on one of the sofas. "It is. I love him and the other men. But when it comes to us, including Ruby, I'm so scared they'll be reckless." Her gaze met Laurel's. "What made you say it's a trap?"

"Because Ruby wouldn't leave the hospital." Laurel stood taller. "She may be eighteen, but she's had more life experience than the majority of thirty-year-old women. And you know how excited she is about the baby."

"And she and Madeline are close," I added. "Their relationship is..." I searched for the right words.

"What I would strive to have if this baby" —Araneae laid her hand on her baby bump— "is a girl." She grinned. "No, no matter the gender. I admire all Madeline has done for Ruby. You're right, Ruby wouldn't have left, not willingly, and there are too many Sparrows for her to have been taken unwillingly."

"It's a hospital," Laurel said. "What about ambulances?"

Neither Araneae or I spoke.

"If somehow Ruby was unconscious, she could have been removed without suspicion in an ambulance."

I began texting the theory to Reid.

"People arrive in an ambulance; they don't leave in them," Araneae said.

Laurel shook her head. "They do leave. Transfers happen between hospitals all the time. It has to do with bed availability, staff, and required specialty. It wouldn't even raise an eyebrow."

I looked up. "I just sent that to Reid. He'll check the surveillance. He'll find her."

"They have to," Araneae said. "She has a little brother to meet."

REID

*A*s the elevator doors closed and the women disappeared, my fist hit the silver wall. Curses and accusations spewed from my mouth and more rang in my head. The impact echoed within the small chamber as nerve endings connected, reminding me of the wound still healing further up my arm.

I didn't give a fuck about my hand or the wound. If I'd been watching the hospital security footage instead of searching the financials of Nancy Pierce, I would have seen what happened. I could have stopped it.

This was my fault.

I would take the blame.

Other questions came to mind.

Where were the Sparrows Mason had scattered about?

What had they seen?

Closing my eyes, instead of thinking about them or Ruby, I recalled the look on my wife's face a few minutes ago. Her expression cut into me deeper than any damn bullet. With Araneae's question, I knew Lorna was remembering something from her kidnapping, and instead of being there for her, I was back on 2. The doors opened and I placed my palm in front of the scanner near the steel door.

Fuck if I wasn't coming up short at every damn turn.

My shoes clipped across the cement floor as I made my way to the bay of computers. This wouldn't be a job for one workstation; I began logging in across multiple computers and servers. First, I needed to scan every damn second of the hospital security feed.

Where did Ruby go?

Why would she leave the room or the floor?

I had one program following the signals Ruby's trackers were sending. According to the GPS, she was currently headed south on Interstate 90. Weekday traffic—I tapped into traffic cams. It was then that I recalled the text Lorna sent as I left the apartment. She could be on to something—more accurately, she said it was Laurel's idea. Credit wasn't the issue. The idea of an ambulance made perfect sense.

Instead of texting, I hit the call button to Mason.

"Do you have something?" he asked as the call connected.

"A theory. First, what are you hearing from Sparrows on-site?"

"Fucking nothing. No one saw her leave the unit."

It was as if she literally disappeared, evaporated into thin air.

Taking a deep breath, I exhaled. "I'm still looking at the security surveillance, and I can't fucking see her anywhere. But Laurel had an idea." I didn't wait for him to respond. "The hospital is on the university campus. Traffic is usually busy, especially this time of day. It's not easy to get to the interstate unless...An ambulance would be able to make it through the city faster than any car."

"Fuck," Mason responded. "We're not far behind where the GPS is saying she should be. There's not a fucking ambulance in sight."

There was a second voice coming from the background.

"We passed one," Mason said, "about three miles back. Fuck, Romero saw it parked to the side of the interstate."

I looked at the screen before me. "But her trackers are still moving."

"Did they slow?"

"I would need to go back to see that." I began hitting keys on the keyboard before me. "You're thinking there was a transfer."

"They might think an ambulance is too conspicuous. We'll keep following the trackers," Mason said. "I'll get capos to check out the ambulance. I have a rough idea of the mile marker."

"Okay. Keep communication open," I said. "Has anyone contacted Sparrow?"

"Fuck. He said he was in meetings today. I'll send him a message."

Neither one of us said goodbye as the call went dead.

There were multiple ideas running through my head. The interstate had cameras that the news stations used for reporting traffic issues. I could work to tap into those. First, my priority was the hospital. Pulling up the surveillance, I began checking the outside bays for ambulances. The emergency room was first and the most obvious. However, it wasn't the only one. There was a side bay.

I looked up as the steel door opened. My gaze met Laurel's. "It's fucking different to see a woman on this floor."

"Sterling offered me the space while on lockdown. I can't do what you do, but since I'm the only one with permission to be here, I'd like to help."

At this moment, I'd take all the help I could get. Often it would be either Mason or Patrick helping from here. Patrick was probably worried sick over his daughter while trying to keep his wife calm. Mason was on Interstate 90.

"Okay," I said, standing and going to Mason's workstation. I hit a few keys bringing up the hospital footage. "You can sit here." I went on to explain how she could move from camera to camera, and also move forward and backward in time. There was one thing about explaining anything to a genius: it didn't take much detail. In no time, Laurel was seated with her eyes set on the screens before her.

My phone buzzed with a text message from Patrick.

Patrick: *"TELL ME YOU HAVE HER."*

It was a metaphoric punch to the gut. I texted back.

Me: *"WE'RE SCOURING THE HOSPITAL FOOTAGE. MASON IS IN PURSUIT OF HER TRACKERS. HOW IS MADELINE?"*

Patrick: *"SHE'S WITH THE ANESTHESIOLOGIST AGAIN. I'M IN THE HALL."*

Me: *"WHEN DID RUBY LEAVE THE ROOM?"*

A rough time frame would help me follow her tracks.

Patrick: *"IT WAS WHEN THE ANESTHESIOLOGIST CAME IN THE FIRST TIME. SHE ASKED US TO LEAVE. RUBY AND I LEFT AND THEN RUBY RECEIVED A TEXT. I FUCKING SHOULD HAVE QUESTIONED HER. SHE SMILED, KISSED MY CHEEK, AND WALKED DOWN THE HALL. THEN I WAS INVITED BACK INTO THE ROOM. I DIDN'T THINK ABOUT RUBY UNTIL SOME TIME HAD PASSED. I KNEW WE WERE BEING PROTECTED BY SPARROWS AND WAS THINKING ABOUT MADELINE. FIND MY DAUGHTER."*

Me: *"WE WILL."*

"Ruby received a text message," I said aloud. "She and Patrick were out of the room because the anesthesiologist was inside."

Laurel turned my direction. "They stepped out of the room and she received a text? That seems convenient. Can we access her text messages?"

"I can." I began hitting keys. As I did, I glanced over at the screen Laurel was watching. Standing, I went to her. "Go backward to a few minutes ago" —I pointed to the view— "on that one, right outside their room." She did. The hallway was empty, similar to how it had been off and on all morning. "Fuck."

"What?" she asked.

I took a step back, my teeth clenching as I slid my hand behind my neck, exhaling. "Patrick just texted and said he was in the hallway."

"He's not there," Laurel said, stating the obvious. "And the time stamp appears right."

"Motherfucker. We're on a goddamned loop."

Laurel's large blue eyes turned to me. In her profession, remaining calm and steady was a learned trait, one that at this moment she'd forgotten. Terror showed in every feature of her expression. "Whoever took her was watching for the right moment."

I nodded.

"And they have the ability to hide it from you."

I nodded again. "They fucking knew we'd be watching."

Laurel's complexion paled as she fumbled for her phone. "It's them, whoever took the other women. I know in my gut."

"Who are you calling?"

"Mason." Her hands trembled as her head shook from side to side. "No. No. This is a trap. I know it is. They want him."

REID

"*A*nswer. Please answer," Laurel spoke into her phone.

I pulled up another program and traced Mason's phone. As I did, the GPS appeared. My gaze went from the map to Laurel as my stomach turned. "Laurel, his coordinates are the same as Ruby's."

Laurel hugged her phone to her chest as she looked at my screen. "Okay. He's busy saving her. That's why he can't answer."

I nodded, hoping she was right.

Laurel's blue gaze met mine. "I'll keep looking at the hospital footage. Let me know when Mason's on the move." She went back to her husband's desk and settled before the screen.

My next quest was to access Ruby's text messages.

Who sent her a text at the time for her to walk away?

We both turned as the steel door opened. Sparrow's dark gaze went from me to Laurel. It seemed as though her presence momentarily stalled whatever he'd been about to say or more accurately, yell.

I lifted my chin. "From here, from what I can see, it appears that Mason is now with Ruby."

He let out a breath, throwing his topcoat onto the weight bench. "What the hell happened?"

"We don't know," Laurel said. "I'm going through the hospital security footage, but we can't see what was happening. There is a nearly an hour loop of the same fifteen minutes in the hallway outside Madeline's room."

"When did it start?" I asked.

"After eleven this morning." She gasped. "It just reverted to real time."

"How can you tell?" Sparrow asked.

"Right here." She pointed to the screen. "See that door? I think it's to a supply closet. It was closed tight and now it's not, but no one has been there."

Sparrow's head shook from side to side. "Who the fuck is out-teching us?" He looked straight at me. "I told you to be sure no one else was in the system."

I lifted my hands. "I didn't see them. I still don't. There's no digital footprint."

The reality settled over us of what we'd believed before.

Sparrow nodded, his jaw clenched, and a vein came to life in his forehead. "Once we have Ruby home, we're headed to DC. I don't believe Walters. The fucking Order is involved and after my people. I want to know why."

"Me," Laurel said. "It's about me."

"With all the shit happening," I replied, "we haven't had time to discuss this, but Laurel, it doesn't make sense that they'd be after you as an endgame. If this is the Order, they have your formula or one like it. Whoever kidnapped Lorna and Araneae have a similar formula."

"Similar," she said, "but not the same and the staying power of what Araneae and Lorna were given appears to be waning. Araneae has almost complete recollection of her time after she woke in that cell. What about Lorna?"

"It's coming back in pieces. Lorna explained it as watching a television show from the end to the beginning. Slowly, the preceding scene is recalled."

"I truly think there's something to the ant venom. It somehow pulled her from the grasp of the pharmaceutical formula."

My phone buzzed. I recognized the name as one of our Sparrows, one I'd recently seen.

"Murray," I said, connecting the call.

"Mr. Murray, this is Sam."

A smile curled my lips at the memory of Sam at the warehouse with the baby. "Sam, what's happening?"

"Sir, I can't reach Mr. Pierce. I'm here with Marsha, near the mile marker he said. We found the ambulance."

"The one on the side of I-90?"

Chicago ranked last of the five largest cities in the United States on the number of ambulances per one hundred thousand people. It didn't make sense for one to be left abandoned.

"Yes, sir."

"Did you find anyone with the ambulance?"

"We don't know. We're near it. Mr. Pierce said to call him before getting close."

My mind went back to the bunkers and how Mason had known they could be booby-trapped. "Sam, hold on a minute." I put the phone on mute and relayed to Sparrow and Laurel that we had Sparrows at the abandoned ambulance. "Mason told them to call him when they arrived. Sam said Mason hasn't answered his call."

"He didn't answer for him either?" Laurel asked, small lines of worry forming around her eyes.

"Put Sam on speaker," Sparrow said.

I hit the button and laid the phone on the corner of the desktop. "Sam, Murray here. I'm also with Mr. Sparrow." I looked at Laurel and shook my head. It wasn't that she didn't matter or that having a woman with us was a weakness—Sam was with Marsha. It was that when you are in the presence of the king, the rest of us are less significant.

"Mr. Sparrow," Sam said, "from a distance, the ambulance looks safe. It's the standard box-like style. The windows in the back and side door are darkened and we haven't gotten close enough to see inside. There's no driver or anyone in the front cab."

Sparrow took a deep breath. "Sam, who's your backup?"

"Marsha, sir."

Sparrow nodded. "Have Marsha take your phone and change to video. I want to see what you're seeing."

"Yes, sir."

I muted the call while projecting my phone via Bluetooth to the large screen overhead.

"Back in Montana," I said as we waited for their video to connect, "Mason knew or suspected that the bunkers were a trap— that they were rigged. I'm wondering if he asked Sam to call because he thinks the same thing is possible about this ambulance."

"It could be," Laurel replied.

"Or simply a decoy to waste our time," Sparrow said.

"We" —I motioned between Laurel and I— "think they used the ambulance to get Ruby out of the hospital. It makes the most sense. What if she's still in it?"

"You said her trackers were with Mason," Sparrow said, "and I sure as fuck don't want to lose two Sparrows to a decoy."

The screen came to life as I unmuted my phone and spoke, "Murray."

"Let me try Mason again," Laurel whispered.

The video feed began. Sam's description of the ambulance was accurate, standard-fare white box with *Chicago Fire Dept.* on the side, red and yellow reflective lines surrounding the back two doors, and one side door near the front on the passenger side. The cab was similar to that of a van. The waning and waxing roar of passing cars came through the speakers.

"Walk around the ambulance from a distance. Don't touch it," Sparrow instructed.

Laurel shook her head, indicating she couldn't reach Mason. "Voicemail."

My heart thumped in my bruised chest as Marsha walked around the ambulance. "Do you have a mirror?" The mirror I was referring to was similar to a giant dental mirror—a mirror on a long stick angled to see beneath vehicles. The secret service used them regularly to check vehicles that came near people they protected.

"No, sir," Marsha replied.

"Fuck," Sparrow muttered.

"Boss, I can check underneath." It was Sam's voice.

Sparrow's head shook. "Sam, you're a big man. You touch a trip wire by mistake and I'm down a fucking good Sparrow, and your wife and kid are down someone they love."

In the midst of all the tension, I had to smile. Sterling Sparrow had literally thousands of people who worked under his umbrella, and yet he knew as much about Sam as I learned the other day.

"Mr. Sparrow," Marsha said, turning the camera around on her. "I can get under there and see what's happening. As a bonus, I'm well versed in explosives."

"First, can you see in the windows?" I asked.

With the camera in hand, Marsha lifted it higher to the windows in the back of the ambulance.

"Hold right there," I said, catching a flash of something within. "Sam, you're taller. Do not touch the ambulance. Tell us what you see."

Marsha stood back and videoed as Sam approached the back doors. The large blue ambulance decal partially hindered the view. His head shook. "Boss and Mr. Murray, there's a body bag in there. It looks like there's someone in it. Either that or it's blankets all bunched up to look like a body. Whatever it is, it's not moving."

"Ruby?" Laurel asked.

"Can you see a face?" Sparrow asked.

"No, boss. The body bag is zipped up tight and strapped to the stretcher."

My eyes shut and images of Ruby floated behind my closed lids. I looked again at the trackers. They hadn't moved from where they were ten minutes ago. "It's not her," I proclaimed. "Her trackers—"

"They fucking knew to take Araneae's and Lorna's shoes." Sparrow said, interrupting me. He turned and spoke toward the phone. "Marsha, there's not much of a clearance to get under the ambulance."

"I can do it, sir."

"She's petite," I whispered. "About Lorna's size."

"Be careful," Sparrow said. "You're also important to the Sparrows. I sure as fuck don't want to lose you either."

"Not my plan, Mr. Sparrow." Marsha handed Sam the phone as she stripped off her outer jacket and reached for the Velcro on her Kevlar vest.

"No," Sparrow said. "Don't take that off."

"It adds bulk. Without it I'll lose at least two inches."

"It fucking saved my life," I volunteered. "Be careful."

We all waited as Marsha knelt down and turned onto her back. With snake-like movements, she crawled where the height was a little greater, beneath the back bumper. Seconds became minutes as time ticked extremely slowly, and silently, we watched the scene unfold.

Finally, Marsha backed out from under the back of the vehicle. Stepping away, she brushed the gravel and dirt from her vest and slacks. "Mr. Sparrow, Mr. Pierce was right to be concerned. The ambulance is rigged. The configuration of the explosives isn't overly sophisticated. It's attached with a magnet. There's only one setup and it looks like a standard VBID with a tilt fuse set to activate when any of the back doors are opened or it's jostled. If someone drove off the road and hit this vehicle, they'd both go up in flames."

"What about the front doors?" I asked.

"They're not triggered, sir, but that tilt fuse could easily ignite with movement from within. Getting a body out of there could cause the vehicle to move and we'd have the same result."

I looked again at the screen showing the trackers. There were none. "What the fuck?"

Sparrow's dark stare came my way in an unspoken question.

"The trackers disappeared." As I spoke, they reappeared, on the move again away from the ambulance. "Fuck, they're back." I ran my hands over my eyes, making sure I wasn't hallucinating. "The interruption could have been a disruption in the satellite signal." Sometimes signals become momentarily blocked by other satellites or even debris floating around in space.

"Do you think that could be Ruby in that ambulance?" Sparrow asked me.

"I wish I could answer that with some sort of certainty. If we could reach Mason..." I took a deep breath. "Without visual, Ruby could be either place or neither."

"Marsha," Sparrow said louder to the phone, "will the explosive device detonate if we wait?"

"Not unless the tilt fuse is activated. Like I said, boss, if a car hit the vehicle or even if what we see in that body bag is a person and that person wakes and freaks out..." She sighed. "Miss Kelly isn't a big person, but if it is her, she could rightfully panic and there would be movement. Sir, I can't be certain."

Sparrow's frustration at the lack of definite answers showed in the strain of his jaw and the way the muscles strained on the sides of his face. He took another breath. "Marsha, I've heard some stories about you. Are they true?" Sparrow asked.

"That depends on what you've heard."

"You said it's a standard improvised explosive device." She'd used the acronym, but that was what she meant. "I don't want to lose you or Sam, but I need to know that isn't my niece in that body bag."

His niece.

"I can disarm it," Marsha replied, the camera moving to her face and showing her determination.

"If it blows, I'd lose both you and Sam and the person inside if there is one."

"I can do it, boss. Let me get a few tools from our car."

"Sam, stand back," Sparrow said, "and keep the video running."

LORNA

"*H*ey," Araneae said, standing in the doorway to her and Sparrow's bedroom as I pulled the sheets from their bed.

"Having trouble concentrating?" I asked.

"Yes. All I can think about is Ruby and Madeline and the hell Patrick must be going through right now." Araneae came in the room and opened the large drawer containing a fresh set of sheets. "I can help. These big beds are a pain in the ass alone."

A grin came to my lips. "I prefer to be in a big bed with a big man."

Her brown eyes met mine as her lips curled. "That wasn't what I meant, but I agree."

Together we went through the motions, stretching the bottom sheet, securing it in the corners, and fluffing the flat sheet as it landed like a parachute over the oversized mattress. As we finished the job, Araneae stepped onto the platform near one side and turning, sat on the edge of the freshly made bed.

I hadn't given it a lot of thought, mostly because this bed had been in the penthouse master bedroom suite since I moved in, but as I looked at my friend wringing her hands as she lay back, it occurred to me how Araneae was taller than me and yet on this bed she appeared small. The bed wasn't only a California king, it was also ridiculously high.

As a means to keep myself occupied, I asked, "Doesn't it bug you how high this bed is?"

Araneae grinned as she sat back up. "Sterling is tall."

It wasn't really an explanation, but it made sense.

She let out a long breath. "I admit it. Besides being worried, I'm jealous."

"You? You're the queen."

"Not much of a queen when I'm sequestered."

"Since we've all been sequestered for nearly the last month, I'm going to guess that you're jealous of the fact that Laurel is down in the man-only zone?" I was pretty certain that was her issue. God knew, the same thought had been rattling around in my head for the last few hours.

"Yes. It isn't even that I want to be down there; I want to know what's happening."

"Have you called your husband?" I asked.

Araneae shook her head. "No. When there are things happening, I'm always afraid to be a bother." She grinned. "Not because of him or his reaction. Sterling's never said that. It's that I know how I get when I'm involved in work. I know what it's like to be interrupted."

"You're the one person who I'm certain Sparrow doesn't mind interrupting him."

"Still, if he's on the phone or with someone..." She looked at her watch, the kind that did everything from emails and texts to steps and heart rate. "I keep checking for a text or something."

Holding on to one of the four posts surrounding her bed, I sighed. "More than being jealous, I'm so damn scared."

Her eyes met mine. "Me too. I don't want Ruby to experience anything we did."

I nodded. "That's what I keep thinking about." My fingers went to my cheek. "Does she know how to fight?"

Araneae shrugged. "Instinct."

"Do you remember the name of her bodyguard when she was with the bratva?" I asked.

"Oleg or Oreg...something like that."

"I bet he taught her."

Stepping down from the bed, Araneae walked to the wall of windows and stared out at the city and lake. "Sterling should have insisted that Ruby have someone with her." She spun toward me. "Garrett or Christian, a Sparrow who the men trust. Hell, there are female Sparrows too."

Coming up beside her, I too looked out at the city below. "Patrick was with her."

"Why would she walk away?"

Unable to answer, my lips came together as I shook my head.

When Araneae turned my way, her eyes glistened with unshed tears. "I was so scared—when we were taken." A tear trickled down her cheek. "I don't want Ruby to be that scared."

For a moment, we stood in silence until our phones both buzzed. "It's Patrick," Araneae said, looking at her watch.

I pulled my phone from my back pocket and read the text message aloud.

"THE DOCTOR WAS JUST IN. SHE SAID WE'RE GETTING CLOSE."

I texted back:

"THANK YOU FOR THE UPDATE."

. . .

I looked up at Araneae. "I wonder what Madeline knows about Ruby?"

"I can't imagine welcoming one child into the world while worried sick over the other one."

"Araneae, Lorna," Laurel's voice came from the first floor of the penthouse.

We both hurried from the master bedroom to the grand staircase. "We're up here. Did you find Ruby?"

Laurel was holding the end of the banister. Her smile bloomed as she nodded. "Yes."

Araneae and I met her at the bottom of the stairs.

"Where was she?"

"First," Laurel said, "she's safe."

"Tell us what happened," Araneae said, leading us all to the living room. "I want every detail of every second."

Laurel nodded. "Well..."

～

Laurel
Forty-five minutes ago in the command center...

"Keep the video running," Sterling commanded, his eyes set on the screen above.

"Laurel," Reid said as we all waited for Marsha to return with the necessary tools. "May I use your phone?"

I pulled it from my pocket, activated the screen with the recognition scan, and handed it his way. "Of course." When it came to anything electronic, I had no reason to doubt Reid. I knew my number was blocked and secured.

I stood beside Sterling with my arms crossed over my chest and my lip secured between my teeth, watching the ambulance with the sounds of interstate traffic in the background. Anxiety and concern emanated from the man at my side. Whether Ruby was in the ambulance or not, if Marsha didn't disarm the explosives exactly right, she would be dead, risking her life for a task Sparrow had requested. She would be another casualty in this recent battle in the never-ending Sparrow wars.

"Is she experienced?" I asked, more to break the tension than receive an answer.

"She is," Reid replied.

"She's not our best," Sterling said quietly. He turned toward me. "That would be your husband."

"Maybe you should wait—"

"No," Sterling interrupted. "You heard what Marsha said about the tilt fuse." He didn't wait for me to respond. "If a person is alive in that ambulance, we can assume he or she is unconscious. If that person wakes and panics..."

"It could cause the explosives to ignite," I said, finishing his sentence.

"Garrett, where are you?" Reid said into my phone. "I need someone I can trust. I'll send you the exact mile marker. Ruby's tracker, Mason's phone, and Romero's phone were in the same spot for over twenty minutes and now they're moving fucking fast, headed south on I-90. If there is a Sparrow closer, contact them and let me know."

There were pauses between his phrases. Though I couldn't hear Garrett, I was certain he was responding. With each phrase, my stomach twisted until I had knots upon knots. I tucked my fingers beneath my arms, trying to regain circulation and warmth. Sterling wasn't the only one stressed.

"She's back," Sterling announced to us. Speaking to the phone, he said, "You could take the phone with you under the carriage. Give us the deets on the explosive; Reid can talk you through disarming it."

I looked over to Reid. Despite Sterling putting him on the spot, he didn't appear concerned. His fingers were flying across a different keyboard. "Marsha, I need as much information to determine how many modules you'll need to disarm," he said.

"With all due respect, boss, time won't be my friend when I get under there. Like I said earlier, the explosive is attached magnetically. It would make it easier to break that bond with a stronger magnet and disarm it out here. I don't have a stronger magnet, and even if I did, the process would certainly trip the tilt fuse." She walked closer to Sam, the camera set on her determined expression. "I've seen similar devices. It doesn't appear much different from the IEDs used in Iraq."

"Most of those were homemade," Reid said quietly.

"If you need anything," Sterling said, "let us know. Sam's going to keep filming. If you think you did something wrong and you have time, get the fuck away."

"Mr. Sparrow, if there's a one hundredth of a chance that the person in that body bag is your niece and Mr. Kelly's daughter, I will not give up."

Looking down, I realized my hands were trembling as the only noises were those of traffic coming through the speakers. I turned to Reid. "If it blows, could it affect passing cars?"

He exhaled. "It depends on the amount and type of explosives. It's not like old bombs with gunpowder. This one probably is a chemical explosive."

I knew enough about chemicals to understand what Reid wasn't saying. It took a lower quantity of a chemical explosive to flash and explode than other materials. The packaging could look small, but it was an illusion. The oxidation process would be rapid and violent. If that occurred we'd never know who was inside, if anyone, and quite possibly, Sam too would be engulfed in the explosion. The Kevlar vest that saved Reid from a slug wouldn't save Marsha as the ambulance and everything around it went up in a flash of flames.

My lip went between my teeth as I watched Marsha crawling under the tailgate of the ambulance. Only her legs were visible as we all waited.

"I fucking wish I could see what she's seeing," Reid said.

Sterling's gaze didn't leave the screen. With each passing second, his neck grew tauter with muscles and cords popping to life. His arms too were crossed over his chest and his breaths were measured.

We waited.

The silence grew heavy around us, thick like a fog when we all took a breath. Marsha's legs moved, inching her out from under the back of the ambulance.

"Fuck, she did it." Sam's deep voice filled the command center as we all exhaled. The moment reminded me of war-room scenes in movies when everyone watching waited for the real players to succeed or fail, knowing they were acting upon the former's orders.

"Now look inside," Sterling said, obviously not yet ready to offer lavish praise.

Even though Marsha had said she'd disarmed the explosives, I held my breath as she and Sam reached for the door handles. The picture was jumpy as they moved about. Much like paramedics would do, once the doors were opened, they pulled the stretcher from the confines of the ambulance. The black body bag secured with the two belts jiggled as the stretcher's legs extended to the ground.

Marsha took the phone as the picture steadied.

A wave of nausea came over me as Sam unzipped the top of the bag.

Dark brown hair was the first thing I saw as I reached for a nearby chair. "Oh God," I muttered. "It is her."

The big man's large hand went into the bag. "Mr. Sparrow, she has a pulse." His head shook. "She's unconscious, but boss, she's alive."

"Call Patrick," Sparrow said to Reid. He spoke to Sam. "Unzip that fucking bag. I want to see that she's unharmed."

Sam didn't hesitate as he unlatched the belts and pulled down the central zipper. He turned toward the camera. "Miss Kelly looks like Sleeping Beauty, sir. I don't see anything to suggest she was harmed."

"I'm going to fucking find out who fed her the poison apple," Sterling said under his breath.

Seeing the intensity in his expression, I smiled, at this moment unwilling to explain the difference of *Snow White* versus *Sleeping Beauty*.

"Marsha and Sam," Sterling said, "you fucking did it. Bring her to the Sparrow tower."

"Yes, sir."

~

Lorna
Present time

I stared in amazement as Laurel finished her story. Hell, my stomach was in knots even though she'd started it with the knowledge that Ruby was found and unhurt.

"Laurel just told us," Araneae said into her phone. "I want her up here in the penthouse. They won't be for a few days. Yes. I love you, too." She smiled as she disconnected and turned to us. "Sterling is having her brought up here. Patrick and Madeline will be at the hospital until at least tomorrow. He also said Renita is on her way."

Shaking my head, I smiled. "I think Mason was right. She needs an office here." A thought occurred to me. "What about Mason?"

REID

"The text message to Ruby was from you," I said to Sparrow as he disconnected his call with his wife. "What the hell?"

I read from the screen before me.

"RUBY, THIS BLOCKED NUMBER IS STERLING. I HAVE A SURPRISE FOR YOUR MOTHER. GO BEYOND THE NURSES' STATION. THERE'S A MAN WAITING FOR YOU."

"From me? I wouldn't send Ruby a message luring her away from her protection," Sparrow said.

"Let me see your phone."

His dark gaze narrowed. "It's never out of my fucking sight."

"Sparrow."

He pulled it from the inside breast pocket of his suit jacket and placed it in my hand. I didn't move. I couldn't access his phone, the same as he couldn't access mine, not without a complicated backdoor option, the one Patrick used on mine when it was left at Maples's house.

Sparrow lifted it from my palm, allowed the retina scan to open his screen, and handed it back. I quickly accessed his text messages. Not surprisingly, there wasn't an outgoing message from him.

I offered him back his phone. "She should have known it wasn't you as your other messages didn't come up."

He took back his phone and placed it in his suit coat pocket. "I don't exactly text Ruby very often. Usually, it's Araneae. Can you track the blocked number?"

"I can try." I began a search, but all I could cross-reference was Ruby's number and the time. I could probably find out where the call originated from easier than the actual number.

"Who else would she trust? Pretending to be you was their best bet to get her to leave her protected area."

Sparrow removed his suit jacket, tossing it onto the weight bench with his topcoat. Undoing his cuff links, he paced the length of the large room and back, the soles of his leather loafers tapping across the floor.

"What was the fucking point?" I said aloud.

"I don't know. To prove they could, like taking Araneae and Lorna."

"It isn't making sense, not if Laurel is the target."

"Have we heard from Mason and Romero?"

I switched to the screen with the GPS trackers. His phone, Romero's phone, and Ruby's phone and shoes had turned around. They were headed north on I-90. Panning out on the GPS map, I realized how far Mason was from the hospital. "Fuck, who is at the hospital?"

"You mean besides Patrick and Madeline?"

"Shit. Yeah. I called Garrett away. Mason and Romero are on a fucking wild goose chase."

"I sent Christian there," Sparrow said, "and Mason had a team of Sparrows."

"Ones who let Ruby get taken right under our fucking noses," I pointed out.

I realized this wasn't exactly the time to point fingers. Hell, I was as guilty as anyone else for not watching the hospital footage and realizing that we were on a loop. Nevertheless, I had a gut feeling this was all a grand diversion. The question was for what purpose?

My phone rang. Garrett's name appeared on the screen. Instead of speaking privately, I hit speaker. "Garrett, Mr. Sparrow is with me. You're on speaker."

"I am where you told me to go, Mr. Murray. There's a dead man in a Camaro. I've called for cleanup."

My gaze met Sparrow's before I spoke. "Is he alone?"

"Yeah, I'd say he isn't very old, young twenties maybe. He's also wearing a paramedic uniform."

"Fuck," Sparrow said. "Garrett, is there any sign of Mr. Pierce?"

"No, boss. And I can't find anything as far as identification on him. No wallet. No phone. His pockets are clean."

"How did he die?"

"The hole in the side of his head would suggest a gunshot." There were some noises, like the opening of car doors. "The revolver is in the car near his feet. It looks like suicide."

I turned to Sparrow. "Call off the cleaning crew?"

Sparrow's nostrils flared. "The scene was set: paramedic steals an ambulance, it explodes, and he kills himself."

"Except it didn't explode." I spoke to Garrett. "What about the rest of the car?"

"Mr. Murray, it's as clean as a whistle, minus the blood and brain matter."

"Ruby's trackers were in that car or at least at that coordinate before Mason met up with him."

Sparrow pulled out his phone. He took a few steps, but before placing his call, he turned back to me. "Let the cleaning crew take care of things. We don't know where the gun came from. It could be a safe one from Mason or it could be a plant by whomever the fuck is doing this. I don't want to take a chance on anything with this scenario coming back on Sparrow."

"Garrett," I said, "follow through on the cleaning crew. Send me pics. I'll try to find out this man's identity."

"Yes, sir."

"Once the crew shows up, please head back to the hospital. I'm worried that this has all been a distraction."

"Yes, Mr. Murray. Pictures coming and I'll secure the cleanup crew. What about the ambulance?"

"We have another crew taking care of it." Fingerprints would be gone. The explosive would be removed and brought back here for Mason to analyze. The body bag and top of the stretcher would be removed in case Ruby's DNA could be discovered.

My phone dinged as Garrett's pictures came through. "Fuck, get his fingerprints. I can't do much with what's left of his face."

"I told you. Cause of death wasn't a mystery."

"Check his hands for residue."

"Will do."

As I hung up with Garrett, I noticed Sparrow, farther away, speaking intently on his phone. From the distance we were separated, I couldn't hear his words. That didn't mean I couldn't read his body language. His dark hair was tousled from his habit of running his fingers through it as he contemplated. With one hand holding tight to his phone and the other grasping the back of his neck, bulging his bicep beneath his light-gray starched shirt with his sleeves rolled up, tension radiated off of him. Like a cloud filled with various emotions, duties, and responsibilities, it surrounded him.

I understood.

He, his world, and his people had been threatened.

In all my years at Sparrow's side, never had anyone or any entity taken the liberty to infiltrate our most secured and loved members. Sparrow had meant what he said when he told Marsha and Sam they were important to the Sparrow outfit. The man I was seeing near the far hallway knew he wouldn't have his power without the devotion of those who served him and believed in his cause.

Recalling Sam's offer and Marsha's determination, I realized something I sometimes forgot or maybe I took for granted. Patrick, Mason, and I weren't the exception; we were the chosen Sparrows, but our dedication and loyalty wasn't ours alone. Sterling Sparrow had employees who were devoted beyond a paycheck. Those men and women on the street did what they did, day in and day out, because they believe in what Sterling Sparrow stands for.

Yes, the Sparrow world operated in the gray of legalities—that area between black and white. However, it took a delicate balance to keep Chicago and beyond operating in such a way that businesses in the shadows of illegality could coexist with the legal ones. It took determination to keep some enterprises like human trafficking away from our city while allowing others to operate.

Earlier, hearing Sparrow relay his concern, as well as his knowledge of both Sam and Marsha, reminded me that while those of us in the tower saw the real Sterling Sparrow, those out on the streets and in the trenches had every reason to believe that as individuals they mattered to the king. They weren't a forgotten name or number nor were they an unknown, disposable commodity. They cared about him—and his niece—because he knew and cared about them.

Sparrow stalked my direction. "Mason is on his way back."

"Where was he?"

"Sounds like a fucking wild goose chase or setup. Once Ruby is safe in the penthouse, we're gathering and getting a fucking handle on whatever is happening."

"I think we should tell more of the Sparrows on the street what's happening. I have the cameras, but nothing beats eyes and ears. Someone is trying to hurt us, and I think Sam and Marsha just showed us that the Sparrows care. We need to involve more of them."

Sparrow pinched the bridge of his nose as his eyes momentarily closed. "It's worth discussing." He looked up. "I want to book a trip to DC and according to Mason, Walters wants you there."

"So Mason will handle the command center or are we waiting for Patrick to get back?"

"Fuck," he muttered. His scowl softened as he looked at the phone in his hand. "Ruby is here. Sam and Marsha are bringing her to 1. We'll get her from there."

"Who else is on 1? I don't think letting anyone see her is a good idea."

Sparrow nodded as he typed a text. "Clearing the entry and hallway to conference room two. You and I will meet them there and take Ruby up to the penthouse."

Other Sparrows couldn't access 2. One also didn't connect to our private garage, apartments, or the penthouse. It was very secure. Of that we had no doubt. No one but one of us four could move Ruby from 1 to 2, and then up to the penthouse.

LORNA

"*R*eid just called," I said, looking up at Laurel and Araneae. "Dr. Dixon is almost to the garage. He's giving her straight access to the penthouse, and" —I felt my cheeks rise— "Ruby is on 1. He and Sparrow will bring her up."

"Is she still unconscious?" Laurel asked.

"I don't know."

The three of us headed upstairs to get a room ready for Ruby.

"There," Araneae said, pulling back the covers on the bed in a spare bedroom of the penthouse. "This is the room where Ruby slept when she first came to the tower."

I nodded. "I think she'll be comfortable." I turned to Laurel. "Have you seen Araneae's nursery?"

Her blue eyes opened wide. "Yes, but not since the furniture arrived."

Araneae smiled as her head shook. "It's not as complete as I'd like, but if you haven't noticed, things have been a little wild."

Sparrow did have trusted Sparrows who he would allow to enter our private residences. They were few in number and always supervised. They were the men and women who brought deliveries —large furniture-type deliveries—all the way to the apartments or penthouse. They were contractors and workers who painted and remodeled. However, it hadn't been one of those people who painted the nursery we'd just entered. They had added a pocket door for access from the master bedroom suite directly to the nursery, but Araneae and I had painted the walls. Just like Madeline and I had painted her baby's new room.

According to their doctor, the paint we used was safe and the painting was done in their second trimesters. Madeline's nursery was a light shade of blue with white trim. Her furniture was white, the crib, changing table, dresser, bookcase, and more.

"Oh, I love it," Laurel said. "My niece's nursery, a long time ago, was green and yellow. It's so bright."

"Since we've decided not to learn the gender of our baby, I wanted something that could be for a boy or a girl." Araneae walked over to the light wood-toned baby bed and ran her fingertips over the soft mint green sheet covered in pictures of sparrows, custom made for the newest Sparrow's arrival. "Every time I get nervous about the baby, I come in here and it makes me feel better." She turned toward the large rocking recliner. "I imagine sitting in that chair, holding our child." She giggled. "And the changing table..."

"Don't tell me," I said, "you imagine Sparrow standing there changing a diaper."

Araneae shook her head. "Even my imagination isn't that good."

"He'll help," Laurel said.

We both turned to her.

"Is that some psychology insight?" I asked.

"No. I saw him earlier as they were opening that body bag. Don't get me wrong. I completely respect all he's done and what he does. The institute is amazing, and I've seen him in public. I mostly see him here. I have heard about Allister Sparrow and also met Mrs. Sparrow."

Araneae's nose wrinkled. "That is why I will forever be known as Araneae Sparrow." She shrugged. "I guess even Mrs. Sterling Sparrow, but that's a bit old-fashioned for me."

"There's no mistaking Genevieve for you, Araneae, or vice versa," I said.

"Back to my theory," Laurel said with a grin. "Sterling has prided himself on being everything his father was and wasn't."

"Isn't that a bit contradictory?" I asked.

Laurel shrugged. "Better than." She looked at Araneae. "Wouldn't you agree?"

Araneae nodded. "Better at the good things and the polar opposite of the bad."

"From what you've been able to glean," Laurel asked, "how was Allister's and Genevieve's parenting skills?"

Before Araneae answered, I asked, "You're saying even with all of Chicago on his shoulders, Sparrow will change a diaper."

Laurel laughed. "I can't promise diaper changes. I can promise that the man I've gotten to know is determined, and when he cares, he cares fiercely. Today, he wouldn't admit it, but he was worried. He was frightened for Ruby and for Patrick. At the same time, he cared about the two Sparrows who were on the scene. And I bet at the same time, he was thinking about Madeline and the baby." She smiled. "He wants to be the father his wasn't." She reached out and gently grasped Araneae's arm. "He may just need you to show him the way."

Araneae took in a deep breath. "What if I don't know what to do?"

"You could call your mother-in-law."

Araneae shook her head.

"May I suggest," I said, "either of your mothers? I know the judge didn't raise a baby, but I bet she knows stuff. Rebecca raised you, and there's always Madeline."

Araneae nodded. "I'm sure I'll talk to my mothers. I do plan on watching and helping Madeline to learn."

My phone buzzed. When I looked up, my chest was as full of

excitement as it had been all day. "Ruby is on her way up." There was another message. "And Renita is waiting in the garage," I said to the other two ladies.

We all hurried from the nursery to the large staircase. As we reached the first floor of the penthouse, we heard the elevator open. All three of us slowed as we stepped back, allowing Sparrow an open path. Ruby was cradled in his arms, her knees bent and face against his chest. Her eyes were closed.

"Oh," Araneae said, her fingers going to her lips. "Is she going to be all right?"

Sparrow's gaze met his wife's. "I won't accept any other answer to that question except yes."

The determination in his voice echoed through the marble entry as he began the ascent up the staircase. Araneae was a step behind, explaining what room she had prepared. Their voices disappeared beyond the second-floor balcony.

My attention went to my husband. "Why?"

His head shook.

"Was it the same people who took us?"

"We don't fucking know. Mason chased down the person who had Ruby's shoes."

"You heard from him?" Laurel said, gripping the bottom of the banister as she took a small step backward.

"Sparrow did. I really don't know much." Reid stepped toward Laurel. "I'm sorry we didn't notify you. We do know he's on his way back."

Her blue eyes shone up at him as she nodded. "Thank you. I've been..." She didn't finish the sentence.

Reid smiled. "What you said earlier is true; Mason takes his role as everyone's protector seriously. I hope he learned something that will help."

The sound of the elevator again garnered our attention. This was the reason we hadn't followed the Sparrows upstairs. We turned as Renita stepped out of the elevator. Based upon her casual clothing, I believed we'd interrupted her in a moment of rare time off.

"Where is she?" Dr. Dixon asked.

"Upstairs," I replied. "We'll take you up there."

"What do you know about her?" she asked as we began climbing the stairs.

"I don't know anything" —I turned back to Laurel— "can you fill her in?"

Laurel began recounting the story that Ruby had been with her parents, the anesthesiologist asked her and Patrick to step out. She received a text message and kissed Patrick and said she'd be back. He knew they were surrounded by Sparrows.

"It appeared as though the text was from Sparrow," Reid said, bringing up the rear of our train.

My gaze went to his. "Appeared? It wasn't, though."

"No. It was a blocked number. I have traced it to a disposable phone purchased at a convenient mart near Northwestern's campus."

"That's near the Women's Hospital," Renita said. "Not very helpful."

"No, especially since it was bought with cash. I'm working on accessing their security to see if I can find the transaction. I do have a time stamp."

"We believe," Laurel went on, "Ruby was rendered unconscious and removed from the hospital via ambulance. I'm going to help Reid continue to search the footage of the hospital to see if we can figure out how she was taken right past Sparrows standing guard."

Renita stilled as we all congregated on the landing above the first-floor entry. "Sadly, there are many patients wheeled around the hallways of hospitals. If the kidnapper was properly dressed and had a badge, there wouldn't be much question."

"Badge?" Reid asked.

"Yes, most doors including shipping docks and ambulance bays require a badge to activate the doors. No one is just wheeling a patient from a hospital without passing security."

"Lorna," my husband said softly. "Sweetheart, I'm going back to 2. I have an idea."

"Do you mind if I come too after I see Ruby?" Laurel asked.

"Honestly, I'm happy to have your help."

Laurel smiled. "I'm happy I can."

As Reid turned to go back down the stairs, I looked to Laurel. "You know, we're a bit jealous. I've lived here a lot longer and I've only seen a small bit of 1 and less of 2."

"Lorna, you're always doing so much for everyone. I'm just happy I can do something—anything."

We all came to a stop outside the room that was Ruby's temporary place to stay. As Araneae tended to Ruby, Sparrow was the first to notice us as he stood back away from the bed with his arms crossed over his chest. "Doctor."

Renita went into the room.

"Thank you."

"Wait until you get my bill."

Sparrow's stoic expression cracked as a smile crept across his face. "I am grateful."

"I know that. Now, Laurel was filling in some blanks. What can you tell me?"

Quietly, I stepped in, Sparrow and Renita's conversation fading into the background as I sat on the far edge of the bed. Araneae was gently clearing Ruby's long dark hair away from her face.

"She looks like she is sleeping," I said.

Araneae nodded.

"Ladies and Mr. Sparrow," Renita said, "if you'll give me a little time alone with Ruby."

We all nodded as we stepped away and Araneae closed the door.

Araneae turned to Sparrow. "I sent Patrick a picture, so he knows she's safe."

He nodded. "Any news on the baby?"

"No." The answer came from all of us.

"Patrick texted me over an hour" —he looked at his watch— "over two hours ago and said it was soon."

"Babies have their own schedule," Laurel said with a grin.

REID

"Would you mind going through the hospital security videos?" I asked Laurel. "The area outside their hospital room is useless, but they had to get her from there down to an ambulance bay. I'm going to work on what Renita said. I think I can access all the badge readers throughout the hospital."

Laurel nodded as she sat at Mason's desk and resumed the task she'd started earlier in the day. For nearly the next hour, we worked in unison. Laurel took notes with time stamps and locations when she saw anyone on a gurney. I began a program that could cross-reference those times with doors restricting entry. Those weren't simply outside doors. Doors to enter the wing where Madeline was situated required a badge or a code. Doors to the actual obstetrics unit required a badge or code. The more I searched, the more I realized that every room, including supply closets, required some form of identification.

"Have you worked in hospitals?" I asked.

Laurel looked up from her notes and the screen. "I've had privileges at the university hospitals in Indianapolis. It was a teaching medical center."

"Northwestern is the same."

"Yes."

"How does that differ from nonteaching hospitals?"

Laurel stood and made her way to the coffee machine. After inspecting the available pods, she reached for one with a sigh.

"Are we missing something?"

"There's no decaf."

"How do you think we maintain our schedule? It's not with decaffeinated coffee."

As she waited for the coffee to sputter out its magic liquid, Laurel contemplated my question. "There are more people at a learning hospital. For example, I had privileges, but I didn't see patients. I was on-site in more of a facilitator role. I oversaw the interns' interaction with their patients. Now, I'll admit, I considered many of those patients mine in the sense that I wanted the best care possible, but my role was to see that the students provided the best care."

"Yet you had the same access that others had."

Laurel nodded. "You're looking into badges. Each one on the medical campus where I worked was unique. For example, I was working with patients in the mental health sector."

"If your badge would have shown up in obstetrics...?" I left the question open-ended.

"Yes," she said, gathering her cup of fresh coffee. "I think it would have worked, but it would have activated a red flag." As she again situated herself at her husband's workstation, Laurel reconsidered. "I take that back. There were more restricted areas. In mental health that included access to medications. A student couldn't access Schedule 3 or stronger medications without the presence of a prescribing medical doctor."

"So their badge wouldn't allow them access?"

"Right."

"And the unit which Madeline occupies was restricted. That

would mean that not every student or staff member would be able to enter."

"Right." Laurel turned toward the screen. "This supply closet has been bothering me." She pointed to the screen. "It isn't filled with brooms, if you ask me. See the scanner?"

Getting up from my chair, I moved closer. "Yes. It's pretty basic."

"And that door is closed right up until someone put this hallway camera on a loop. When the loop ends, the closet door isn't shut tight."

"They don't lock up brooms and mops?"

Laurel shrugged. "I can't answer that for sure. In my experience, the answer would be no. It would depend on what cleaning solutions are present. Even so, this door is restricted. My gut is saying that whoever took Ruby did so while accessing this closet. I don't know if they took her inside it or they were hiding within, waiting for the right moment."

I took a deep breath. "Either way, they had access."

"Can you find the data for this closet?"

"I sure as fuck can try."

I couldn't be sure how much time had passed. I'd compiled a list of badge numbers that had accessed that particular closet in the last ten hours. I'd cross-referenced it with badges that had entered the unit. They didn't all match. My mind told me there were practical reasons for that discrepancy. As an example, I often entered 2 with one of the other men. One of us scanned our palm or retina for entry and two or more of us entered. We had no way to record each person, only the one who used the scanner. In other words, the kidnapper could have entered the secure unit at the same time as someone else. That made sense for entering the wing, not the closet. The first person would most definitely realize they weren't alone in a closet.

"I think I found something," Laurel said. "Here. The time

stamp is 12:04. See this orderly wheeling this gurney out to a waiting ambulance. And there's a paramedic waiting."

Quickly, I reviewed the footage Marsha and Sam had sent us. "The number on the back of the ambulance where they found Ruby was forty-eight."

"Bingo," Laurel said with a grin. As she did, the steel door opened, and her husband entered. Laurel stood and ran toward Mason. He caught her mid-lunge as her arms wrapped around his shoulders.

"Hi," he said after they separated, a tired grin on his face as he hung up his jacket. "I didn't expect to see you down here."

"Laurel's been helping," I replied. "Sparrow gave her entry, and I'm recruiting." Laurel smiled in my direction. "It just so happens that she's perfect for the job of detective."

Mason tugged his wife closer and laid a kiss on the top of her head. "My doc is perfect for anything she puts her mind to."

Laurel took a step back and swatted Mason's arm. "Return my damn calls."

His smile morphed to a guilty smirk. "I was going to after I got back here." He walked near his workstation. The picture on the screen caught his attention. "That's him."

"Him who?" she asked.

"The man who had us speeding down I-90."

"Suicide or assisted?" I asked.

"Tomayto-tomahto. I heard you sent Garrett to check." Mason pulled up a second chair and sat. Leaning back, he stretched his arms over his head before relaxing them. "Cleanup crew was Sparrow's idea."

It wasn't really a question, but I nodded.

"Not necessary," he went on. "I left the scene as clean as it needed to be."

"Did he have ID on him when you got to him?"

Standing, Mason went to the jacket he'd taken off as he entered the floor and hung on a series of hooks. Next, he pulled out a plastic bag. "It's all here."

"The gun?"

"His. Technically, legit suicide. We got the information we could from him" —he looked my way— "I'll share more when Sparrow gets down here. We gave him the choice to let his employer know he compromised the situation or take another alternative."

"Oh my," Laurel said, "so he killed himself?"

"Doooc," Mason said, elongating the nickname. "He knew it was an easier road than what would have happened if his employer found out he fucked up."

"What did he fuck up?" I asked.

"I have it all in the evidence room on 1. In the car was a box lined with a special polymer. I think it is how they blocked the signal of Lorna and Araneae's shoes." Mason tilted his chin toward my computer station. "Look and see if you see Ruby's shoes and phone on 1."

I pulled up the GPS. "No."

"I want to do some more investigation on what they're using." Mason ran his fingers through his hair. "The box was in the back seat. If the kid had used it, we wouldn't have been able to follow. To give the kid a break, he was fucking freaked out. I don't think he knew what he signed up to do. It was just some extra cash. Once we caught up to him, he tried to run." Mason laughed. "He pulled the fuck over and bolted into a damn field. Fucking playing tag in a cornfield." Mason shook his hair. "Damn tassels shed everywhere."

The steel door opened. "Welcome back. How was Indiana?"

"Didn't quite make it that far."

"What made you turn around?" Sparrow asked.

"Jimmy boy had strict instructions to take Ruby's shoes and phone to a drop-off. The closer we got to that drop-off, the more my gut was telling me not to go. With just Romero and me and no other backup, I had the feeling" —his green gaze came to me— "it was a trap. The kid did his job. I'm starting to believe that his getting caught was part of the plan. I decided that the two of us weren't walking into an ambush."

Sparrow nodded and looked at Laurel. "Thank you for your help down here. In case you want a break, Ruby is awake and talking to her parents."

Laurel stood. "Oh, that's great news."

Sparrow smiled. "Ruby wanted to meet her little brother in person, but seeing him via FaceTime is the next best thing."

"He's born?" I'm not certain if one or all of us asked at the same time.

Sparrow turned to me and Mason. "They didn't call earlier because they wanted Ruby to be the first one to meet him. It sounds like they'll release Madeline tomorrow or the next day. When they do, the fucking flock of Sparrows around them will be so goddamned thick, no one is getting close to the Kellys."

"Do we have a name?" Laurel asked as she stood near the steel door.

Sparrow shrugged. "It's not one I'd pick, but Ruby was excited."

All of our attention was on Sparrow.

"Well?" Mason encouraged.

"Edward Oleg Kelly."

We all scoffed.

"Fucking rolls off the tongue," Mason said as Laurel disappeared beyond the steel door.

"Now, give me the details you didn't want to say in front of your wife," Sparrow ordered.

LORNA

"What can I get for you?" I asked as Ruby laid her iPad on the bed.

Her blue eyes glistened. "I wanted to be there."

Araneae reached for her hand. "I'm so sorry, Ruby. I know there's nothing we can do to make that up to you, but you'll be the first one to hold Edward when he gets home."

"Why did this happen? Why?"

Araneae and I looked at one another with the same uncertainty in our eyes. When she didn't speak, I tried to articulate what truly had no good answer. "There isn't a good reason. Why were your aunt and I taken? All we can say is that we're all happy that you're home and unharmed."

Ruby pulled the covers higher over her chest. "I'm scared. What if that would happen when I'm away at school and Uncle Sterling or my dad couldn't get help to me fast enough?"

I sat on the other edge of the queen-size bed and smoothed the comforter beneath my palm. "Ruby, do you remember what you said to me after Araneae and I came back from Montana?"

"To talk to people."

"Exactly," I said, "talk to us or your mom or dad. I can't promise any of us have answers, but we can all talk and more importantly listen."

She shrugged her slender shoulder. "I remember getting the text from Uncle Sterling. I now know it wasn't from him, but I guess I wasn't thinking. I was so excited for the baby." She grinned. "He has a name. Edward." Her chin fell to her chest as a tear streamed down her cheek.

"Ruby," Araneae said, "it's okay to be disappointed. It's not okay to focus on that. Your brother is healthy and will be home as soon as the doctors discharge him and your mom."

"I wish I could go back to the hospital." She dabbed her eyes with the corner of her sheet. "I hate living in a cage."

My chest inflated as I inhaled, wondering how many times I'd thought the same thing. "You don't."

Her head fell back to the headboard. "Sometimes it feels like it. Why can't we just be normal?"

"Because we're not," Araneae answered. "None of us are. You're not. Your mom and dad aren't. And do you know why that's a good thing?"

"Why?"

"Because if we were all normal, your parents wouldn't have found each other again."

"Maybe if we were normal," Ruby replied, "they never would have been separated."

Araneae and I shared a glance.

"Tell me," I said, "about your brother's name."

"You know that Edward is Dad's middle name."

Araneae and I looked at one another and both shrugged.

"You didn't know that?" Ruby asked, a bit more excitement to her tone. "How? You've known him longer than I have." She sat taller and smiled. "Well, it is. When Mom first mentioned it, I thought it was because she liked Edward" —Ruby looked at us for recognition— "from *Twilight*."

"Oh," Araneae and I said together.

"I guess I thought someone like your mom," Araneae said, "being in the Ivanov bratva, wouldn't have time for pop culture."

Ruby rolled her eyes. "In a lot of ways, it's like being here. Time was one thing we had in abundance. I think Mom was late to the party. She read them after she saw the movies on television. Then she went on and on about how much better the books were than the movies and wanted me to read them. Of course, since I'd already seen the movies, the characters in my head when I read the books were the actors and actresses." She pulled her knees up to her chest and wrapped her arms around them. "It would have been neat to imagine them with just the descriptions in the book."

Araneae grinned. "So Madeline is Team Edward. I can't wait to bring that up in conversation."

"Don't bother doing it around the men," I said. "I'm confident Reid has no idea what Team Edward versus Team Jacob is even about."

I noticed the way Ruby was smiling. "What?"

"Dad does."

"No way," Araneae said. "Your dad is clueless on things like that."

She slowly shook her head. "He surprises me with all the stuff he knows. You'd think doing whatever he does for Uncle Sterling would take up most of his time and headspace. He's good at seeing people—everyone. He always knows what to say or do." Her smile faded. "I should have told him where I was going."

"You're right about your dad," I said, trying to deflect the conversation's direction. Standing, I asked, "Now, is there anything I can get for you? Dr. Dixon said you need to drink plenty of fluids." I tipped my chin at the barely touched water bottle on her bedside stand.

Ruby turned to Araneae. "Would it do any good for me to talk to my dad to overrule Uncle Sterling?"

"About?" Araneae asked.

"Going back to the hospital?"

We both shook our heads.

"I don't know if the original decision came from your uncle," I said, "or your dad, but I'll place money on the fact that the two of them agree on keeping you as safe as possible."

Ruby sighed. "Will they catch these people?" When neither of us responded immediately, Ruby went on, "It's been almost a month since you two were taken. And now me." She laid her chin on her knees. "It was scary when Mr. Hillman did all those things, but I knew it was over."

"They're working very hard to find out who is behind this," Araneae said.

"I don't remember anything except the text message," Ruby said. "I went to the nurses' station. I thought it would be flowers or something." Her eyes grew wide. "I remember now. There was a guy with flowers. He was wearing scrubs like he worked at the hospital. I went to him, and he asked me if I was Ruby Kelly. I said yes and he had a clipboard with a paper for me to sign. When I reached for it" —she lifted her hand— "something poked me. He apologized and said he'd get me a Band-Aid." Ruby shook her head. "I started following him. The next thing I remember, I was here."

"If you remember more..." I began.

"...And I want to talk, I have plenty of people to talk to."

"I think you should tell Sterling, Reid, and Mason what you remember," Araneae said.

"That's about it."

"Okay, Ruby, if you won't tell me what to bring you, I'll be back up with six glasses of various beverages and five different sandwiches."

She lifted her chin and grinned. "I'm good with water." Turning toward the gray Chicago sky, visible through the windows, she added, "Hot chocolate would be nice. I promise I'll drink water too."

"And to eat?" I prompted.

"Pizza sounds good."

I nodded. "It does. I'll be glad to make all of us pizza for dinner. How about something for a snack?"

A few minutes later, I left Ruby and Araneae alone. As I was walking down the stairs, I sent a text to Reid.

"RUBY REMEMBERS A MAN DELIVERING FLOWERS AND A PRICK WHEN SHE REACHED FOR A CLIPBOARD. YOU SHOULD TALK TO HER."

I put my phone back in my pocket, uncertain my text would get a reply as my thoughts went to the salad Ruby had decided upon for a snack. In my head I was going through the list of ingredients. We were due for a grocery delivery; even so, I was certain I had everything I needed.

When I entered the kitchen, Laurel was there, sitting at the long table with a cup of coffee before her.

"Hey, have you had lunch?" I asked as she looked my way. "Ruby's awake."

"I went up, but you were all talking. I came back down."

Her voice seemed flat, not like herself.

Bypassing the salad-making for a minute, I went to the table and pulling out a chair, I sat with one leg beneath me and leaned over the cool granite. "What's the matter?"

She looked over to me with a faraway expression. "This is all my fault. You and Araneae and now Ruby."

"It is not."

"I never should have started recreating my formula. They told me not to."

Instead of replying to what she should or shouldn't do, I asked the question that has been bugging me. "What does my mother have to do with your research?"

"What?" She looked my direction.

"My mother. Whoever took us had her at that bunker. How does she fit into the equation?"

Laurel wrapped her fingers around the warm cup. "I don't think that she does. She's an outlier."

"What if she isn't?" A new thought occurred to me. "Could she have been in one of your trials?"

Laurel shrugged. "I doubt it. I know she hasn't been to the institute, and my original trials were in Indiana."

"We're in Chicago. Indianapolis isn't that far away."

"All of my participants were vetted. Remember me telling you that we had to ask questions to determine where in the brain the traumatic memories were centered?"

"Did you personally talk to each participant?"

"No," Laurel said, looking down into her cup. "My partner Russ did some and so did my assistant." She looked up, her eyes wide. "Shit."

"What?"

"My assistant was the one who was after my formula. She killed Russ, but she died, so it can't be her." Laurel's head shook from side to side. "What traumatic memories would your mother have had?"

Scoffing, I stood and went to the refrigerator to find the fixings for Ruby's salad. "I honestly couldn't tell you. I would assume if she had any, it would be a relationship gone bad."

"A breakup?"

"You know she was a prostitute? Those weren't usually long-term relationships."

Laurel stood, coming to the edge of the breakfast bar. "Did she have a pimp? Maybe a customer or boss who was abusive? We had multiple victims of domestic violence and rape."

I pulled the bag of romaine lettuce hearts from the crisper. "That would be karma."

"Prostitutes sell themselves consensually for money or product. That doesn't mean they're immune from sexual assault."

"Her name was Nancy Pierce. I don't believe she was ever married."

Laurel's lips pursed as she exhaled. "I have my old data, but participants were assigned numbers. We didn't use names."

"Did you have some consent form? They would've needed to sign their names then, right?"

"This feels farfetched."

Tearing the freshly washed pieces of lettuce, I laid them to dry on a paper towel before looking up. "Ruby asked if the men will catch the people who took us." I shrugged. "I have total faith in all of our men. I also know Araneae and I were taken from your home. Ruby was taken in the daylight from a busy hospital that not only has its own security but also was and is crawling with Sparrows. Someone is showing us that they can get us anywhere anytime."

"Is she frightened?"

"She is. Honestly, so am I."

Laurel tapped her fingernails on the granite breakfast bar and hummed. "You think there's a connection to your mother and all of this?"

"I didn't, but if there wasn't, why was she there?"

Laurel slapped the top of the breakfast bar. "You know what?"

"What?"

"When I went upstairs, I heard Ruby say something about living in a cage. If we're being honest, I've felt the same way. That's why I went to 2, to do something. I think what you're proposing is a wild goose chase, but after I go see Ruby, I'll go downstairs and look for the old flash drives with the data from my original research. It will be a needle in a haystack."

"I guess that will give you something to do."

Her smile grew. "It will. Did I ever tell you what Reid said about your cooking when you first married?"

"What?" I asked, thinking it was an odd change of subject.

Laurel smiled. "He said you have always made a great parmesan chicken and I agree."

For a millisecond, my thoughts went back to when we were first married. "It was all I knew how to make back then. My grandma taught me."

REID

"Why?" I asked, staring across our dining room table at my wife and lifting a piece of homemade pizza from my plate.

"Because I want to ask Anna what she knows about my mother."

Taking a bite of the pizza, I stalled, trying to come up with the words to tell Lorna that we were all working overtime on everything happening. We didn't have time for a field trip or a family reunion with the daughter of the man I gutted and the sister of the woman Mason tortured.

Tilting her head, Lorna pursed her lips, her green gaze simmering. "Are you going to answer me?"

"Didn't you say something about Anna being estranged from her father and sister?"

"Reid, I don't know. The last time I saw her was the morning after that ball in New York. Mason came to the motel, and hell, he already had my stuff packed. I never went back to my apartment, much less the motel. That was almost ten years ago. Things change in ten years."

Things had begun to change today, for the better. While Ruby's abduction was inexcusable, it gave us insight we'd been lacking. The kid in the Camaro—Jimmy Dole—wasn't a paramedic. He was the son of one. He'd borrowed his father's uniform and somehow managed to steal the ambulance. If we'd left him for the authorities to find, we might know more about the family. As it stands now, the ambulance has been found, explosive free and cleaned by our crew. The Camaro was still sitting along the side of I-90, tagged for impound. However, Jimmy Dole won't be found. His family will never know how he died, or when. He will forever be missing.

Before Jimmy had passed, he'd run his race through the cornfield, only to be tackled by Mason and immediately threatened by Romero. According to Mason, Jimmy began singing as soon as his body hit the ground.

His explanation to Mason and Romero was too twisted to have been made up on the spot.

The young man admitted that he was in debt to a loan shark, one we knew and one who had Sparrow's permission to operate in Chicago. Being Sparrow-approved meant we received our cut, so in fact, Jimmy was in debt to us.

When he was approached by a tall black-haired man for a one-time job, Jimmy saw it as his ticket out of debt. He had no idea the girl would be put into the ambulance unconscious, or so he claimed. He was told he'd be helping someone—a hospital patient—escape from an abusive relationship.

Once Ruby—he didn't know her name—was brought out of the hospital and he was instructed to put her in a body bag, Jimmy said he sensed that something wasn't right. Yet the payoff was too enticing. With the promise of cash, Jimmy drove away from the hospital as he'd been instructed. Stopping at an abandoned shopping mall, he moved Ruby into the body bag, taking her shoes and phone.

His next task was to stop on I-90 at a certain mile marker. When he did, the dark-haired man was waiting in a black Ford truck. He expected the man to take the girl. Instead, the man checked on her. He then put something under the ambulance and drove Jimmy to a nearby rest stop where Jimmy's car was waiting.

Jimmy claimed to repeatedly ask the man what was happening and who would get the girl. He was told she would be taken care of. The only other task was for Jimmy to drive the shoes and phone to a preset destination as fast as he could without attracting the attention of cops.

When Mason asked him about the box in his back seat, Jimmy claimed he didn't know its purpose and feared it was something that could harm him or his car. His suspicion of the dark-haired man was growing. Jimmy swore the man never told him to put the shoes and phone in the box.

That was the part of Jimmy's story that caused Mason to believe the drop-off point was a trap. If the dark-haired man had wanted the shoes and phone, he'd have kept them. If he didn't want them traced, he'd have told Jimmy to put them in the polymer-lined box. The dark-haired man wanted Jimmy to get caught and for Mason or another Sparrow to follow the breadcrumbs.

I did a quick search of Jimmy's family. His father currently worked for an ambulance service, one that serviced the greater Chicago area. He wasn't a direct employee of the hospital.

That meant that Jimmy couldn't have accessed the restricted unit. The man Ruby recalled with the flowers was someone else. When we showed her a picture of Andrew Jettison, she shook her head and said the man was younger.

Studying the hospital footage, we found the man with the flowers. He was good at avoiding cameras with a direct frontal image of his face. Nevertheless, I had a facial recognition program running.

Granted, we weren't ready to apprehend Andrew Jettison yet, but we were closer than we'd been twenty-four hours earlier. In confiscating Jimmy's phone, we had the contact number he'd called.

Much like the number that texted Ruby, this one went to a

disposable phone purchased at the same convenience store as the one that sent the text to her. We didn't have the full picture, but we were connecting dots. Mason also confiscated Jimmy's wallet and his one-thousand-dollar cash payoff.

"Reid," Lorna said as she stood, taking her glass into the kitchen.

I shook the thoughts of Jimmy soaking in acid away as I feigned a smile to my wife. "I don't think visiting Anna is a good idea. It's not common practice to introduce ourselves to family members of recent murder victims."

"Is it really introducing when we know one another, or we did?"

My eyes closed as I savored the pizza. We may live in Chicago, but Lorna's specialty pizza was New York style. "This is great. You don't make pizza often."

"Ruby requested it."

"I didn't talk to her for long," I admitted. "We just showed her a few pictures, like Patrick and Laurel did you and Araneae. How is she faring?"

With her water glass refilled, Lorna placed one fist on her hip. "She's scared, Reid. This has been going on too long and whoever these people are aren't scared of the Sparrows. It's like they're purposely poking the wasp nest."

I let out a long sigh. "We made some progress today."

"Did you, or did you make the progress they wanted you to make?"

"Why would you say that?"

"Laurel said that Mason was on a wild goose chase and then some kid shot himself." Her head shook. "Ruby doesn't want a head at her feet either."

My teeth clenched. There was a reason we kept our discussions private. Thankfully, Laurel hadn't heard everything. I smiled. "Really, sweetheart, no one is laying a head at her feet." I didn't say that the reason was because there wouldn't be much of one left.

Lorna shook her head. "We want this to end."

"Everyone does." I pushed my chair back from the table. "Don't you get it? You're right, someone is purposely going after our people—not our people, our *women*." I lifted my hands. "And don't give me some bullshit about not being made of glass. Damn it, Lorna, I know you're strong. Hell, Ruby is and so are Araneae, Laurel, and Madeline. We all know that you are the strongest, most beautiful, and intelligent women in the whole damn world." I reached for her shoulders. "There is only one reason why you're being targeted."

She looked up with her bright emerald eyes. "Tell me."

"To get to us. We don't know if it is to get to Sparrow or to Mason, or to bring down the whole fucking outfit. Is this about *you*?" My voice rose. "Fuck yeah. It's about all of us and we're not stopping until it's safe for you to go out when you want to." I nodded. "Yes, bodyguards will be necessary, but damn, you all deserve more freedom than you have while this Andrew Jettison and some partner of his are out there."

Lorna's brow furrowed. "Partner? Do you mean the blonde woman?"

It was my turn to be surprised. "You haven't mentioned her before."

"I did. I just hadn't remembered what she looked like. That just came to me recently. Araneae and I both recall her. She was petite but in charge. Araneae recalled her wearing gloves. I remember one of her hands was..." Lorna searched for the right words. "...different. The skin reminded me of Mason's, what it would look like without the tattoos."

My gut twisted. "Are you saying it looked burnt?"

"Scarred."

Fuck.

"I need to go back down to 2." I turned to the table. It had been the first meal we'd eaten with just the two of us in a while. It's not like there were candles lit and a bottle of wine opened, but nevertheless a pang of guilt came over me. "I'm sorry, Lorna."

She shook her head and standing on her tiptoes, kissed my cheek. "Don't apologize for making the world a better place."

Images of barrels with acid came to mind. "I'm not sure some would agree with your assessment of our goals."

"If the world is safer so that Ruby can go back to school and not be afraid, then it's a better place."

I wrapped my arm around Lorna's waist and pulled her closer until her small breasts pressed against my chest. The bruise was still there, but not having Lorna near wasn't an option I was willing to take. "I fucking love you."

"I love you, too. I still want to visit Anna."

Inhaling through my nose, I nodded. "Let's deal with one disaster at a time."

"How do you know they're not the same disaster?"

"Because that doesn't make sense."

"Exactly."

REID

*T*hree days later, the cabin of the plane filled with the rush of outside air as the plane slowed until the wheels touched down with barely a bump. Marianne kept us moving until we came to a stop at hangar one at Ronald Reagan Washington National Airport. It was the area of the airport not seen by many, exclusive for VIPs and their private planes.

I met my brother-in-law's gaze as Sparrow continued his conversation on his phone. He wasn't talking about what we were doing or why we were away from Chicago. Instead, he was dealing with a metaphoric fire at Sparrow Enterprises, having something to do with contractors maintaining the construction schedule and fulfilling obligations to investors. From the one side of the conversation I was hearing, Sparrow wasn't happy, and the person on the other end of the call was getting an earful.

When the plane stopped, I unfastened my seat belt and stood. Reaching for my suit coat, I shrugged it on, fastening the buttons. Our meeting required more than my normal blue jeans wardrobe. Beyond the windows, Washington DC was experiencing an unseasonably warm day. Unlike the clouds we'd left in Chicago, the sky in our nation's capital was bright and clear.

Keaton appeared from the aft of the plane. "Sirs, is there anything I can get for you before you deplane?" He tilted his head toward the opening door. "Your cars are waiting."

Without a closing salutation, Sparrow disconnected his call and slipped his phone into the inside breast pocket of his suit coat. "Tell Marianne to refuel. We won't be here long."

Neither Mason nor I spoke as we each took our turn, ducking our heads to fit through the doorway. At the top of the stairs, I took a moment to scan the tarmac. Despite the claim of exclusivity, the airstrip was filled with planes in varying colors and sizes. I also took note of the insignias, many indicating visitors and dignitaries from around the world.

Washington DC was in full legislative session as well as a popular tourist destination. This was the season that created full schedules for our lawmakers.

As I descended the stairs a few steps behind Sparrow and a few before Mason, my lungs filled with the warm autumn breeze. Over time, breathing was less painful.

Once again, we had a cover story for our visit to Washington DC. Sparrow's assistant at his Michigan Avenue office had him booked for another meeting with Edison Walters, senior legislative aide. With an exasperated sigh, Sparrow retrieved his phone and read a text message. When he was done, he nodded toward the car, the one driven by Garrett, our Sparrow who had flown ahead to coordinate much of our schedule as well as the other Sparrows. "Ride with me," Sparrow said as both cars pulled forward. "We have a few things to discuss before our meeting."

Granted, I was less experienced at our out-of-the-tower logistics, but after our last trip to DC, I knew the three of us riding together went against our normal protocol. The same unspoken recognition was in Mason's gaze as almost imperceptibly, his head shook.

Beside the fact this was against protocol, together we'd spent a great deal of our time over the last two days preparing for this meeting. There wasn't much we needed to discuss that hadn't already been said. Nevertheless, without acknowledging the second car, we all walked toward Garrett's SUV.

Opening the doors, Mason sat in the front seat, riding shotgun, while Sparrow and I sat in the back seat. It wasn't until we were moving that Sparrow spoke. "Good call, Garrett."

His head shook. "Gut feeling, boss. I don't have anything else other than he's new."

"Who?" I asked.

"The driver of the other car," Garrett replied.

The sounds of the city disappeared within the reinforced vehicle.

"How new?" Mason asked.

"Mr. Pierce, he's been vetted, I can vouch for that. He came to us from Hammond. It's that he wasn't our first choice for this trip. We have a few men down with illness. I prefer to have our new men and women prove their capabilities in a less hostile environment."

Looking beyond the windows at the pedestrians and monuments, nothing seemed hostile. However, we understood Garrett's meaning. Washington DC held more unknown variables than travel around and near Chicago.

"Will you send me his intake information?" I asked, curious if I could find any oddity.

Garrett's eyes met mine in the rearview mirror. "Yes, Mr. Murray. I can get his file to you by tonight."

"Stay with this vehicle, Garrett," Sparrow said, "and let the other driver know we don't need him today. Romero is in the suite. Christian is overseeing the hovering Sparrows. Have the driver report to him."

Garrett nodded. "Yes, boss."

"There's too much shit happening right now," Sparrow went on. "We're not taking any unnecessary chances." He looked toward me and Mason with a smirk. "This just means that the two of you will have to miss the splendor of the hotel lobby and join me in the employee elevator."

"Well, damn," Mason said. "I wore this monkey suit for nothing."

That wasn't really true. Our attire was more for the man who called this meeting than for a show of wealth in the hotel common areas. Sunlight disappeared as Garrett pulled the SUV into the parking garage of the Mandarin Oriental Hotel. As we'd done before, a flock of Sparrows arrived last night to set up and secure the hotel suite.

Unlike any of our previous meetings, this gathering had been called by Top himself. He'd communicated through the private secure network of the Order. His message had gone to Mason, saying he had information and wanted to meet in person. The two of them worked out a date and time. That was two days ago. The birth of Edward Kelly along with the abduction of his sister caused us to delay the meeting until today. If there was good news to share, it was that the entire Kelly family was safe at home in the glass tower.

With Mason and me on each side or in front and back of Sparrow, depending on where we were, we navigated our way to the back elevator. A Sparrow was waiting with the necessary access code to escort us up to the same suite we'd used nearly a month before.

As we approached the double doors, they opened inward.

"Walters just arrived," Romero said as he reached for the second door to the suite. "He's inside."

Sparrow's neck straightened. "The meeting isn't for another forty minutes."

"I'm aware, boss. I sent a text to Garrett, and he said you were on your way up."

Sparrow's nostrils flared as his dark gaze came our direction. His voice lowered. "Well, fuck. Walters asked for you, Reid. And

Mason" —he took a breath— "I know Walters has the ability to push your buttons. No matter what is said, my word is final."

It wasn't exactly a rousing pep talk before a ballgame. There were no high fives or shouts of impending triumph. By arriving early, Walters was asserting his dominance in a game where mutual admiration was the only means to victory.

Mason and I both nodded as Romero opened the second door leading to the suite.

As we filed inside, Edison Walters stood, tugging his suit coat and straightening his shoulders. Each time we met, I assessed his appearance, noting that he appeared older than the time before. Today it was more than wrinkles or gray hair. There was something in his composure that seemed a bit off even given my inexperience with the man.

"Mr. Walters," Sparrow said, walking toward him and extending his hand.

Shaking his head and not accepting the customary handshake, Walters cleared his throat. "Senator Jackson will be expecting the donation to his PAC that was mentioned by your assistant."

Sparrow stopped, squared his shoulders, and took a deep breath. "That isn't the reason for this meeting. We're here because you called us."

"My schedule has your name on it, Mr. Sparrow. That's a precarious closeness to a known criminal that I'm not comfortable maintaining."

What the fuck?

"Mr. Sparrow is a renowned businessman, *Mr. Walters*," Mason said, emphasizing his name. "If your secretary incorrectly identified him as anything other than such, the problem is with your office, not Mr. Sparrow."

Walters reached for his phone. "I will assume you haven't seen the news coming from Chicago." After pulling up the story he wanted, Walters handed his phone to Sparrow. "This coming to light the day of my meeting with you is unfortunate."

Sparrow read the news brief. With each passing second, an icy chill of emotionless composure emanated from his being. I knew Sterling Sparrow well enough to know that his lack of display was hiding a fury within.

His chin rose. "You're right. I hadn't seen that." Sparrow handed the cell phone back to Walters. "When did this story break?"

"Thirty minutes ago," Walters said. "I came over here immediately."

"I can assure you that story has no bearing on our meeting nor is it accurate."

I was usually the person with the information. I was the one who scoured the internet and news feeds. Being on the outside, literally and figuratively, as the one without knowledge and uncertain as to what they were discussing was not a place I enjoyed inhabiting.

My phone within my breast pocket vibrated. From his reaction, I believed Mason's had too. My skin crawled with the desire to check my phone, to know what was being said, yet that wasn't our role. Instead, Mason and I remained silent and still.

"The donation, Mr. Sparrow."

"You'll have it after we receive the information we want."

REID

$\mathcal{W}$alters put his hands in his pockets and took a few steps to the French doors. "Son, this is a fickle town." He turned. "I suppose Chicago is the same."

"Hardly, Mr. Walters," Sparrow replied. "You see, Washington DC changes direction depending upon the wind. For two or four years it will blow one direction and then it changes, sometimes for good and other times for worse. Chicago has been under steady leadership for nearly the last decade."

Walters's lips curled. "I believe the government on a city level also has its changes."

"Yes, it does. I'm not talking about the government. I'm talking about me."

"Very good, Mr. Sparrow. As I was saying, this city is fickle; I am not. The men and women who come here, or I suppose to your city, want to put their fingerprints on our country. Here, those individuals are simply the show that is Washington DC. They're the acts that keep the news media ratings high. Whether they are for the people or against is inconsequential as long as the buck stops with me."

Sparrow nodded. "I strive for the same. That article that you saw is only loosely based on truth. I'll have ten retractions as soon as our conversation is over."

"You believe you hold that much power?"

Sparrow took out his phone, sent a text, and put it back in his jacket pocket. "I do. The retractions will be out before we're done."

Walters nodded.

"Chicago," Sparrow said, "isn't the only city that has a similar power structure. I have counterparts throughout this country in cities large and small. We are the ones who make the tough decisions. Now if we're done with this philosophical discussion of power, who holds it, and who wields it, we're ready to hear what you have on Andrew Jettison and Stephanie Morehead."

"Both of the agents you named are deceased."

"So was I," Mason said.

Walters nodded. "Let me rephrase. Jettison and Morehead worked on the same team upon their inclusion into our agency. At that time, they were assigned new identities. As you're aware, Morehead was given an unusual assignment. Rarely do we deploy agents into a long-term mission." He looked at Mason. "The orders are to usually get in and get out, as I'm sure to which you can testify."

Mason nodded.

"In the meantime, Jettison served in a more traditional role."

"As for Morehead, you're aware that she decided to forget her pledge to the Order and to serving the republic to pursue financial compensation beyond that which was granted to her."

"We're aware," Mason said, "that Morehead double-crossed the Order."

"We were also told by you," Sparrow said, "that she died in the house fire on the ranch in Montana."

Walters took a deep breath as his finger curled near his chin. "Hmm. Did I say that?"

"You said," I began—I'd recently reviewed the audible tapes of that meeting, "and I quote 'we planned on apprehending her as she left the country. Instead, her body was discovered by our team.'"

"Yes, Mr. Murray. I do believe that was what I said."

"She's alive," Sparrow said. "And so is Jettison."

"They are no longer part of the Order."

"You let them go?" Mason questioned. "After what Stephanie Morehead did against the Order?"

"No, Pierce, I didn't." Walters pushed his hands back into his pockets. "Morehead was injured in the fire at your home. As I said, her body was discovered. She was not, however, deceased." His voice rose. "After the betrayal that she'd shown, I demanded that she be returned to one of our training sites." He turned to Sparrow. "The Order has soldiers in the war for this country. Betrayal is treason. Dying was too easy. She was nursed back to health. Considering her burns, it was a painful recovery."

Mason stiffened beside me.

"She came through," Walters continued. "Her memory was of our soldier, our agent. She did and said all the things that make a repentant soldier. She and Jettison were reunited on a mission. It was her first assignment back. I had my reservations, but I'm certain you know how difficult it is to recruit competent soldiers. And when I considered the resources we'd already used making her what she was, I wanted to believe she was true to the Order."

"What happened?" Sparrow asked.

Walter's head shook. "The mission involved infiltrating a stronghold. There was an explosion. It wasn't fire this time. The escape tunnel collapsed. According to our operatives, the two of them as well as one other were buried under tons of rubble."

"When you met with us last time," Sparrow said, "you knew that Jettison was alive. We told you we found his blood."

"I wasn't sure," Walters said. "Now I am. I have never asked for anyone else's help in a matter of the Order." His neck straightened. "I'm not doing that now. I'm offering our intel to you in an effort for both of our organizations to work together to rid us of these rogue operatives."

"Your intel?" I asked.

"Yes, Mr. Murray, Morehead and Jettison were not the only ones we lost on that mission. There was another, named Lawson. All three were reported buried and deceased in the rubble. Over a year ago, Lawson was located stateside, hospitalized as a John Doe, and suffering from delusional episodes. The Order found him and has since relieved him of his mental incapacity."

"Now Lawson is really dead," Mason clarified.

"Yes, Pierce, he is. You see, his delusions weren't figments of his imagination. No one survives who tells our secrets. A red flag came about when he named a deceased terrorist. Think of it as someone admitting to killing Hoffa. To the good fortune of the medical team, he wasn't believed.

"After our last meeting, I went back and read through the entirety of Lawson's file. It was incredibly comprehensive. With the information I gleaned, I have come to the conclusion that the three of them, Lawson, Jettison, and Morehead, planned their demise because of one particular connection they shared."

"What was that?" Sparrow asked.

"It's noteworthy to mention that all three received the same medication Pierce received," Walters said. "And even upon Morehead's recovery from the fire, she had no recollection of her life before the Order. It's my theory that her interest in you" —he turned to Sparrow— "is not you or Chicago, other than to cause problems, diversions, and interruptions. You welcomed Pierce back after he was granted a release from the Order few others have obtained. That makes you her enemy.

"It was discovered too late that she was in DC recently. You see, Morehead has an unacceptable flaw for an agent of the Order. She wants recognition. The Order isn't about the individual but the republic. I believe the continued woes you're facing are because she wants to be appreciated for her ability to disrupt your world. You mentioned that your wives had been given a pharmaceutical similar to what" —he turned to Mason— "your wife created?"

"Yes."

"It was a calling card. Morehead worked closely with your wife for years on that formula. She wants you to know it's her."

"You said that Laurel was to stop her research," Mason said. "It sounds as though Morehead isn't following that order."

Walters nodded. "One of her many transgressions."

"How does this connect to Jettison?" I asked.

Walters turned to me. "It is my assessment that Morehead's motivation is twofold. The first is her crusade." He turned to Mason. "She has deep-seated resentment regarding your wife. In her mind, your wife escaped her plan. Even more motivating than her need to complete what she began by killing your wife, Morehead and Jettison want to learn how you did it."

"How I did what?" Mason asked.

"How you regained your past. Morehead knows that you did, and I believe that is the true motivation behind her obsession. She wants to remember."

"I researched Jettison with his DNA," I said. "Couldn't Morehead do the same with her own?"

"Yes, Mr. Murray. What did you learn?"

"Jettison was a member of TACP, tactical air control party specialist, with a long list of commendations."

Walters nodded. "What else?"

"He was married and upon his death he left behind parents, siblings, and a child he probably never knew existed, born roughly nine months after his last leave and six months after his death." I shrugged. "His wife may not have even known she was pregnant until after she received word of his death."

"Everyone has a past, son," Walters said. "It's one thing to read about it, like a history lesson. It's another to recall it." Walters addressed Mason, "If we'd told you, Pierce, that you had a mother and sister, how would that have made you feel?"

"With all due respect, Top, neither you nor the Order," Mason said, "gave a shit about what I felt or how any of the operatives feel."

"That's true. Why?"

Mason's feet were spread, his back and neck straight, and his hands holding each other behind his back. Without the expensive suit, cowboy boots, and long hair it was easy to see he was a soldier in his very blood, in a way the rest of us never were. "Because those emotions would interfere with the current mission or the next one."

"Exactly. Morehead doesn't want a biography; she wants to remember. She wants memories. She wants what others take for granted, to hear a song and recall a dance or a feeling. She craves the small things that don't come about in a report: the first time she was kissed, if and when she was in love. She wants to recall even insignificant particulars that she may never have shared with another soul."

"How do you know this?" Sparrow asked.

"I don't," Walters said. "I have no concrete proof. I have over fifty years of service, including watching and manipulating the lives of others. There were clues in Lawson's ranting, but the conclusion is mine."

"Why are you willing to work with us even after that news story?" Sparrow asked.

Walters lifted his hands before bending down to retrieve a briefcase. "Do not fear. Your men thoroughly checked the contents prior to allowing me entry." He pulled out a plain manila envelope and handed it to me. "Mr. Murray."

Everyone watched as I bent the small clip and opened the flap. Tilting the envelope, a picture fell into my hand. It was a simple snapshot. The colors had faded over time. As I stared, my heart beat faster and a lump the size of my fist formed within my throat. It had been a long time since I'd seen his picture, yet I had no doubt that the smiling man beside a younger Edison Walters was, in fact, my father, Rendell Murray. I looked up at the man across the room. "Thank you."

"Pierce," Walters said, "emotions don't work in war and we're constantly in a war. Once you had those back along with your past, you were no longer a resource the Order could control. It's the medication that works to create our finest team. They are focused and loyal."

"*Most of them*," I wanted to say but didn't.

Walters tilted his chin toward me and the picture. "But there was a time I had them, a time when entering the Order was a decision based solely on patriotism. With each loss of a good man or woman, a good friend, it doesn't require a pharmaceutical to relieve a person of emotion or memories; it's a conscious choice. In my opinion, it's better not to have the memories or the emotions." Walters took a breath and looked at Sparrow. "It's my theory that Morehead wants that pain of remembering. As I said, I believe she's a hell of a lot better off without it, but that isn't why I'm willing to help. I'm willing to offer you what I can because Jettison and Morehead are deserters. In hindsight, I should have authorized Morehead's death after the fire. I didn't. I made a mistake and I want to rectify that." He smiled at me. "And she made a mistake I can't overlook."

"What was that, sir?" I asked.

"She went after Rendell's daughter-in-law. That is unacceptable."

LORNA

"He's beautiful," I said, staring down at the small baby boy in my arms. It was difficult not to pry his little fingers open and marvel at his small hands and count his fingers and his toes. I was certain I wasn't the only one who had done it; I knew the answer was five fingers on each hand, five toes on each tiny foot, yet I couldn't stop myself.

"We think so," Madeline said, sitting on the other sofa with her daughter at her side. Their similarity was striking as Ruby leaned into her mom. Both of their dark hair was piled on their heads in messy buns. Even after giving birth, Madeline could be mistaken for Ruby's sister instead of her mother. Their only glaring difference was their eyes. Ruby's were from Patrick and based on what I knew of Madeline's biological father, hers must have come from her mother. As they sat, they were in constant contact, one placing her hand on the other or tipping her head to the other's shoulder. I would suppose after what happened at the hospital, they both needed and wanted the connection their close proximity provided.

"Don't you just want to hold him all the time?" I asked.

Madeline grinned, her green eyes shining. "I do." She reached out to Ruby's knee. "When Ruby was born, she was so small that I could hold her for only a few minutes at a time. I spent two weeks sitting outside her small bassinet, watching her every move. I'd reach in and let her hold my finger. To have Edward be bigger, I have to remind myself to share him with the rest of his family."

Edward's small fingers closed around one of mine as she had described. Smiling, I looked up. "He has a grip like his sister."

Ruby beamed.

"How is Dad doing?" I asked.

"He's downstairs working in the command center while everyone is at some important meeting." Madeline sighed. "When it comes to Edward, Patrick's a natural."

"He hasn't changed a diaper yet," Ruby announced.

Madeline patted her daughter's knee. "He has. You forget time passes when you're asleep."

I imagined Patrick helping in the middle of the night. "You know, these men work all hours. Maybe it was all training for three a.m. diaper changes and feeding."

"I appreciate that Patrick doesn't want to leave the tower. It makes me feel..." Madeline sighed.

"Safer," I said, finishing her sentence. "Believe me, I get it. I'm so accustomed to Reid being near, even when things are tense." The baby in my arms stretched, his little arms moving above his head as his legs straightened, and still he slept. I couldn't stop a chuckle. "Obviously, Edward isn't concerned about the newest Sparrow fire."

A cloud passed over Madeline's green eyes.

"Are you all right?"

She patted Ruby's knee again. "Could you go make me a cup of coffee?"

"You're trying to get rid of me. You know the kitchen is right over there."

"Maybe you could make it in the penthouse?"

After kissing her mother's cheek, Ruby pulled a pair of earbuds from her pocket. "Talk, pretend I'm not here."

"I really would like that coffee," Madeline replied.

As Ruby walked away, Madeline met my gaze. "Edward will though, one day. I mean, I know that. Is it ridiculous that as a mom I'm scared for what my four-day-old son will become, the decisions he'll face, the choices he'll have?"

It was difficult to look at the innocent little baby and imagine that one day he could be a Sparrow in the dangerous sense of the name.

"You know, there are other options. Maybe he could work at his uncle's real estate company."

Madeline nodded. "You're right."

As Ruby returned with a mug of coffee, her head bobbed to whatever tune was playing within her ears. Setting the mug on the table, she plucked an earbud from one ear. "Is it safe? Are you done talking about Edward's future in the Sparrow mob?"

"It's not a mob," I replied.

"Oh, okay," Ruby said with a grin.

It was clear this teenager was too knowledgeable for her own good. "What are your thoughts, big sister?"

"I think I'll teach him Russian to broaden his prospects."

"*Ya lyublyu tabya*," Madeline replied. Looking at me, she added, "Bilingual isn't a bad thing."

I peered down at Edward. "You know what, Edward Kelly, you have a world full of prospects, and I'm certain that no matter what you choose, your dad, your mom, your sister, your aunt, your uncle, and everyone here in this tower will be there to cheer you on."

After all we'd been through, sitting in Madeline and Patrick's apartment with Edward in my arms and Madeline and Ruby right next to one another felt like a dream. Staring down at his little sleeping face with the fine dark peach fuzz on his head, I knew that we would all be all right. We'd have our hurdles to jump and times when we were tested, but we, the Sparrow family, would survive.

For only a moment, I thought back to the day Mason brought me to this tower. Tears prickled my eyes as I recalled how insecure

I'd been, how scary Sparrow seemed to me. If I'd been asked after we were told Mason died if I'd be here nearly a decade later, I would have laughed or maybe I would have cried. Looking up at the bond Madeline and Ruby shared, it was almost impossible to deny the fact that despite our last names or the blood in our veins, we were family.

I looked back at Madeline. "So, has Uncle Sterling held Edward?"

Ruby giggled. "He did."

"Really?"

"Araneae," Madeline said, "may have encouraged it, but he did it without arguing."

If I knew Sparrow and Araneae's relationship as well as I believed I did, the arguing occurred upstairs before they came for the visit. And if that's the case, it was pretty clear that the king had not won. Then again, maybe he was willing from the beginning. After all, he needs the practice.

"He didn't want to give him up," Ruby said. "I think it's funny to watch all these big men melt when they hold a baby."

She'd summed it up. Our world was changing for the better. Our family had grown and was growing.

"You won't believe who called to congratulate us," Madeline said, reaching for the mug of coffee.

My eyebrows rose as I considered the possibilities. "Someone from Detroit?"

She shook her head. "Mrs. Sparrow."

"Oh, I'm assuming you don't mean Araneae."

Madeline's lips formed a straight line and cheeks rose as she suppressed the grin. "You would be right. After I got over my shock, I decided it was a move in the right direction."

"The best direction to go."

Ruby had her phone in her grasp when her countenance changed. "Oh shit."

"Ruby," her mother scolded.

"What is it?" I asked.

"There's a breaking article that says the FBI is raiding Sparrow Enterprises."

"What?" we both replied.

"It says that they're following up on an anonymous tip regarding tax evasion." Concern showed in her blue eyes. "What does that mean? Will Uncle Sterling go to jail?"

"It means nothing," I said with all the confidence I could muster. "Your uncle prides himself on his abilities to outdo his father. I will put money on the fact that Sparrow Enterprises is as squeaky clean as it could possibly be. Sparrow Enterprises and the Sparrow Institute are completely legitimate. The FBI can look, but they won't find anything."

Ruby was back looking at her phone. "Yeah, it says here that via his personal assistant, Mr. Sterling Sparrow has issued a statement denying any wrongdoing and welcomes the FBI's efforts to thwart this attempt to delegitimize his name and company."

"Don't worry, Edward," I said, looking again at the beautiful boy in my arms. "Everything will be waiting for you one day. In the meantime, rest, eat, and grow."

"You forgot poop," Ruby added.

"That's what babies do."

The phone in my back pocket vibrated. Holding Edward against me, I reached for it and swiped the screen. It was a text from Reid. After reading it, I looked at the women on the other sofa. "Reid said their meeting went well, and they're on their way home."

"Did he mention the news article?"

My nose wrinkled. "He didn't, but if the media has a statement from Sparrow, I'd assume they're aware. Let's take one victory at a time." I looked down and up. "No, we have more than one victory. We have all of us here. You, Ruby, are safe. This little guy is healthy, and so are you, Madeline, and the men had a good meeting. We have a lot of victories."

REID

"Where's Sparrow?" Patrick asked as Mason and I entered the command center.

Mason shook his head as he peeled away his suit coat and hung it on the hooks. His tie was already MIA. I believed he'd placed it in the pocket of his suit jacket as soon as we boarded the plane. Looking up, he replied to Patrick, "At Sparrow Enterprises."

"He has nothing to worry about," Patrick stated calmly. Or maybe the adverb was tiredly, the jury was out. "Sparrow Enterprises' books are clean. Sparrow is obsessive and has a team dedicated to this kind of shit. I just finished taking a broad overview at the last seven years and like I said, nothing sends a red flag. This is just another jab. In theory, these probes and raids aren't unexpected; it just seems like right now we're getting fucked from all directions."

"It's her," Mason said, walking closer to the computers. "Top confirmed Stephanie Moore, a.k.a. Morehead, didn't die. Lorna remembered a blonde with a burnt hand in the bunker." He tipped his head back as he entwined his fingers at the nape of his neck and stretched. "Oh shit." He looked at me. "Didn't Zella say something about a blonde woman wearing gloves?"

"That's what Araneae said too," Patrick added. "She recalled a petite blonde who seemed in charge. Araneae said it was weird that she wore a glove. Only one, you know, like Michael Jackson without the dancing."

Mason went to his workstation and began typing. It took a minute or two for him to jump through the needed hoops, blast past the firewalls, avoid a few snares, and land himself within the dark web. Once he was there, he accessed the message Walters sent after our meeting.

"What's with the five million?" Patrick asked.

I nodded. "If you're talking about the donation to Senator Jackson, the answer is it was a promise to fulfill for today's meeting."

"Sounds like a bribe."

"Since it is earmarked for Jackson's environmental PAC, it can be justified. Sparrow is on record as a supporter of the mission statement."

"I hope it's worth it," Patrick said.

Mason leaned against the back of his chair, his eyes wide as he stared at his screen. "Fuck. He's handing them to us on a silver platter."

"Are you looking at Walters's message?" I asked as confirmation.

"Fuck yes. Top has logged her location over the last forty-five days. Shit, it goes back further than that. She and Jettison were in DC. Theoretically, she's poking the Order's wasp nest too."

"If he can come up with that data, why didn't the Order take them out?" Patrick stood and reached for the back of his chair. "Tell me again, why do we trust him?"

My thoughts went to the picture in my suit coat pocket. "I don't know him like Mason does," I said. "You're right. Walters is either for real or he's setting us up."

"There's no reason for him to set me up," Mason said. "I didn't defect from or betray the Order. I left with his blessing."

"Unless," I said, "you consider the part where he said you became no longer useful."

"I could be fucking useful."

Patrick and I both nodded. We'd seen him in action. However, what Walters had said made sense. To live the life of an agent or operative for the Order or even to have lived Kader's life required the ability to block away emotions, to see people as either targets or assets, and to carry out a job or an order without question or reservation. A split second of regret could mean losing your nerve or being killed.

"Wait a minute," I said. I turned to Patrick. "Have you listened to the audible of our meeting?"

"Yeah, Romero sent it as soon as Walters left."

"Okay, I've been thinking about what Walters said, and in my mind, I've been dividing the world up into targets and assets. Right now, Stephanie Morehead and Andrew Jettison believe the Sparrow world is a target. And yet they haven't taken a fucking A-bomb and wiped us off the map. Instead, they've picked and picked. Right now, Sparrow is on Michigan Avenue overseeing his own FBI raid." I began to walk as I talked. "Stephanie could have killed Araneae and Lorna." I turned to the other men. "Why didn't she?"

"She didn't want them. She wants Laurel, just like we thought," Mason said.

"But not for her formula."

"From the recording," Patrick began, "if Walters is right, Morehead wanted Laurel dead before you brought her here, long before you married."

"She hired me to do it," Mason admitted. "I didn't know it was Morehead. Those jobs didn't come with a calling card."

"And when you didn't do it," Patrick went on, "Morehead went to your ranch to do it herself."

"You saved Laurel again," I said.

"The Sparrows helped," Mason replied.

I kept going, "And Stephanie has a grudge."

Mason inhaled, his nostrils flaring. "She fucking killed Jackson."

"Yet she didn't kill Lorna or Araneae," I said. "Technically, she didn't kill Nancy either."

Patrick shook his head. "Cause of death was a combination of things, co-morbidities. Nancy Pierce's body was worn out. Her organs showed signs of deterioration, in some cases severe. Her liver was working at less than forty percent, and her kidneys were at sixty. It happens when the body is fighting other battles. She also had stage-two lung cancer, which she may not have even known. Laurel and Renita and I debated on the cause of the cancer. While there's always her history of smoking, Nancy also showed signs of asbestos poisoning. Many of the places she called home over the years were probably decrepit old buildings, the kind with not only asbestos but also lead paint. And it didn't take a doctor to see that she was also malnourished. The lack of nutrients gave the organs more reason to shut down. The malnourishment could have been Stephanie's doing."

"According to Zella," I said, "The man and woman bought Nancy from Maples over a year before we found her. What the fuck was Stephanie doing with her for that long?"

Mason jumped up from his chair. "Fuck, what if she was experimenting on her?"

"What do you mean?"

"Somehow, she found out that Nancy was my mother. I never put that on any of my military forms. I only listed Lorna, but that shit isn't that hard to find if you know where to look and dig deep enough. Anyway, if Top is right and Stephanie is trying to find out how I recovered my memories, what better person to try theories and shit on but a relative?"

"She didn't do anything like that to Lorna," I said, grateful to be able to say it. "And she's your sister."

"What are we going to do with the information from Walters?" Patrick asked.

"I say," I began, "we don't react. We spend the next twenty-four hours or more verifying. I fucking want to trust the man. Walters knew my father better than I did. But I can't trust someone I barely know and someone who advocates for wiping people's pasts to make them better soldiers."

Mason turned to Patrick. "The next time you're on the street or in a situation that requires you to pull the trigger, will you do it?"

"Fuck yeah."

"So having a kid doesn't make you soft?"

"I have *two* kids," Patrick corrected as he stood and made his way to the coffee machine. "And to answer your question, the fucking opposite." He straightened his shoulders, standing taller. "Jettison was involved in Ruby's abduction. The less sane part of me at this moment, you know the part that has awakened to a crying baby multiple times a night, yeah, well that part wants to read that fucking message on your computer from Walters. And then that part wants to not do what Reid just said. I don't want to verify. I want to get a flock of Sparrows and ambush their asses. And if you don't think I want to be the one who pulls the trigger simply because I now have two children, you'd be sadly mistaken."

"So you think Top is wrong about emotions and following orders?" Mason asked.

"I'm not sure that there is a right or wrong answer to that," I replied. "I believe it's up to the individual. It's why, even with the Order's magic memory blocker, people like Morehead and Jettison still go rogue. It's independent thought. Taking away a person's memory doesn't take that away." I lifted my hand toward Mason. "Look at you. Even before Laurel, you and Jack had said enough is enough. They took your memory of who you were, but they couldn't take that independence from you. Even Kader was independent."

"He still followed orders," Mason said.

"And if I'm right about what you've told us, he also was in control of his own life."

"My guess," Patrick added, "is that Morehead fit that bill, like you're saying. She was strong and independent. Wasn't she Laurel's assistant?"

"Yeah," Mason said, "in hindsight, that status in the university wasn't her choice; it was her placement from the Order. She had the credentials to exceed beyond that rank, but wasn't able to pursue that due to her assignment. I think that situation added to her dislike of Laurel."

The steel door opened, and we all turned, expecting to see Sparrow. Instead, it was Laurel carrying something small in her hand.

"Hi, I won't bother you for long, but I thought I could explain this better in person." She lifted a flash drive. "Lorna got me thinking the other day." She looked around. "Wait, I'm interrupting, aren't I? I can bring this to you later."

"No," Mason said with a sigh. "We were just talking about you."

"Oh, that's never good."

"And about your assistant," I said. "Stephanie Moore."

Laurel lifted the flash drive again. "It's interesting that you'd mention her." She walked up to Mason. "May I show this from one of your computers?"

He went to his workstation and brought a computer to life, different than the one with Top's message. "Here you go."

Laurel inserted the flash drive and sat in Mason's chair. Pulling up what appeared to be a file of PDFs, she turned to all of us. "I know I'm somehow connected to what's been happening." Laurel lifted her hand. "I don't need anyone to sugarcoat it for me. I'm assuming it is because I've been working on my research without permission from the agency Mason worked for."

"That's not—"

Interrupting her husband, Laurel continued. "I want to help in any way I can. A few days ago, Lorna asked me how I was connected to her mom. I was her daughter-in-law, but she never knew that, so after Lorna's and my discussion, I started going through all my original research."

"Laurel, we have—"

"Mason, let me finish. This won't take long. It's funny that you mentioned Stephanie Moore. I found this." Laurel turned and clicked on a saved document, a scan of a document. It appeared to be a consent form from the university where Laurel worked. The form had been filled out by hand and the writing wasn't exactly neat or clear, but as we all stared up at the screen, Laurel explained, "I don't recall meeting her. I don't believe I did." She moved the cursor. "But as you see, I wasn't the one who did her intake."

"Nancy Pierce was a participant in your study?" I asked, a bit dumbfounded.

"No," Laurel said. "She was a volunteer, but based on our criteria, she wasn't chosen."

Patrick stepped closer, looking up at the screen. "And Stephanie Moore did her intake." It wasn't a question but a confirmation. The evidence was in scrolling signatures high above. "What exactly was involved in the intake process and why wasn't she selected?"

"Being as we were in the early stages of our clinical trials," Laurel said, "in an effort to minimize extraneous variables, we had strict guidelines."

"So a coked-out whore wasn't your participant of choice?" Mason asked.

Laurel laid her hand on Mason's arm. "Honey, I think you may have some resentment issues regarding your mother you need to work out. Let me know when you're ready. I know a great counselor." She turned to me and Patrick. "I don't have Stephanie's notes; they weren't scanned. However, in the normal procedure, we did a medical history, including live births. We also ran blood tests and did a comprehensive psychological evaluation."

"Stephanie had the credentials to do all of that?" I asked.

"We had a phlebotomy team to collect the blood samples. As

for the psychological evaluation and medical history, they were simply forms with questions and answers. Stephanie as well as Russ's assistant, Jennifer Skills, both worked to complete the forms. Then those of us more qualified, Russ, Eric Olsen, and I, would go through and analyze the answers. This process ensured that our decisions were based on uniformly taken information, not our impression of the volunteer."

"I bet you paid your volunteers," Mason said.

Laurel exhaled. "Yes, all volunteers received a stipend, and if a person was chosen, they received additional payments at different checkpoints throughout our trial."

"This is big," I said, "Stephanie met Nancy." I looked at Mason. "You said you never mentioned Nancy on your military forms." I pointed up at the screen. "This is the connection."

"Stephanie died," Laurel said.

"No," Mason said as he crouched near Laurel's knees and placed his large hand on her thigh. "We thought she did. The evidence was mounting up that she could be the brains behind Andrew Jettison's brawn. And yet the fact that she was dead kept interrupting that theory. Earlier today we had a meeting in DC with someone from my old agency. He confirmed that Stephanie Morehead—her real last name—lived through the fire at the ranch."

Laurel's face paled. "How? The office was locked."

"We don't know the details. We'd been told they found a *body* in the office. What we weren't told until today was that the body was not deceased. She suffered burns."

"Like you?"

"From what Araneae and Lorna described," Patrick began, "not as severe. One hand and one side of her neck and face were affected."

"The office was locked tight and reinforced," Mason said. "I had built it like a fucking fortress. The entire room was steel enforced. With the fire, I'd assume the temperature was too extreme to support life. Somehow, she was found. Maybe it was before the fire was out. We let the original report stand on its own and never questioned it."

"What else did you learn?" Laurel asked. "You believe Stephanie is the one who took Araneae and Lorna. What about Ruby?"

"Jettison was involved, the man both Araneae and Lorna have called Jet," Mason answered. "And Maples's daughter also described both of them."

"And," I added, "we have unofficially identified Jettison regarding some problems we've been having here on the streets of Chicago."

"What does Stephanie want?" Laurel asked.

"The man we spoke to believes she has two goals," Mason began. "First, let me say, you being a decoy is out of the fucking question. We have more information now. We will take both of them down and track down any accomplices."

"What are her goals?" Laurel repeated.

"She wants to find out how my memories returned."

Laurel's eyes narrowed. "She doesn't want my formula or any other formula...she wants the antidote." She sighed. "I had never thought of that."

"Why don't you go back upstairs?" Mason said, standing and gently tugging his wife from his chair. "Your information is helpful. Thank you."

"Mason, what aren't you telling me?"

"We can talk about it later."

Laurel looked our direction. "Reid? Patrick?"

Mason reached for her hand. "Laurel, the man we spoke to believes that Stephanie wants to finish what she started at the ranch or before."

Laurel's chin rose. "She wants me dead."

LORNA

I watched from within as the SUV drove through a neighborhood outside of Chicago. The houses weren't new, but they were well maintained. The green lawns of summer were replaced with the drier autumn version. Trees that could canopy the streets with their foliage were mostly bare, leaving a few brown leaves holding on through the Chicago wind.

With my hand in Reid's, I turned his way. "It feels so strange to be out of the tower like this."

Reid lifted his chin to the front seat. We had Romero and Christian in the SUV with us and Mason and other Sparrows were in another car, following close behind. "You're safe, sweetheart. I wouldn't risk it if you weren't." He squeezed my hand. "You were the one who said you wanted to do this."

I nodded as I swallowed. "From what you and Mace said about Maples's house, Anna seems to be doing better if this is where she lives."

"She no longer manages the motel where you two worked."

"She doesn't?"

He grinned. "She started a public relations company, working from home. It's one of those ones where you pay to improve your online persona. If you have bad reviews, she will flood you with good ones. It sounds a little shady to me, but I guess..." He grinned. "...glass houses and all."

I smirked. "I'm actually nervous to talk to her."

"It's not going to be a surprise. She knows we're coming."

My eyes widened. "Isn't that dangerous? What if she has the police there to arrest you?"

"We've had her on full surveillance since she was contacted. She hasn't made any attempt to do that."

"Can you be sure?"

Tugging me closer, Reid kissed my forehead. "When it comes to you, I wouldn't take a chance if I wasn't one hundred percent sure." He reached for a lock of my hair and running it through his fingers, smiled. His voice lowered to a whisper. "I guess my days of fucking a brunette are over?"

Warmth filled my cheeks knowing that one or both of the men in the front may hear him. "Shh."

"Now, Mrs. Murray, that isn't an answer."

He was right. I couldn't add the length back to my hair, but I could find the right dye to return it to very close to its natural shade of red. "You, sir, are stuck with a redhead from now until forever. Besides, I thought Anna would recognize me better with red hair."

His thumb and finger captured my chin. "You could be bald and it would be your stunning eyes and gorgeous smile that will forever remain in anyone's memory."

I fluffed the side of my still-short hair. "So you're recommending a clean shave." I grinned. "Maintenance would be easier." I grinned. "I'll make you a deal. I'll go bald but only if you do, too."

"I want you to do whatever you want with your hair. However, if I get a say, I fell madly in love with a redhead and I like seeing her again."

As the SUV pulled into a parking space on the side of the road, I looked around at the homes and lawns. Compared to our castle in the sky, they would pale, but I wasn't seeing them through that perspective. My mind went back to Gordon Maples's house.

"I think she made it."

"Made it?" Reid asked.

"I guess we'll see."

My stomach twisted as Romero opened Reid's door and we both scooted from the back seat. The slacks and sweater I wore beneath my overcoat were nicer than my normal around-the-tower attire, but in no way ostentatious. I smiled up at my husband. He too was dressed for this occasion. His pants were tan and instead of a casual shirt or shirt and tie, he also wore a sweater. I liked the way the maroon wool pulled across his wide chest.

Lifting my hand, I cupped his cheek. "I love you. Thank you for supporting me with this."

"I don't know if it will help us find Missy," he said. "Hopefully, it will answer some questions about your mother."

I nodded.

Reid's large hand went to the small of my back as we walked across the street. My heeled boots clipped the cement as we grew closer to the yellow house with white trim and a white door. The lawn was free of leaves and the flower beds were cleared. There was a pumpkin on the porch and a wreath made of colorful silk leaves on the door.

Out of the corner of my eye, I saw the second vehicle, the one with my brother inside. I'd convinced him to let me do this without him. Anna and I had a past, but we also had a connection of being young females in the same home.

As we came to a stop on the small concrete porch, Reid nodded.

Taking a deep breath, I lifted my hand to knock, but before I did, I saw the doorbell. When I pushed it, chimes rang from within the house.

As soon as the door opened, I recognized Anna. She'd been my manager for over a year at the motel, and while we had that connection, as our eyes met, I felt an unexpected kinship. "Anna, thank you for seeing me."

"Lorna, I can't believe it's you."

"It is."

The woman before me had the same light-brown hair I recalled. It was shorter now, a stylish cut. Her eyes were the same gray, yet they seemed clearer. Her complexion was light and healthy, as was her body. While she had a few more curves than I did, she wasn't overweight by any means.

Anna smiled at me and then at Reid. "Hello" —she extended her hand to my husband— "if you're Lorna's husband, I'm sure you've heard all sorts of terrible stories about me."

"Yes," I said, "this is my husband, Reid."

Reid shook her hand and gracefully sidestepped addressing her comment. "I hadn't heard much of anything until recently."

Anna opened the door wider. "Please come in."

The scent of vanilla filled the front living room. It was then I saw the burning candles on her mantel. The glass doors of the enclosure were closed on her fireplace, yet by the presence of the fake logs within, it appeared as if the flames worked, not unlike ours, with a push of the button. The floor was hardwood and her furniture was neither bad nor good. My first thought was that it was much cleaner than I recalled Maples's house.

"May I take your coat?"

While this reunion was going better than I'd imagined, I hesitated, unsure how long we would stay. Finally, I shrugged the wool coat from my shoulders. Near the door was a brass hall tree. Anna hung it there. The whole incident struck me as quite possibly the first time Anna had ever done anything for me.

When she turned, she asked, "How are you doing, Lorna?"

I smiled. "I'm doing well. We've had a lot happening, and I wondered if you could help me learn a few things."

"I still can't believe you're here." Anna gestured toward the sofa and chairs. "Please, have a seat." As we did, she continued, "As you can imagine, I was a bit stunned to receive the call from..." She didn't finish the sentence.

"An associate of mine," Reid volunteered. "You mentioned stories, and I suppose I didn't want Lorna walking into unfriendly territory."

Anna had taken a seat in a nearby chair. "You're a good man."

I reached for Reid's hand. As his fingers encased mine, I agreed with Anna's assessment. My husband was a good man, actually, the best man.

"If anyone should be or has the right to be unfriendly," Anna said, "it should be you, Lorna. I think time and life have given me a bit of perspective. If you came here to hear me apologize, I will. I treated you horribly. I'm sorry."

A lump formed in my throat. "I think we could both apologize for things in the past, but let's move beyond that."

She sat straighter. "What is it you want to know?"

"My mother."

Anna flinched. "What about her?"

"What do you think we're about to ask?" Reid questioned.

Anna's head shook. "When we worked together, I was married to Justin. He wasn't a bad man" —her nose wrinkled— "but I admit to having set a pretty low bar where men were concerned. Justin never balked at raising Julie. That was his best trait."

"Your oldest?" I asked.

Anna nodded. "We had two others." She grinned. "Julie is taking classes to be a vet tech. I'm so proud of her. And the other two are still in high school. Do the two of you have children?"

I shook my head as Reid squeezed my hand. "No, we don't. We've been married for nearly ten years."

"Congratulations. Someday I may hit that milestone. You see, I'm no longer married to Justin. I think it is my current husband, Steve, who opened my eyes to so many things. He's a great dad even though he doesn't have to be." She scoffed. "He even gets along with Justin, for the kids. I never knew life could be like this. As you know, I didn't exactly see it growing up."

I waited.

"Steve and I went into counseling before we married. I wanted him to know what a mess he was getting by marrying me." Her gray eyes moistened. "He said he didn't care. The kids and I were worth weeding through some issues." She took a deep breath. "Some issues is a kind way to say a lot of BS.

"I had to come to terms with the difference between decisions I made and the ones that were made for me. I tell Julie all the time to make her own choices.

"Anyway, being mean to you, Lorna, was a choice I made. It was wrong."

"We both came out on the other side."

"Is that what you came here to hear?"

"No," I admitted, "but it was nice to hear. I'm happy for you, Anna. I really am. The reason we came is that I have a few questions. Do you see or did you see..." I wasn't certain how to title Gordon Maples.

"My father" —Anna took a breath— "and Julie's father." While I knew that was the case, I didn't respond. "I haven't seen him since Julie turned ten." Sitting taller, she swallowed. "I wouldn't let him be around her." Anna stood. "I'm sorry. May I get you two anything? This isn't an easy subject. I'm being honest because I know you know the truth."

I nodded. "I'm not trying to bring up old memories. It's the more recent past I'm interested in."

Anna nodded, taking her seat again.

"So how long has it been...what? Eight years?"

"Longer. It was back when we first began to work together. I still hadn't come to terms with everything, but I knew I had a responsibility to my daughter."

My lips pursed. "I'd say that makes you a good mother. And with that timetable, I don't believe you'll be able to help me."

"What did you want to know?"

"We have reason to believe my mother returned to your father's house in the recent past. I wondered why. I also was recently told that my mother had received payments. I can't ask her, and I am grasping at straws."

"I never saw Nancy, but Zella told me she was there."

"You were in contact with Zella?" Reid asked.

"Am, I guess." Anna shrugged. "I haven't heard from her in a couple weeks. I'm afraid she got messed up in whatever happened with our father. The police said that drugs were found. It doesn't take a genius to assume our dad tried to skim from someone who didn't like the idea. I know it sounds terrible, but when I was told he was dead, it was more of a relief than a shock. Until Julie turned eighteen, I was always afraid he'd try to claim custody. I think even Zella will agree we're better off without him. That is, if she gets and stays clean. She and little Gordy can have a better life. I know that for a fact."

"Maybe Zella could answer my questions," I said, knowing that wasn't possible.

"Don't take this wrong, Lorna," Anna replied, "but she wouldn't give you answers even if she could. Zella and I took different paths. Our communication is usually spurred by her need for cash or food for little Gordy. When it comes to her, I can't say no. It's something I'm working on. It's also one of the few things Steve is adamant about. He is okay with helping little Gordy, but he does not want drugs around our kids."

"Do you know if Nancy lived with your father recently?"

Anna nodded. "She was there for a while. I only know what Zella told me and none of it was complimentary. According to her, Nancy didn't have any money. She still held out that her tried-and-true commodity was of value."

I nodded. I wasn't here to defend my mother's choices.

"Zella also said she had forgetfulness issues."

"Forgetfulness?" I asked.

"The way Zella talked, Nancy was like one of those highs-and-lows people. One day she'd be real sullen and the next she would rant about all she'd lost and beg for...anything and everything. Given her surroundings, I'm going to assume she was either high, coming down, or looking for more. It's the cycle.

"Zella never said anything nice about her or anyone." Anna shrugged. "I wish I could tell you more, but I have the feeling it wasn't a great environment. My dad wasn't the only psychopath in our family. Zella has a mean streak. It's the reason her ex got full custody of her older kids before they were adults." Anna shook her head. "I know she isn't a good person. I also know I'm worried about her and little Gordy."

"Anna, did you hear anything about Nancy receiving payments?" Reid asked.

Anna's lips came together as she paused to give his question thought. "I don't recall specifically. I think there was a time Nancy was receiving some money." She looked at me. "It was when you were younger, but it ran out when you got older."

"That could just be SSI," I said, a bit disappointed.

"Yeah, it could," Anna replied, "but for some reason I think it was more. I can't say for sure. I'll be honest, Lorna, I never liked her. Well, until the night she clobbered my dad with that baseball bat."

I sat taller. "You knew about that?"

"I never said anything. After you all left, I cleaned the bat. When dad woke he thought he'd fallen. I was glad all of you were gone."

It made me laugh. "I was glad too." I looked over at my husband. "I think that's it."

We both stood.

Before I could put on my coat and say goodbye, Anna asked, "Is Nancy still...alive?"

"No," I replied, placing my arms in my overcoat. "I hadn't seen her in nearly twenty years. I was eighteen, right before my graduation from high school, she got in the cab of a semi-truck, and that was it."

Anna stood and walked to a table near the door. It was covered with small framed pictures and had an oval mirror over it. She opened the drawer and pulled out an envelope, an everyday letter envelope. When she turned, her expression was one of uncertainty. "I debated about this."

"What is it?" Reid asked.

Anna shook her head. "A few months ago, Zella brought this to me, asking me to give her money for it. She said it would be valuable because one day you or Nancy would come to get it."

It was my turn to shake my head. "I have no idea what you're talking about."

"That's the thing. When I got the call from" —she tilted her chin toward Reid— "your associate, I remembered this necklace."

"Necklace?"

Anna unfolded the envelope, opened the flap, and shook the necklace into the palm of her hand. "It's not fancy." She shrugged. "It seems cheap." Anna lifted the gold-colored chain. The pendant was shaped like a wispy leaf with small green gemstones. "Does it mean anything to you?"

"No."

"It's so odd that Zella predicted you or Nancy would come here." Anna grinned. "I'm glad it was you."

"Keep it," I said. "Maybe Zella is right and you can get money for it."

She extended her hand toward me. "I don't want money. I mean, everyone does but not for this cheap old thing. You can take it. Maybe it was Nancy's."

I reached for the chain and dangled the pendant before me. "How about Julie? Does she like jewelry?" I asked.

Anna shook her head. "Julie doesn't need anything to tie her to that world. Keep it. Throw it away. Sell it. I really don't care." She smiled. "You know for the first time in my life, I'm content and" —

she nodded toward the necklace— "I don't want anything tying me to the past."

Nodding, I placed the necklace in the pocket of my coat.

"I don't know," Anna said, "but looking at the two of you, I get the sense that you're content too. I think we're both much better off than we could have been."

"I agree."

Her countenance fell. "Didn't I hear that Mason died?"

"You might have heard that," Reid replied.

"I'm sorry."

"Thank you again, Anna. I'm glad we came even if we didn't learn much."

Anna looked at Reid. "Your associate has my number. I think it would be nice to stay in touch."

I smiled. "We'll see."

As Reid and I settled into the back seat with our Sparrows in the front seat and in the car behind, I sighed.

"Sweetheart, I'm sorry you didn't learn more."

"But I tried." I leaned over and kissed his cheek. "And for that, I'm thankful."

Once we were on the highway headed back to the city, I asked, "Where is little Gordy?"

REID

"I think he's better off with a stranger," Mason said.

"It's not your decision to make."

Mason ran his hand through his hair as he paced to the weight bench and back. "You have one meeting and suddenly you think Anna will make a great parent? Her sister sure as shit didn't. They were raised together."

"Anna said she was worried about Zella and Gordy. Zella will never be found. Anna can assume she took off or she is messed up with whoever's drugs were found at her father's house. I don't give a shit what she thinks. She should have the option to take on little Gordy." I was arguing my wife's point. The more I spoke, the more I saw its merit.

"And if she doesn't want him, she sends him to DCFS. My way, we guarantee him a good home."

I shook my head. "A home with money to buy a kid isn't the guarantee of a good home."

Mason stopped near my desk and picked up the gold necklace Anna gave to Lorna. "What is this?"

"It's the necklace Lorna mentioned last night."

Mason's eyes narrowed. "I'm not a jeweler, but it looks like cheap costume shit."

"It probably is."

"Tell Lorna not to wear it. It'll fucking turn her neck green."

"I told her I'd try to find out what I can. I figure the age of the metal and design of the pendant will tell me if it might have been something that mattered to Nancy."

Mason let out a long breath, dropping the necklace to the desk. "I need to get the fuck out of here. I've spent the last two days going back over traffic cams, security footage, and anything I could access to verify or nullify Top's information."

The steel door opened and Sparrow and Patrick entered.

"How are the FBI?" I asked.

Sparrow's dark stare came my way. "Fucking great. I'm having lunch catered to them today."

"Laced with a side of arsenic?" I asked.

"If only it were that easy."

"They won't come up with anything," Patrick reassured. "The way I see it, they should be done by today."

Sparrow's head shook. "I fucking hope so. Instead of them taking shit out of the building, we were able to push back and let them stay in the office space. At the time I thought it was a good idea. That way they couldn't add shit that wasn't there. Now I'm sick of their fucking faces." He shook his head. "Give me county, city, or state cops. I fucking hate the feds."

"Sorry," Patrick began. "I know you all needed me last night, but man..." He ran his hand down his face. "I needed some sleep."

It was pretty funny considering Patrick and well, all of us, were used to working with minimal slumber.

"Did you get some?" Mason asked.

Patrick sighed. "Four straight hours. I think it's a fucking record."

"We're good," Mason said. "I spent most of yesterday verifying Top's information."

"And?" Sparrow asked.

Mason shrugged. "It's verifiable."

"You sound enthusiastic," I said in observation.

"You're wondering if you can trust him or if this is a setup," Patrick said. "I'm wondering the same thing."

Mason lifted his own coffee mug and leaned against the counter, his cowboy boots crossed at his ankles. "Hear me out."

Sparrow and Patrick sat as we all turned to Mason.

"We're listening," Sparrow said.

My brother-in-law's expression was somewhere between angry and defeated. That alone had my attention. He lifted his coffee to his lips and then set the mug on the counter, crossing his arms over his chest.

"Fucking believe me that this has been the only goddamned thing on my mind. First, I'm damn good." He lifted his chin toward all of us. "We're all damn good. We had already discovered bits and pieces of the information that Top sent, but ours was not compiled as succinctly. What he sent...it's all right there. There's a pattern of behavior that I didn't pick up on." He took a deep breath and ran his fingers again through his hair. "Maybe I'm stuck on something he said the other day in DC. I admit, I can't separate my emotions for Laurel and Lorna, and from everyone in this case. I think I should confess to all of you that I screwed up." He turned to Patrick. "Fuck, my inability to see what was right in front of us could have resulted in Ruby's death. There's not a damn thing I can ever do to make that up to you, Madeline, or Ruby."

Sparrow stood, his brow furrowed. "Is this a resignation speech?"

Mason exhaled. "No, it's—"

"Good," Sparrow interrupted, "because unlike the fucking Order, I won't accept it. You're still useful to me whether you think so or not. You think you've screwed up on this? You think it's entirely your fault that we're not celebrating Morehead's and

Jettison's demise?" He didn't wait for Mason to answer. "Get the fuck over yourself."

"She was trained by the Order," Mason refuted. "I was too. I should have known she wasn't dead. Everything starting with the damn canister in the ventilation at the ranch screamed the Order and I didn't figure it out."

Sparrow turned to me and Patrick. "Which one of you had this entire debacle figured out, or was it both of you? Did you decide it was a fun pastime and you'd keep the information to yourselves?" Before we could respond, Sparrow turned back to Mason. "It wasn't only you. It's them and me too. Listen, I can handle another outfit. I can handle shit on our streets and gang fighting. I'm pissed as hell at the gun supply and that is fucking going to stop. Patrick made a trip to Dino's yesterday. The owner was given the choice to sell and get the fuck out of my city or stay and watch his business go up in flames."

"What?" I asked, hitting a few keys on my keyboard. "Fuck," I muttered, remembering a news story. The picture appeared before me with the caption of Dino's Liquor and the address. "He chose flames."

Sparrow lifted his chin. "It's a fucking message. I'm done messing around. My city. My rules. Fucking comply or you're done." He turned to Patrick. "Any news from the capos?"

Patrick nodded. "Yeah, I got a report down on 1 about an hour ago. Word is spreading fast, and six newly declared gang lords" —he shook his head— "who rule over maybe five people each, have gone to our capos asking for protection."

"From us?" I asked.

Patrick shrugged. "We protect our own. They pledge fidelity to Sparrow, turn in the firearms, and rat out others, and we'll find them a place."

Sparrow went on speaking to Mason. "Maybe Morehead understands better than most how to get to us. Hell" —he tipped his head up— "Walters was right about something. Those women up there…" He grinned at Patrick. "…and that little boy, yeah, they've fucking changed my perspective. They haven't made me weak or any one of you weak. They are what I always knew they'd be and why I fucking fought Lorna in the beginning. They're our Achilles' heel."

I lowered my chin, not wanting Sparrow to see my grin caused by the confession I'd known for over nine years.

"Reid, you're an asshole," Sparrow said.

Looking up, I saw his grin. "Everyone in this room is." I looked at Mason. "Don't tell us what we or you should have done. That time is over. Your gut was telling you it was the Order on the ranch. Walters misled us regarding Morehead's demise. Now we have that information. What do we need to do? What conclusion did you come to when you were going through Walter's information?"

Mason took a step away from the counter. "I think the reason I'm so pissed is that throughout this entire fucking time, she's been a step ahead or ten. Hell, she had my mother for over a year. She infiltrated my ranch." His head shook. "Jettison hurt Lorna." He looked up. "Ruby was taken right under our fucking noses. She wants us to know it's her. Like Top said, the memory thing with Lorna and Araneae was a calling card.

"When I would take on a job by myself, I would study my target. I would get to know that person. It's not the way it is in the Order. There, you're given a command, you do it. No research is necessary. It's the operative's job to trust the research was done. The timing was right. The only goal is completing the mission."

"Morehead has moved beyond being that operative," I said. "She's independently researching and testing us."

"I think if I put myself in her place," Mason said, "she hasn't done all of this for small rewards. She wants a big prize."

"What?" Patrick asked.

"Like the song says, she wants it all," Mason replied.

"She's not getting my city," Sparrow said. "Supplying a few small factions and subsets of gangs won't get her that."

"I'm not sure she wants the city," Mason said.

"She just doesn't want you to have it," I said to Sparrow.

His eyes narrowed. "Over my dead fucking body."

My pulse raced as we all stared at one another. The answer was right before us. In reality, it was above us. "Take out the tower. Make a show of killing Sterling Sparrow and anyone he held dear."

Mason nodded. "Fucking cartel 101."

Sparrow's head shook. "No, nothing above 1 is accessible. They aren't even on the blueprints. These floors don't exist."

Patrick began working on his computer. "We need to be sure there isn't something giving us away."

"Do you mean like a beacon?"

"She could have implanted something in Nancy or the women," Mason suggested.

"No," Sparrow said, "she would have known the women would be thoroughly examined, x-rays, ultrasounds, whatever we could safely do. They're clean."

"She won't give up as long as she is alive," Mason said.

"Maybe one of our deliveries?" I suggested.

"They're made by trusted capos and checked," Patrick said.

"What could she possibly think would be allowed in our fortress to show her exactly where we are located?" Sparrow asked.

Mason's green gaze met mine before I looked down at the necklace lying next to my keyboard. "Fuck."

LORNA

*L*ifting my face to the warm spray, I soaked in the shower's energy. Since Madeline had become occupied with Edward, I had begun setting my alarm for earlier. It was only a little after five in the morning and still, I woke to an empty bed.

The scents of bodywash, shampoo, and conditioner filled the humid shower stall as I prepared for the day. As I ran the loofah over my skin and down my torso, I noticed that the soreness was mostly gone. The bruising had disappeared and even the tenderness had improved. It was my breasts that ached.

It was as I dried myself that I thought about the time that had passed since our abduction in Montana. While in the beginning it seemed that days lasted for weeks, more recently time has accelerated. Edward would be a week old in another day. The tower was adjusting to the presence of a baby much like we'd welcomed Ruby.

Heck, as I thought about it, I took that timeline back further, as we'd welcomed Araneae, Mason and Laurel, and Madeline and Ruby. In some ways it seemed that it wasn't that long since Mason had brought me here, and in other ways, I felt this was my one true home.

Wrapping the towel around my head, I reached for my robe as I felt a new twinge in my abdomen. I rolled my eyes at the mirror, recognizing the sign. I never suffered too much from menstrual cramps, but that didn't mean I avoided them all together. That was probably the issue with my breasts. Hormones were a bitch.

How long had it been since my last period?

"Lorna." Reid's deep voice came from beyond the bathroom door as it simultaneously opened inward.

A smile came to my lips as I fastened the sash on the robe and I took him in. From his head to his toes, my man was all I ever dreamed of. Handsome beyond measure and exactly what Anna had said—a good man.

"You arrived too late. The robe is tied," I said, hoping he'd take the bait.

His fingers splayed around my waist as he pulled me close. My breasts flattened against his chest and my hips fell perfectly lower than his. "I love you."

Lifting my chin, I met his dark stare. "I set my alarm a bit early. I might have a few minutes to spare."

"Sweetheart, I want more than a few minutes with you."

With the tenor of his cadence and his strong hold, my core twisted; unlike before, this was wanton desire and I wasn't ashamed. Pushing up to my tiptoes, I pressed my lips against his. Firm and inviting, our faces turned and our tongues found one another.

As Reid pulled away, I saw the concern in his expression. The small lines near his eyes deepened as did the furrow of his brow. "I promise you, I will ravage you and make love until neither of us can move."

"But...not now?"

He shook his head and stepped back. With a tug of my hand,

Reid led me to the bedroom. "I need to tell you something. Just know, we don't have a lot of time. So listen very carefully."

My heart pounded in double time. "Reid, you're scaring me."

His palm came gently to my cheek. "That's exactly what I'm trying not to do. We're all working so you won't be scared anymore."

My gaze narrowed. "What is happening?"

Reid tilted his head toward the bed. "Please sit for a second."

I wrapped the robe tighter around me as I walked barefoot to our bed and sat on the edge. I didn't say a word as for the next few minutes, Reid laid out what was supposed to happen. Although there were huge gaps in his plan, things he wasn't telling me, I concentrated on one. "I don't want to leave the tower, Reid, and neither will any of the other women."

His lips formed a straight line. "Forever? Do you want to be stuck here forever?"

I stood, crossing my arms over my chest. "That's not what I meant."

"We've been compromised."

My stomach dropped as I stumbled backward to the edge of our bed and sat. "How?"

Reid came to me, crouching, and rested his large hand on my knee. "Sweetheart, we had no way of knowing. It wasn't until yesterday that we knew for certain. I want to believe Anna didn't know, but it might be too late to save her."

I stood and my head shook as I recalled our reunion. "What are you talking about? Anna isn't the bad person here. You met with her." Stepping around Reid, I walked to the windows and back. As I did, I pulled the towel wrap from my hair and shook out my damp tresses. "No. You may not kill Anna."

A smile threatened his stern facade. "You're cute when you give orders."

"I'm not being cute, Reid. I'm serious. Gordon Maples was a

piece of shit. Even Anna was relieved when she found out he was dead. Nothing says you're a great dad like your kids rejoicing at your demise." Dropping the towel, I slapped my robe-covered thighs. "Zella." I shook my head. "According to Anna, she too was a psycho. So, fine, she's dead, but not Anna. You saw her and her home. She's happy that her daughter is taking classes, and she has two other children. She's married to some guy named Steve and she's happy." My chest ached as I considered her dying because she met with me. "Please no. What about little Gordy? She would take care of him."

"Or everything we saw and heard was a fucking act."

"Or it was the truth."

Reid gripped my shoulders. "The necklace she gave you is a tracker. You and I carried that necklace into our private garage, up our private elevator, into our apartment, and then I took it to 2."

It felt as though the floor had just dropped out from beneath me as I staggered toward my husband. "Are you saying it was *me*? I compromised us all?"

"It was *us* and it wasn't intentional."

"Maybe Anna wasn't involved intentionally either."

Reid took a deep breath as his chest filled with air. "It wasn't intentional, but we have worked out how to use this to our advantage."

"What are you saying?"

"Sparrow has it worked out. Hurry and get dressed. Don't worry about breakfast. This change of plans is out of our norm and should be able to proceed without anyone realizing what's happening."

"Who is anyone?"

Reid didn't answer. Instead, he went on, "Garrett, Romero, and Christian will take all six of you to the airport. Marianne and Keaton are waiting. Her flight plan is for Texas, down to Ruby's place in South Padre. If our plan works as well as we hope, Marianne will be able to change the flight plan and circle back."

"And if it doesn't?" I asked.

"Then you will vacation in the Gulf surf while we deal with things here. The weather here is getting cold. This trip is not unusual."

"Edward isn't even a week old," I said, my volume rising. "No one takes a week-old baby to a seaside vacation."

"Technically, it's his family's home."

"No. Hell no," I said, breaking free of his grasp. "I don't want a vacation. I went to Montana, and that didn't work out well. I don't want to leave you again, and I think the others will agree."

"It's all been worked out."

All worked out by the men without our input.

I huffed and exhaled. "I don't understand why we can't stay here. Ever since I arrived in this tower, I've been told it's safe. Hell, you once left me alone on lockdown for five days. I was scared to death about what was happening to you and the other men, but I never worried about me. You and Sparrow and Mason, hell, even Patrick, all of you have preached about this tower's ability to keep us all protected."

"All of that is true," Reid said. "We're going to give them a window. It's a trap and maybe it won't work, but we have to try, and we sure as fuck aren't trying while any of you are here."

"A window? What the hell is a window?"

"An opening. The people we're fighting know we exist. And now they have confirmation that this is our castle—our stronghold. They should suspect we have everything well monitored. Our plan became accelerated because in the last twenty hours, there have been multiple systematic attempts on the power grid supplying this tower. I've watched and verified that the hits on the grid weren't from the city or the power company. I believe that these people now know where we are and are going to try to disable our surveillance and infiltrate our home."

I was trying to comprehend. "You're going to let them?"

Reid swallowed, his Adam's apple bobbing. "It's a good plan, Lorna. Christian will accompany you to South Padre Island. Garrett and Romero have intricate roles to play here. We have to make this seem like a normal day. That's why it's imperative that you and the others leave soon."

REID

The mood was unusually somber as I opened our apartment door and carrying an overnight bag for Lorna, the two of us were met by everyone in the common area. Everyone wasn't an exaggeration. It was barely six in the morning, and everyone, including Edward who was covered by a blanket and quiet in a car seat, was present.

By the expressions on all the ladies' faces, I wasn't the only husband who received pushback. Lorna walked away from me and stood by Araneae as Sparrow began to speak.

"Thank you."

His unusual spoken gratitude was met with less-than-receptive murmurs.

"There isn't much I can say that you haven't already heard. I" — he cleared his throat— "we all understand your apprehension. Fuck, I..." He looked at Ruby and grinned. "...this plan is foolproof in the sense that you will be safe, every one of you. The house staff on the island has been made aware that guests are arriving. We reached out to our trusted Sparrows in Texas and they are sweeping the house, the ventilation, every damn inch to assure that you will be safe. If we can take care of business here in a speedy fashion, you'll be rerouted. If not, I want you all to know you're not in jeopardy while away."

"What about you?"

Sparrow's dark gaze went to the woman who asked the question, the only one who would. Instead of answering right away, he took a few steps until he was nose to nose with his wife. In front of everyone, one of his hands went to her arm while the other went to her enlarged midsection. For a second, there was no one else as they stared at each other. "We discussed this."

"Sterling." Her voice cracked with just his name.

His lips came to the top of her head before his head ducked, whispering something close to her ear that no one else could hear. I didn't know what he'd said, but I watched as for a moment, her anguish turned to blush and a smile emerged.

Backing away, he reached for Araneae's hands. "I promise you and our child" —he looked up at the entire group— "and every one of you that we will all be back here together. We will be here, we'll be in fucking Texas, Montana, and Canada. The threat we've been facing is about to end. Our lives will go on." He smiled at the car seat. "Better than before and a hell of a lot better than the shit we've been dealing with."

Patrick tilted his head toward the elevator. "The cars are waiting. I'm riding to the airport with Romero, Maddie, Ruby, and Edward. Garrett and Christian will take Araneae, Lorna, and Laurel. The SUVs are reinforced for chemical as well as trajectory assault.

"We have room for one overnight bag per person." He scanned the women. "Did everyone leave their phones in their apartments?"

They all nodded.

"When we get to the cars, you'll all remove your shoes. Garrett has slippers and flip-flops." He lifted his hand. "I'm sorry. We didn't have time to get you all untraceable shoes.

"When you're at the airport, pretend to be excited. There is no reason for our current problems to be watching, but there could be someone. If word gets out that you were seen boarding the Sparrow plane, it should appear that you are celebrating an impending vacation."

"At six in the morning?" Ruby asked, before laying her head on her mother's shoulder.

Patrick's lips pursed as he nodded. "You can do it, Ruby. I've seen you in action."

"Yeah, yeah."

"We'll go down first," Patrick said, scanning the elevator. "Then you can ride down next."

As Madeline and Ruby entered the elevator, Patrick followed carrying the car seat.

Lorna left the ladies and came back to me. As she did, all three of them went to their husbands.

"I'm so scared," Lorna said, her stunning emerald eyes staring up at me.

I couldn't not reach out and hold her. As I lifted my hands to her waist, Lorna's arms came up around my neck and I pulled her against me. A thought came to mind and grinning, I went with it. "Do you remember when we had to sneak around?"

Lorna nodded.

"I was never a rule breaker until your bad influence."

A tear slid down her cheek. "You're a good man, Reid, the best. I love you and I don't want to lose you. You promised me fifty or sixty more years and I want every minute."

"I also promised to ravage you until neither of us could move."

Her closed-lip smile grew and her green gaze glistened. "I want that too. I want it all."

It was what I'd said about Morehead.

"I'll spend every minute," I said, "of my life making sure you have it all."

"Make sure you have lots of minutes."

The elevator returned. Over Lorna's head, I saw as Sparrow walked Araneae and Mason walked Laurel to the threshold.

Lorna's small hand came to my cheek. "I have it, you know? I have it all. You have given me everything I never knew I wanted. Please let me continue to share it with you."

I reached for her hand and walked her toward the elevator. Handing her the strap to the bag she'd packed, I let her walk away. "Lorna." She turned back. "Fifty years."

"I want sixty."

The doors closed.

After the elevator had deposited all of our loved ones to the garage, it came back with nothing but shoes. It was a strange and unnerving feeling to take each woman's shoes to their own residence. For a moment, I recalled the heels Lorna had worn the night we met. If I looked, I believed I'd find them in our closet.

My heart wouldn't let me look. Not yet.

Mason looked up from his phone as I continued to monitor multiple fronts.

"Patrick said they're all on board. He, Garrett, and Romero will wait until Marianne completes the checklist and the bird takes flight."

After his announcement, Mason also went back to his computer screens. Together we were not only watching the systematic attack on the power grid, we were running backup programs we'd installed but never imagined needing. All of our information was secure from the world, but not from here. If this floor of the tower was infiltrated, someone with Morehead's skills could quite possibly access data that was better left hidden.

Sparrow's books at Sparrow Enterprises were spotless. Last night, the feds had announced that they would conclude their probe—the term they used. The media called it a raid—later today.

That was his legitimate business. It would be another story altogether if our information that we had here was to become known, either by the feds or media or anyone. We'd begun the process sometime during the night.

Slowly, but surely, we were backing everything up to a securer new cloud and deleting the original from our files. It would be a pain in the ass to recover. Nevertheless, the risk of exposure would harm more than what would remain of the Sparrow world.

We had information on both friends and enemies of the Sparrows, a significant amount dating back to when Allister Sparrow shared the reign of this city with Rubio McFadden. There was intel on government officials, elected and appointed, local and federal, as well as judges on all levels of the courts. Name a branch of government and we had something. Move beyond that to local, county, city, and state personnel. Leave the acceptable world and enter that of the counterparts Sparrow mentioned to Walters: kingpins, dons, godfathers, cartel bosses, and mob bosses to name a few of the titles.

Our fortress held secrets belonging to people around this state, country, continent, hemisphere, and globe. As Mason, Patrick, and I worked on moving information, it became a real possibility that accessing our network and files would benefit Morehead and propel her as a controlling player if she were to overthrow the Sparrow world.

"I believe Top wasn't completely correct in Morehead's goals," Mason said as the clock continued to tick.

"What do you think he missed?"

"World domination."

It made me grin. "That's Sparrow's goal."

Sparrow had left the tower to make an appearance at his Michigan Avenue offices. In different times, that wouldn't have been necessary. With a half dozen FBI agents going through his networks, it was essential.

"Yeah," Mason replied. "I think Top has been either in power or isolated for so long, he underestimated Morehead's thirst for supremacy."

"The other two goals?" I asked. "Memories and Laurel?"

"He's on target with those. The thing is, I couldn't tell her how I did it—how I regained my memories. I could tell her it was Laurel, but that would only make her more determined to kill my wife."

"There wasn't any drug or pharmaceutical involved, was there?"

Mason shook his head. "No, just a blue-eyed stare and a woman who saw through me." He smirked. "Fucking blew me out of the water. The more I saw her, talked to her, got to know her, the more I wanted."

As he spoke, I thought of Lorna, my wife and his sister. "I want it all."

"Patrick's back," Mason said, watching a subdivided screen. He, Garrett, and Romero, entered the elevator. Garrett and Romero would end up on 1. We had determined our most vulnerable spots. One was it. It was the floor most frequented by others. The other was the direct elevator to the penthouse. Though it was rarely used, and never by any of us, it existed. I had control of its ability to ascend and descend as well as stop it and operate the doors. Nevertheless, it remained a possibility.

"They're fucking getting close with the power grid," I said.

"The generators will kick on," Mason said. "And Morehead knows that. She'll know her window to bypass our security is limited."

"Ten seconds if we're lucky," I said, "and thirty to forty if she is."

Forty seconds seemed like a fucking lifetime when it came to what she could do. And though we hadn't discussed him, Jettison too had been trained by the Order.

"I have confirmation of Jettison two city blocks from the garage entrance," Mason said.

My stomach twisted.

"Fuck," I looked at the surveillance. "Sparrow just entered the tunnel."

"Jettison is literally seconds behind."

"Lock the garage entrance and call Sparrow and Patrick."

LORNA

Half an hour earlier

I wasn't sure how jovial we appeared leaving the cars, walking across the tarmac, and climbing the stairs to the bird plane. I'm sure it had some official name and make and probably numbers. We all referred to it as the bird plane. Painted on the outside to resemble a giant sparrow, it was big, luxurious, and ostentatious.

Bypassing the front room with the round table, most of us made our way to the center section and found seats for takeoff. The last person in the Sparrow parade was Madeline. Patrick carried Edward's car seat as he followed her up the stairs. It was a few minutes later when Patrick entered the area with the rest of us. Since all the chairs were facing the huge television screen, he had our full attention as he took the car seat to a chair near the windows and strapped it in, as it had been in the car.

"I've asked Christian to carry Edward," he said, "but if he has business, would one of you? The weight of the car seat exceeds what Maddie should lift."

Ruby's hand went up. "I've got him."

Patrick went to her and cupping her cheeks, tilted her head forward, and placed a kiss on the top of her hair. "I'm not giving up my hot chocolate."

Ruby smiled. "Get us back home, Dad. Mom and Edward need you."

"You don't?"

She sniffed. "I do, too."

My wide eyes met Laurel's and then Araneae's as they filled with tears and a sob bubbled up in my chest. Pushing it all away, I called out as Patrick started to leave. "Hey, Patrick."

He stopped and turned. "Lorna?"

"We all do."

Instead of addressing my sentiment, he said, "Christian is in the cockpit with Marianne." With a nod, he disappeared toward the front. It was another few minutes when Madeline entered. We could blame it on hormones or postpartum issues, but whatever the reason, she was having a difficult time. Red blotches covered her neck and cheeks as she dabbed her nose with a tissue and went to the seat beside Edward.

Ruby unbuckled from where she'd been sitting and moved over by her mother and brother.

I couldn't be sure how much time passed. Keaton came and went, promising us all breakfast once we were at a steady altitude and offering everyone a bottle of water, complete with his standard dehydration and flying speech.

By the time we left the ground, my head ached and my stomach twisted.

We climbed higher and higher until we cleared the cloud deck and bright sunshine streamed through the windows. I wanted to think of it as a sign that the darkness from the early morning would clear and a bright, glistening dawn was on the horizon waiting for all of us and ready to deliver a bright new day.

Keaton returned. "Ladies, you may unfasten your seatbelts if you want to move around. It's a good practice to keep them buckled when seated. The bedroom suite is available, and I'll have your breakfast in another fifteen minutes. Would you like to eat up front?"

When no one responded, finally Araneae did. "Thank you, Keaton. The table up front would be perfect."

He grinned. "Very well, Mrs. Sparrow."

The way Araneae cringed at that title made me snicker.

"Madeline," Araneae said, "have you been on this plane before?"

"No," she said with a grin. "I can honestly say, I've never flown in a big bird before."

"Let me show you the suite. Maybe you and Edward can rest."

When Araneae began to unbuckle Edward's car seat, Ruby intervened. "What? You're pregnant. If you don't have weight limits, you should."

Araneae smiled as she stepped back. "I'll need you around when this one is born."

Ruby lifted the car seat. "Deal. Show us this fancy bedroom."

Once we were alone, Laurel turned to me. "I don't like any of this."

My somber mood returned. "Me either. I am scared."

"Mason has never fully explained the organization he worked for while he was Edgar Price. I have picked up on a few things, I know the name, but mostly, it sounds unbelievable and dangerous. I know it's dangerous because I watched the dean of my university campus die in front of me. I saw Russ." She took a deep breath. "I'm scared too."

Araneae came from behind us. "They're going to settle in the suite for a while. I told Keaton to take their breakfast in there." She looked from Laurel to me and back. "If you're up here spreading negative thoughts, I'm going to say, as *Mrs. Sparrow*" —she enunciated the name in a mocking manner— "I command you to stop."

Laurel nodded. "You're right. Our attitude plays an important part in our decision process. We need to believe our men will be safe and in turn so will we."

"A little prayer wouldn't hurt," I said, thinking of my grandmother.

"That's better," Araneae said. She laid her hand over her midsection. "I'm carrying a little princess or prince and he or she will know their daddy. I refuse to believe otherwise." She looked my direction. "And I followed your directions, Lorna."

"Mine?" I asked confused.

Araneae reached for one of the chairs as the plane wobbled and hummed. "I don't think I'd been in the tower for long. Shit, it might have been day one or two. Anyway, you mentioned that you always tell your man you love him every time you part. I think I responded with a comment about not really knowing Sterling and that love was a strong word." She shrugged. "That's probably not exact, but I have pregnancy brain and am allowed a little creative liberty. Anyway, that as well as many other tidbits of advice you've offered over the years stuck. I told Sterling how much I loved him before we went to the apartment level. I told him again before I got on that stupid elevator. I may have said a few other things in the penthouse, but the important thing is that he knows I love him." Her light-brown eyes filled with tears as she shook her head. "Nothing is going to happen to any of them. I absolutely forbid it."

REID

*T*he program watching the power grid appeared as a series of boxes and light. I understood it better than I could explain it. The important factor was that the number of lit boxes was decreasing exponentially. That meant that Morehead or Jettison was getting closer and closer to the right combination and the ability to shut down the building's power supply. It wouldn't be for long, but long wasn't needed.

"To make sure we're on the same page," I said, "when the power is interrupted, they won't physically need to enter our building or floors if they can install a backdoor entry allowing them access in the future."

"Essentially," Mason replied. "I fully expect and hope to God that they make the physical entry soon. If they don't, we're left in limbo. Unless, with such a small opening of time, between the three of us, we are able to locate the intruding counterprogram. Now, if it's a virus, that changes things."

"A counterprogram is a virus," Patrick said. "And our antiviral software is better than anyone else's."

"I mostly agree," Mason said, watching the monitor as Sparrow rode upward in the elevator. "Fucking make it," he muttered.

"Why only mostly?" I asked.

"I'm not fucking full of myself," Mason said as a countermeasure. "Morehead has gotten this far in and out of the Order because she's smart, very smart. And other than knowing about Jettison's flying skills, we don't know what he's capable of. Our antiviral software can stop anything that's commonplace, most, if not all, of what is exceptional. I'm worried about what we've never seen before."

The lit boxes were down to one or two dozen, out of hundreds of thousands. The muscles in my neck and shoulders pulled tight as I alternated my attention between the power grid and the elevator. Up it moved. We watched the monitor feed from outside our steel door. Finally, the doors opened.

I held my breath until Sparrow stepped forward and placed his hand in front of the scanner. The steel door began to move at the same time the boxes went totally dark.

"Fuck," Mason yelled as he bolted toward the door, throwing himself between the door and jamb.

"Stop," Sparrow yelled from the other side. "It will fucking cut you in half."

Patrick and I gripped the door as the powerful motor did what it was supposed to do, close. My fingers ached as we both pulled. The door hesitated and before we knew what happened, Mason managed to get out of our command center and to the man he'd sworn to protect.

Patrick and I released the door before losing our fingers. It slid shut.

"Fuck." It was the only word I could articulate as I hurried back to the monitors and program. The screens flashed, but our battery backups wouldn't allow them to crash. The lights throughout the entire building blinked off and then on.

The roar of cooling fans accelerated. "The generator kicked on,"

Patrick said. As he did, the steel door opened and Sparrow and Mason entered.

"Ten seconds tops," Mason said.

"Did you think I wanted to tell your wife or your sister you were cut in half for a door?" I asked.

"I didn't do it for a door." Mason walked toward his workstation. "We have ten fucking seconds to search and I mean thoroughly. Something happened. We need to know what it was."

Alarms began to sound.

"What the hell is happening?" Sparrow asked.

"Fire in the residential garage." It wasn't our private garage, but one for the other people who lived on any one of the over ninety floors. "The sprinklers are working."

"Fire in the overflow garage," Mason said.

Sparrow paced back and forth as small fires erupted only to be put out. One was in an office suite fifty floors up. There was another in a sandwich shop on the second floor. More alarms sounded.

"Fucking distractions," Sparrow said. He turned to Patrick. "Tell me you have 1 covered."

"It's covered."

Alarms.

Sirens.

Flashing lights.

Every small incident was immediately countered by the safety systems installed in the building. The local news was reporting that the fire department had been called.

"Check the fucking back door," Sparrow said. "Morehead wants our attention on this shit. What is she doing?"

"Shit," I said, my heart dropping. "Two fucking possibilities. We had a welcome team on 1 and they fucking chose door number 2."

Everyone gathered behind my chair as Morehead, Jettison, and two men I didn't know rode up the exterior elevator to the penthouse.

"Fucking make it stop."

My fingers feverishly moved over the keyboard. "I can't. I have no control."

Patrick sat down at his workstation and also typed.

"They're moving higher."

"Another thirty seconds and they're to the entry."

My teeth ached as my jaw clenched. "No fucking way am I this close to the man who hurt my wife and I'm sitting here."

As I opened a drawer near my desk and reached for my gun, Mason stood in my way. "Fuck no." He pointed his finger at my chest. "Where is your vest?"

"I don't have time." I looked over at the screen. "The damn doors are going to open and they'll be in the fucking penthouse."

"No, they won't," Patrick said. "I overrode it." He let out a sigh as the elevator began to descend.

"Hold them a little longer," I called as I went back to the locker room for my vest. Sparrow and Mason were a step behind. "Make them think they have control."

"Let me do this," Mason said. "I owe Morehead the honor of dying from my bullet." He turned to Sparrow. "Your place is in this fucking control room. What makes you think you're putting on a vest?"

"It's moving," Patrick yelled.

"Because they took my wife, that is my home, and that bitch has been fucking with my world."

The three of us wearing our vests rushed back to the command center.

Patrick looked up from the monitors and keyboards. "I think I can delay them another minute, but not much after that. I'll let you know where they are."

The steel door opened with the scan of my hand. Our forward movement stopped as we approached the elevator doors. "If they have any control, they could lock us in there. Come here," I said, leading the three of them to the emergency fire stairs we'd never used.

"Fucking forgot these existed," Mason said as we pried the door open.

"We won't be able to enter the penthouse," Sparrow said. "I had a fake panel installed."

"I remember," I said looking at Mason. "I'm a bit bruised, but I would say you and me together could knock the shit out of the panel." I called Patrick. "Turn off the alarms in the stairwell."

Emergency lighting activated as we stepped onto the metal stairs, but no alarms sounded. Cobwebs crisscrossed from stairs to ceiling as we kicked up dust with each step. We stilled at the first-floor penthouse landing. The stairs continued up to the second floor of the penthouse.

"Where does this come out?" Mason asked, looking up.

"Upstairs, it's in an extra bedroom," Sparrow answered. "Ruby's bedroom. Shit, I just remembered on the first floor it's in the library. There's not only a panel but a fucking bookcase too."

Mason and I looked at one another and both began running to the second floor. Pulling the fireproof door toward us brought us face-to-face with the backside of decorative paneling. Mason grinned. "It'll fucking be easier than a bookcase."

With Sparrow a step behind, we both rammed the paneling with our shoulder.

"Motherfucker," I muttered as pain shot down my injured arm and torso.

"I have a better idea," Mason said. Pushing me back, my brother-in-law held to the door as he brought the heel of his cowboy boot to the center of the paneling. As if it were nothing but pressed wood, the barrier splintered. I joined him, kicking away our obstacle. Soon we had an opening large enough for each of us to get through.

Once we were standing in what was sometimes Ruby's room, I reached for my phone. Instead of using the cell service from before,

I switched to our direct line, calling Patrick. "Where are they?" I asked, knowing he was doing his job, putting out literal and figurative fires while watching everything unfold.

Patrick responded immediately. "They're in the penthouse. First floor. Jettison is headed up the staircase toward you. The other two men have split up. Fuck, Morehead is going to the elevator."

"She's figured out that is where Laurel should be," Mason said.

"Let her enter the elevator. Try to keep her trapped for a while," Sparrow said. "We'll take care of these men first."

"Jettison is mine," I said with my heart pounding against my bruised breastbone.

Mason turned. "Sparrow, will you please let us handle this?" He tilted his head toward the hidden stairs. "Command center is safest."

"No. I'm not letting you handle this alone. You three have fucking backed me up. It's my turn."

Mason's green stare met my dark one. We didn't have time to argue. All we could do was what had been our job ever since basic training—clear the way and protect the king. Of course, Sparrow wasn't a king back then. If you'd have asked Mason back then, he'd have said Sparrow was a spoiled rich kid from Lincoln Park.

That was a long time ago.

The three of us moved in unison as Jettison crested the grand staircase. His gun was poised as were ours. Shooting him would alert the people below and minimize our opportunity. Hell, we had no way of knowing if Morehead had found the elevator.

Instead of heading our direction, Jettison went down the hallway toward the master bedroom suite and nursery. Rage radiated from the man behind me. I didn't blame him. His castle was under attack.

Sparrow looked down and pointed to our shoes. Mason and I were both wearing boots. He had his prissy Italian loafers. Without words he was saying he could sneak up on Jettison better. Mason shook his head, but that didn't stop Sparrow. With the two of us now in the rear, we followed, ready to shoot.

As we turned into the second hallway, we saw the door to the master bedroom was ajar. As silently as possible we approached. From the doorway we saw the back of Jettison as he pulled open a drawer in Araneae's closet containing her jewelry.

Seriously? Petty theft?

The marble tile of the hallway gave way to lush carpeting in the bedroom. Without waiting, Mason went forward. The butt of his gun came down hard on the back of Jettison's head.

With a thud not much unlike the sound of a cracked egg, Jettison collapsed. I lifted my gun as my wife's bruised face appeared in my memory.

"No," Mason said, reaching for my hand. "You can do it." He pushed my hand and gun lower. "Not in Araneae's closet. And one bullet will take him out of his misery. I'm going to tie him up." He looked behind me. "Sparrow, get me belts or something to bind him."

My hands shook. "I fucking need to kill him."

"You can. You will. I told you once if you want to fuck with him, give him those memories if for only ten seconds, then you can blow his brains out."

When Sparrow appeared, he had multiple lengths of satin-covered ropes and scarves. He smirked. "Shut the fuck up. They work. Tie him up."

A ridiculous and inappropriate desire to giggle threatened as Mason and I went to work tying and gagging Jettison with supplies less like those used by our capos and more like those used with a four-poster bed—oh, shit that's right, Sparrow had that too.

When we were done and had taken all of Jettison's weapons, Mason patted Sparrow on the shoulder. "I suggest you buy a new stock."

Sparrow shook his head, his attention on the unconscious man in his wife's closet.

I switched on the two-way direct function again. "Tell us what's happening, Patrick."

"Morehead is in the elevator. She's stopped at the apartments."

"What about the others?"

"Still on the first floor. One is nearing the office; the other is in the front den."

In a V formation, we descended the staircase. Mason and Sparrow went right toward the office while I went left. It would be more exciting to describe a Western-style shoot-out, but that isn't what happened. We knew the terrain. Years ago, it was a village in a desert. Today it was our home.

My man, the one in the front den, fell as my bullet hit him between the eyes. Seconds before he hit the floor, I recognized him as the man with the flowers at the hospital.

All in all, it was rather anticlimactic.

I heard a second shot.

After taking my man's gun and ensuring lack of a pulse, I headed toward the office. Their man was also down, his brain matter splattered on the tall windows overlooking the city of Chicago with some upon Araneae's glass desk.

"We'll need a cleanup crew," Sparrow said.

"Patrick?" I asked, speaking into my phone.

"She's in your apartment, Reid."

"That was where we'd broadcast the signal from."

"Can we take the elevator?" I asked.

"Hurry," Patrick replied.

REID

"**W**rong apartment, Ms. Moore," Mason said, his gun extended.

Morehead turned with her gun also pointing our way. "I could shoot you right now and your wife is next. Or maybe I'll let you watch her die."

A shot rang out from behind me, hitting Morehead's hand as her gun fell to the ground.

"Fuck," she screamed, reaching for her injured hand with her gloved one.

Sparrow stepped forward. "Let me introduce myself. I was told you didn't give a fuck who I am. That's what you told my wife." He pointed his gun at her forehead. "I'm Sterling Sparrow. You kidnapped my wife, and your crew is gone."

Morehead laughed. "You won't be rid of me anytime soon. You can go ahead and shoot, but I promise you'll remember me as you're sitting in prison, Mr. Sparrow."

~

Later that night on 1, in two separate conference rooms, we learned more of the plan. It wasn't from Morehead. She was well trained and too fucking gone on her own power. Sparrow was the one to pull the final trigger. After what had happened to Araneae, he wanted that.

Patrick and I had other plans for Jettison.

When we entered the conference room where he was secured, I set down my laptop and started with a story, one about a soldier, a member of the TACP, and a married man.

The marriage was where I got his attention.

And then I began the slideshow, pictures of a beautiful bride, parents, and siblings.

He stayed quiet until I brought up pictures of a little five-and-a-half-year-old boy with jet-black hair.

"No," he repeated, closing his eyes as if it could make my pictures disappear.

"Talk to us, Jettison," Mason said, "or we're going to keep you here and bring in that boy." Mason turned to me. "Should we let the kid watch his father die or would it be more appropriate to let Jettison watch his son die?"

I admitted defeat when it came to the tactics Mason displayed without hesitation. That didn't mean I couldn't stomach them. I believed that whatever my brother-in-law was capable of years ago, he wouldn't do what he was saying. Nevertheless, Mason had done his own homework. Slipping a flash drive into my laptop, he brought up a video of one of our men ringing his widowed wife's door. A little boy ran up behind her, holding onto her legs.

"I'll tell you everything," Jettison said, "and when I'm done, kill me. I want this to end."

It was almost too easy of an ending for him, but when the time came, Mason stepped back. "He's yours." Mason looked at me and Patrick.

Sparrow had his arms crossed over his chest, watching.

Patrick was the first to come forward. "Your son, how would

you like me to put him in a body bag before I delivered him to your widow?"

Jettison's dark eyes looked up at Patrick. "I didn't..."

Patrick's fist connected with Jettison's jaw.

Long ago, this had stopped being only business. Morehead and Jettison had made it personal, taking my wife and Sparrow's wife, threatening Mason's wife, and taking Patrick's daughter.

"No one fucking touches my daughter," Patrick said as blood dripped from Jettison's lip.

It was only the beginning as he stepped back, allowing me to take his place. Using my fist, I hit Jettison's jaw, once, twice, and a third time. Blood oozed from his nose and lip, yet he didn't speak. I hit him again. Each time I envisioned Lorna's injuries and her road to recovery.

"Fucking use the gun," Jettison finally pleaded.

"I want you to know who the fuck I am."

"I know who you are."

"And my wife?" I asked.

"The redhead."

I lifted the gun to his temple. "She fucking fought you off, you piece of shit."

His eyes raged. There was something he wanted to say. Not that anything could have stopped what was coming.

"This is for her." I pulled the trigger.

There weren't words to describe the sense of relief.

A weight lifting.

That was how it was often described.

However, as Jettison's body twitched in the chair where he was tied with black satin bindings and blood dripped from the brain matter splatter on the plastic sheet attached to the wall, I would say the feeling was different.

It was like walking into the fucking early morning sunshine after a long dark night. It was raising your face to the sky and feeling the warmth on your skin.

It was the dawn of a new day.

Of course, this ordeal wasn't fully over. It would take time to find all the traps and snares Morehead had laid for Sparrow and Sparrow Enterprises. Jettison had given up what he knew and given us a good idea what to look for. His kid would be fine, but Jettison didn't die with that reassurance.

"They landed at the private airport near South Padre," Sparrow said, stepping forward.

"I don't know about you," I said with a sigh, laying my gun on the nearby table, "but a beach sounds fucking nice."

LORNA

A few weeks later

The SUV pulled up in front of the Four Seasons Hotel on Delaware Place in downtown Chicago. I turned to my handsome husband. "Is this a romantic getaway?"

Reid shook his head. "Not quite. It's a meeting, but after that, we'll see what happens. I still have more ravaging left to do."

My smile bloomed as I recalled our few days down in the sunshine of South Padre Island, more accurately the nights. The entire resort was reinforced as only a Russian bratva could do. The suite the two of us used had a balcony that overlooked the Gulf. At night we'd leave the glass doors open and listen to the surf as we reveled in the knowledge that we were safe and together. We found comfort and solace in one another. While we were nearing our ten-year anniversary, the recent events reminded us that each day and each night is precious. Our time together wasn't guaranteed, and it was up to us to live and love to the fullest.

In each other's arms we found pleasure, reassurance, and the love that had been with us since the night we first met. Obstacles had tried to deter our connection and yet we were together. With the surf crashing on the shore, the ravaging began.

To this day, not one of the men had given away the details about what exactly happened in Chicago. We knew the basics: our castle had been infiltrated. We also knew that each and every one of our men promised it wouldn't happen again. The precautions from now going forward would be greater, the guards readier, and the locks stronger. The invisibility cloak Araneae joked about would be denser. Our tower would forever forward remain our safe haven.

Their next promise was the one we all clung tightly to. They promised the threat we'd faced was eliminated, never to be faced again.

I wasn't certain if my pleasure at hearing that people had died made me a bad person or not. Nevertheless, as we all gathered on the beachfront, I was happy. I was pleased that the promises that had been made to me over the last decade had come true, not only for me but for all of us. We were safe. Our men were safe, and our children.

Edward was growing more every day, Ruby had returned to her school in Michigan until the approaching holiday break, and our newest addition was only six weeks away. Araneae and Sparrow's baby would arrive next, and after theirs, in approximately seven and a half months, Reid's and my child would join us. The doctor confirmed my pregnancy not long after we returned to Chicago.

"You don't mind being ravaged, do you, Mrs. Murray?"

"Not as long as it's by you." Romero opened the back door, allowing Chicago's cool, crisp breeze to infiltrate the warmth within the interior. "What is this meeting about and why am I here?"

Reid offered me his hand. "You were specifically invited."

For only a moment, I stared at the incredibly handsome man waiting for me. Nearly a decade before he was my Prince Charming. Seeing him now, the love and desire in his brown eyes and the tenderness in his touch, it filled me with love knowing that tonight and always he'd remain my happily ever after.

I placed my hand in his.

Tonight we were both dressed to impress. I knew I was impressed by him, and from what he'd whispered off and on in my ear, I believed the feeling was mutual. In a black suit, red shirt and black tie, my husband radiated power and influence.

Not to be totally outdone, under my long wool coat, I wore a black mid-length Sinful Threads original dress with a red sash and tall black shoes that were supposed to say *Fuck me*. As I stepped from the SUV, I hoped they would send their message before I tripped and fell.

My hand went to Reid's elbow as we entered the posh foyer. Reid led me past the front desk. "I thought we were getting a room?"

"We already have that. First, our meeting."

Others smiled and some stared as Reid escorted me to the elevators. I couldn't blame them; we were an incredibly handsome couple.

"Our meeting is private," he said as we entered the elevator.

My curiosity grew as we rode upward, higher and higher. When the elevator stopped, my husband led me past a few double doors. Finally, we came to a stop by the one with *Presidential Suite* embossed on the plate beside the doors.

As Reid lifted his hand to knock, the door opened inward.

I don't know what I was expecting, but a well-dressed older gentleman wasn't it. The man greeting us reminded me of a black Alfred Pennyworth. Perhaps my husband was planning to take on a side job as the new black Batman.

"Son, it's good to see you." Creases surrounded the man's eyes as he smiled at me. "Mrs. Murray, it is a pleasure."

"Thank you."

The man gestured inside. "Please come in." He spoke to Reid. "I'm sure you know that your men have verified that everything is as it should be."

Once inside, the man bowed. "Mrs. Murray, my name is Edison Walters. May I take your coat?"

As Reid helped me with my topcoat, I searched my memories, certain I'd never heard the name Edison Walters before.

Folding my coat, Mr. Walters laid it across a chair and led us farther into the suite. Beyond the tall windows framed with heavy draperies was the city of Chicago all lit up for the upcoming holidays.

"Your husband and I recently became acquainted." Walters tilted his head toward the sofa and chairs. "Would you please have a seat and be so kind as to indulge this old man a story."

I had no idea what I was about to hear. There was no way I could.

Reid reached for my hand as we sat.

Mr. Walters took a seat opposite us. "As I said, I'm old." When I started to comment, he waved my words away. "Please, Mrs. Murray, I want to be as candid as I possibly am able. Let's get the obvious out of the way. I'm an old man."

I smiled. "I like you."

"Well, that's good. I think I could like you too. You see, I was a bit shocked when I met your husband. It had been over thirty years since I'd heard of him."

It didn't take a math genius to know that time frame would have been when Reid was six years old or younger. "How had you heard of him back then?"

"Well, that's what I came to Chicago to talk to the two of you about. Without compromising what I cannot, I hoped I could share what is possible." When neither of us spoke, he went on, "I wanted you both to know that I had the unique pleasure of having a very good friend. We'd met early in our military careers. It wasn't until things began to change in the world around us and I found myself working for an organization that had the potential to be a significant positive influence to the world to right wrongs and correct mistakes that we reunited and our friendship rekindled."

"Who was your friend?" I asked.

"Your husband's father."

My head snapped toward Reid. By his stoic expression and intense attention on Mr. Walters, I determined this wasn't news to him as it was to me.

"You see," Mr. Walters continued, "life doesn't always give us an easy journey. Sometimes paths converge and other times they take us astray. All we can do is our best, what we believe our best can be, striving for that goal that helps not only ourselves but others. During that journey there are decisions that must be made. With power comes seclusion. I've found that oftentimes it's a lonely journey. When you have the opportunity to share that journey with someone you care for, it makes everything else better."

I squeezed Reid's hand.

Mr. Walters spoke to Reid, "Rendell loved you, Reid. I hope that learning his choices won't cause you to doubt that fact. He cared deeply for your mother and her mother. He also had a calling to the republic. An opportunity arose where he was able to make a difference, something that not many patriots can truly say. Of course, we all want that, but the opportunities aren't always at our fingertips."

Reid stiffened at my side. "My father chose the republic over his family."

"No, son, he chose the republic *for* his family. It may take years to understand that, but it's the truth. And I can testify that I was a witness to the sacrifice he made and the doors he opened for everyone in our great country."

Mr. Walters turned to me. "I heard about what occurred a few months ago. I want you to know that I'm deeply sorry that happened to you, Mrs. Murray. I believe in some way I could have prevented it and I didn't. We all have decisions we later regret. This is one of mine."

"I-I..." I wasn't certain what to say. "How do you know anything about what happened?"

"Old men often know more than young men give us credit for." He took a breath. "I was wrong and while it won't make up for what was done to you, I found a way I might be able to give you something, something I have recently been made aware that you were seeking."

I looked from Mr. Walters to Reid and back. "I appreciate your gesture, Mr. Walters, but I can honestly say I'm content, more than content, I'm happy. I have a wonderful husband, great friends, and family." I didn't know this man enough to include our pregnancy. "I'm not seeking anything nor do I lack for anything."

He leaned down and moving a magazine with a photo of this hotel, he revealed a manila envelope. "Mrs. Murray, your light shines bright. Seeing your hand in Reid's and looking in your eyes, I see the dawn of a new day. The goodness within you shines." He sighed. "I couldn't be happier for Rendell's son."

He handed the envelope my direction. "The information in this envelope is for you to do with as you wish. You may never pursue it, and that is your choice. You may pursue what I have given and it might not end the way you want or maybe it will. Knowing the future is not a gift I possess. I do, however, know the past, and I believe we can all learn from that."

While the envelope was light, its significance felt weighty. I looked up to his eyes. "Do you want me to open it now?"

"No." He stood. "I can't tell you what a pleasure this has been. I have business I must attend, and I'm sure you have better things to do than converse with this old man."

Reid and I also stood as I held tight to the envelope.

Mr. Walters's hand came to Reid's shoulder. "Your father is proud."

"Is?" Reid replied.

"I believe that those who made the ultimate sacrifice never truly leave us. They work continually on our behalf in ways we never know and in ways reason defies. They send people to intervene when it's appropriate. I can't come up with another plausible reason why after all this time, I'd come face-to-face with Rendell's son." Mr. Walters turned his attention to me.

I offered my hand. "Thank you, Mr. Walters."

Mr. Walters took my hand and turned it. With a bow, he brushed his lips over my knuckles. When he stood erect, he nodded. "It has been a pleasure, Mrs. Murray." He moved us toward the door and reached for my coat. Fluffing its length, he held it for me to put on.

"Thank you," I said again as I placed my arms within.

"I hope you will know," he said with a shimmer in his eyes, "the pleasure has been mine."

For our entire walk toward the elevator, neither Reid nor I spoke. It wasn't until we entered, Reid hit the button for another floor, and the doors began to close that I found words. "That was odd."

Reid grinned. "I don't know what's in that envelope. I could take it back to the tower and assure you it's safe."

"I don't get the feeling the man invited us there to poison us with anthrax or something else."

Once we arrived to our suite, Reid opened the door. Soft music filled the room. On the table were a huge bouquet of red roses and a chilling bottle of champagne. "Champagne?" I asked.

"It's alcohol free."

Placing my hand on his wide chest, I lifted myself and kissed his cheek.

"It's my turn to help you with your coat," Reid hummed near my ear. "And then your dress and then..."

The warmth of his breath on my neck sent chills across my skin and a twisting deep within.

"Our dinner is scheduled to arrive in thirty minutes." He grinned. "In this time frame, it won't be full-out ravaging, but I'm willing to give it a go."

I took a seat at the table and pushed aside the two champagne flutes. "I want to know what's inside this envelope."

"There's only one way to find that out."

My fingers trembled as I laid back the clip and opened the flap.

"Sweetheart, it's only an envelope."

"It feels like more." Inside was a folder. Pulling it out, I laid it on the table and opened the cover. Tears filled my eyes at the top picture. It was black and white and taken from a distance.

It had been twenty-five years and yet I knew in my heart who I was seeing. "Oh my God."

Reid was immediately at my side. "Fuck. Is that Missy?"

I couldn't speak. All I could do is nod as I moved the picture and began reading the report. Finally, I found words. Looking up at Reid's anxious stare, I swallowed again. "She's alive. My sister isn't dead. Not only is she alive, she's married and has two children. I'm an aunt. A real aunt."

Reid took my hand and led me to stand. As I leaned into the security of his embrace, he asked, "Are you sure it's her?"

"I am, Reid. In my heart I am." I pulled away and looked down at the information and turned another page. "Here is all her contact information."

"Are you ready to call her?"

I shook my head. "No. Not yet. Let me think about this. I understand what Mr. Walters meant. I have to decide what to do with this information. Even if I do nothing, I now know." I threw my arms around his broad shoulders. "Missy's alive."

Reid laid his hand over my stomach. "You know, she might want to know the same about you and Mason." He grinned. "After all, she's going to be an aunt too."

EPILOGUE

Reid

Late summer of the following year

I paced outside our apartment in the common area waiting for the doctor to allow me reentry. Dr. Stevens, the Sparrow family's obstetrician, was inside our apartment with Lorna. After what had happened to Ruby during Edward's birth, the decision was to deliver future children at home, as long as there were no concerns. I wouldn't say I was currently in a no-concern status.

It wasn't the noise or chaos around me that had my attention. Honestly, it had become commonplace in the same way that ten years ago, stillness had prevailed. While it would be me who was let into the apartment and extra bedroom, the one currently set up with everything that was needed for a home birth, I wasn't alone.

"She's going to be fine," Laurel said, wrapping an arm around my waist.

Our gaze went to the two small children playing on the floor.

According to the mothers and experts, they weren't really playing together. It was called co-play and perfectly normal for their ages. Edward was now eight months old and while not yet walking, he pulled himself up on everyone and everything he could find. He jabbered nonstop. And with dark hair like his mother, he had Patrick's eyes. I imagined he was a male version of his older sister.

Near him with various toys hanging over her from a little contraption was the tower's princess. Officially, she was Jacquelyn Goldie Sparrow. Word was that as a Sparrow she needed a stately if not pretentious name. Since naming her for Sparrow's mother Genevieve was quickly nixed—honestly—by both parents, they began a search for a name they both liked. While our Sparrow princess was named Jacquelyn, it was Araneae who came up with the middle name Goldie. After all, her father was Sterling. If he could be silver, their daughter was gold.

Now with a wavy crown of silky blonde hair, rarely was the name Jacquelyn uttered. To everyone who loved her, she was simply Goldie. If memory serves me, as a teenager, there would be a time in her future when her parents would use all three names—usually when she was in trouble. At five and a half months, the smiling blonde with her daddy's dark brown eyes was everyone's Goldie.

I leaned toward Laurel. "I believe she will. Lorna's had a great pregnancy."

Laurel smiled. "I always love to hear men say that."

"Don't lump me or any of the men here in that group. You know we would move heaven and earth for any one of you."

She nodded. "I know that, Reid. I've watched you do that. I just want you to know it's okay to be nervous."

"I think I'm more nervous about what comes next."

"Next?"

Madeline's and Araneae's laughs filled the air as Edward investigated Goldie's hanging toys.

"Listen, I know I can function on little sleep, but I know my wife. That woman loves her eight hours."

Laurel laughed. "You two will work it out, and if you need a break, Aunt Laurel and Uncle Mason are right next door."

I knew that. I knew Lorna and I weren't in for this change alone. Simply seeing all the women present, utilizing the space that forever seemed to sit unnecessarily between our individual entrances and the elevator, let me know Lorna and I were surrounded by family and friends.

The elevator doors opened as Sparrow, Mason, and Patrick joined the rest.

"Am I an uncle?" Mason asked above the din.

"Yes," came from both Araneae and Madeline.

"As for Lorna," I said with a grin, "not yet. The doctor is checking on progress and told me to take a break."

Mason looked around the room. Goldie was now off the mat and lifted high in the air in her daddy's hands while Patrick was sitting on the floor in his thousand-dollar suit building block towers so Edward could knock them down. "Is this what she considers a break?"

With Goldie on his arm, Sparrow came closer. The joyousness of the occasion seemed suddenly lost in his expression. "Nothing to be concerned about," he began, "but Patrick found some irregularities with some recent reports coming from the institute. We're watching everything like hawks. There was an instance before we stopped Morehead with a concern of a security breach. I wouldn't have put it past her to have planted something to get the institute caught up in an audit."

I grinned. "We've shut everything down she's thrown at us. If this is something left behind by Morehead, we'll shut it down too. Araneae's project, Laurel's life's work, and Madeline's passion will be safe. You know we're watching your back."

Sparrow grinned as Goldie reached for his nose. "You always have."

"Reid?"

I turned as Dr. Stevens opened the apartment door. "Lorna is doing well. We have some time before baby Murray joins us. Come on back and sit with your wife." She looked out over the crowd. "Goodness. You're all here. It's all right with me if you want to come back one at a time."

While Patrick and Sparrow shook their heads and the ladies all nodded, I looked at Mason. "Come back."

"Childbirth isn't really my thing."

"Doesn't have to be. She's your sister."

"She's your wife."

I laughed, recalling the same conversation on the way to Montana. However, this time, it seemed that Mason was emphasizing my role over his. "Come back for a minute."

Together we walked through the living room, passing the man at the dining room table and a woman at the breakfast bar. They looked our way. "Slow day?" I asked.

The man grinned. "Glad to help."

"Nothing like having your own medical staff on hand," Mason said as we entered the hallway.

"He's the anesthesiologist and she's a labor-and-delivery nurse Renita suggested."

"It's nice to have connections."

The bedroom in use wasn't ours, my office, or our newly decorated nursery. It was the room across from the office. I peeked my head in.

Propped up on the special bed—it was more than a hospital bed. It broke down to a delivery bed when needed—was the most stunning redhead I'd ever seen. Her red hair had grown out and was now long enough for a ponytail. But when she looked up, it was her emerald gaze that caused my heart to skip a beat. "Hi, sweetheart, are you up for visitors?" I asked.

"Anyone except Mason," she said with a smirk.

"I heard that," Mason said, stepping into the room.

She lifted her hand, beckoning him closer. "And I saw you behind Reid."

Mason took her hand and stepping closer, kissed the top of her head. "Are you all right?"

"Well, I'm about to push an approximately eight-pound baby out of me." She tilted her head and after flashing her gaze toward me, she added, "I'm great."

"There's a whole room of people out there who want to see you."

Lorna held tight to her brother's hand. "Mace, stay a minute."

"Don't get mushy on me."

"Me. Never." She took a deep breath.

"Are you all right?" he asked again. "Because if you're not, I'll kill the guy who knocked you up."

Though I knew he had the skills, I wasn't concerned.

Lorna's grin faded as she reached to her midsection. "Even with the epidural, I think the contractions are getting stronger." After a moment, she looked up at her brother. "Reid and I have been talking about names."

He nodded. "It is about time. I think Mason Murray has a nice ring."

"It does. We were talking about maybe Edison."

Mason didn't respond.

"Hear me out. Now that I know who he is, I think I owe him a debt of gratitude. Honestly, I owe him more than that."

"You don't owe him anything."

Her eyes glistened. "I do, Mace. He gave me both of my siblings back. I know you lived through hell, but, Mace, you made it back. What if they hadn't taken you? What if you would have died here in Chicago? I remember how tense of a time that was. Allister's or McFadden's men could have killed you in the hospital, and you wouldn't be here. Edison's organization saved you."

Mason scoffed. "Saved." He took a breath. "It's not his organization. He is just currently the top."

"He is also a connection to Reid's father."

Mason took a deep breath. "Sis, have I ever told you that you see the world through fucking rose-colored glasses?"

"And there's Missy."

"We haven't contacted her."

That was Lorna's decision. Nevertheless, we'd checked on her, since Nancy had mentioned she'd told *them* about her. Her history was another story, but she was safe.

"But we have the option." Lorna squeezed her brother's hand. "Edison gave us that too."

"Don't you think it will be a little weird having two Eddies around here?"

His question made me chuckle. "We talked about that. Just like Goldie isn't Jacquelyn, we'll call our boy Jackson."

Mason took a step back, his green eyes going wide. "Jackson?"

"Unless you and Laurel want that name."

Mason smiled. "Use it, sis, who knows what the future holds for Laurel and me. I believe Jackson would be proud to have a strong little boy named after him." He grinned. "I guess the ranch will be going to..." He paused. "Will it be Jackson Edison or Edison Jackson?"

"It's Edison Jackson," I said. "Our Jack."

"They both brought you back to me," Lorna said.

"Mason would have been easier," Mason said with a smirk.

"But then we'd have two Masons."

During the next few hours, people came and went, each one excited about our growing family. And then finally the doctor made her declaration: it was baby time.

"Talk to me, Reid," Lorna said as the pains intensified and the doctor and nurse prepared for the birth.

Holding onto my wife's hand, I stared down in awe of our connection, her small pale hand in my large dark one. Barely a chicken nugget and she was everything, not only to me, but to all of us. Truly Lorna was a wonder of a woman, and that showed every day in her continued strength and ability to love, to even love and admire Edison Walters and another man named Jackson, a man she never knew.

Lorna's capacity to feel affection had no bounds. It was evident during the unofficial ceremony she held for Nancy on the shores of Lake Michigan. With all of our family present—and a few dozen Sparrows on watch—she gave a tribute that in my opinion was more than Nancy deserved as Lorna emptied her ashes into the water. It was also evident in her persuasive efforts to reunite Anna with her nephew, Little Gordy. While they were still in the midst of their custody pursuit, with the Sparrow influence, soon Steve and Anna would have a new son.

Lorna cared for everyone in this tower. I believed in the depth of my heart we wouldn't be the family we were today without my beautiful, courageous, and giving wife.

"Reid."

I swallowed, trying with all my might to be half as strong as this tiny woman and wishing I could take away her pain. "I fucking love you."

"I love you, too."

"Lorna, we need to push," Dr. Stevens said. "Three rounds of ten seconds."

Lorna gripped my hand with the force of a three-hundred-pound man as the doctor counted to ten followed by ten seconds of breathing. Another ten of pushing. More breathing. The final ten.

"Very good. Let's rest."

Did this doctor think this was a team sport?

All of her directives sounded as if she too were having a baby.

"Reid, can you tell me a story?" Lorna asked, her green eyes only on me. "Like I heard you telling Goldie."

Goldie's story was different. It was about a beast who pursued a beauty.

This was Jack's story. "Once upon a time," I began, "in a land far away, there was this quiet boy who never dreamed of what life had in store. And then one evening, once he was grown, he met a beautiful princess."

Lorna shook her head. "She wasn't a princess. She was nothing more than a cleaning maid."

"She wore a crown, so the man was certain she was of royal blood."

"She thought the man was royal," Lorna added. "After all, she'd never been to a ball."

"And from the moment the man saw the beautiful woman, he gave her his heart. But then the clock struck midnight and he was certain she would be forever lost. After all, even with her shoe in hand, what were the chances their paths would cross?"

"And then they crossed."

I grinned. "They crossed and intertwined as this beautiful woman with flowing red hair agreed to live in a glass castle high in the sky. And through the years, that simple maid infected even the king and queen with her love. Her caring and giving couldn't be contained. It spread to all the inhabitants of the kingdom. The man who first saw her was simply happy that every night, her love was reserved for only him."

"Lorna, push."

Tears rolled down Lorna's cheeks as she squeezed my hand and she bore down.

"Your son is almost here. Come on Lorna, another big push."

Cries filled the room as the doctor held to our son.

Was there any way to prepare for this moment?

If there was, I'd failed miserably.

Lorna and our son weren't alone in their tears as my eyes filled with salty moisture. Holding tightly to her hand, I peppered her red hair with kisses. "I fucking love you."

The nurse brought our son closer and laid him skin to skin on Lorna's chest. Even covered in the goo that hadn't yet been cleaned, our little man settled at the sound of Lorna's heartbeat.

"Hi, Jack, I'm your mommy."

I ran my finger over his sparse red hair. "I'm your dad." My gaze met Lorna's. "Do you want to hear the rest of the story?"

Lorna looked up at me. "I know the rest. They lived happily ever after."

And they lived happily ever after

Thank you for reading *DAWN*, the conclusion of Reid and Lorna's story, *Dangerous Web*.

If you'd like a little more of the Sparrows, please go to https://dl. bookfunnel.com/4d1290dwmz
to enjoy a deleted chapter from DAWN and sign up for Aleatha's newsletter to stay up to date on all things Aleatha.

If you enjoyed *DAWN* and want to know more about our other Sparrow men:

Web of Sin, Sterling and Araneae's story, is complete with *SECRETS* (FREE*), LIES*, and *PROMISES*.
Tangled Web, Mason and Laurel's story, is also complete with *TWISTED, OBSESSED*, and *BOUND*.
And *Web of Desire*. Patrick and Madeline's story, is complete and ready to binge with *SPARK, FLAME*, and *ASHES*.

It's time to binge Sparrow Webs!

Are you ready for a new dark and dangerous romantic suspense by Aleatha Romig?
Get ready for the heat and humidity of New Orleans as Emma North learns her fate from the mysterious Everett Ramses in FATE'S DEMAND, prequel coming March 2021.

Live release: To receive a text alert of FATE'S DEMAND release, text "Aleatha1d" to 21000

Pre-order today:
DEVIL'S DEAL – full-length novel with Everett Ramses and Emma North coming May 2021.

Following the Acknowledgments, check out a peek at FATE'S DEMAND and **DEVIL'S DEAL**:

ACKNOWLEDGMENTS

A special thank-you to my beta readers: Sherry, Angie, Val, Ilona, and Mr.Jeff, my editor, Lisa Aurello, and my sensitivity readers, Renita McKinney and Yulanda Bolton, for their dedication to my Sparrow Web world, the array of characters, and to making Reid and Lorna's story the best it can be.

You are all greatly appreciated. Please know, I couldn't do this without you.

Another special thank-you to my publicist Danielle Sanchez for never giving up on me and encouraging me to keep going, day after day.

Thank you to my readers. Whether you've been with me since *Consequences* or *Dangerous Web* was your first dive into the worlds of Aleatha, I thank you for giving me your time and energy and allowing me to take you away with words.

Finally, my family, I love you beyond measure and couldn't pursue this dream without all of your constant support. And to our beautiful granddaughter, you may read Grandma's books after your thirtieth birthday if your mom and dad approve.

Thank you.
Aleatha

FATE'S DEMAND

Synopsis

Stepping into the city limits, the vibes of New Orleans infiltrate the thoughts and feelings of each unsuspecting individual.

Twinkling lights.

Copious amounts of alcohol.

And

Ghost stories of lore.

As Emma waits for a business meeting, those ingredients are there, in the heavy air and circulating through her bloodstream. Until everything changes.

Everett Ramses is tall, dark, and mysterious.

He's more than that.

According to him...he is Emma's fate.

And he has a demand.

Will she run, or will she find out what fate's demand has in store?

"FATE'S DEMAND" is an intriguing meeting to whet readers' appetite for more of an all-new dark-romance world by New York Times bestselling author Aleatha Romig. Get ready to love and hate, to swoon and swear...Rett Ramses will bring out all the emotions.

"FATE'S DEMAND" first appeared in the Bookworm Box anthology *ONE MORE STEP* as a short story entitled "THE DEAL."

"FATE'S DEMAND"- EXCLUSIVE EXCERPT

From the side of the courtyard, leaning against a stone archway, a strikingly handsome tall man with a dark gaze stared unblinkingly my direction. I turned from side to side, wondering if I was truly who he was looking at.

With broad shoulders that tugged at the seams of his white shirt, he remained still, a statue immune to the influx of patrons. The sleeves of his shirt were rolled up near his elbows, revealing powerful forearms. The top buttons were undone, showing a thick neck. His skin was dark, either tanned from Louisiana sun or perhaps his natural pigment. His dark hair was longer than short and shorter than long. It was combed back in soft waves. Unlike most of the men wearing shorts or blue jeans, this man's long legs were covered with gray dress pants, as if he'd made his way from the business district directly to the happenings of the French Quarter.

"Yeah?" a voice came from the bar.

I spun back, my heartbeat unexpectedly racing and my lips dry. "I'd like to order some food."

The bartender nodded, reaching for a pad of paper.

"I'd like an order of—"

Two large tanned hands and muscular forearms came to either side of me, gripping the bar and caging me. I was trapped between the sticky surface and a solid chest. Heat rose from the ground upward, warming my already-heated skin. The deep voice vibrated his chest as his timbre rumbled through me.

"The lady is mistaken. She's dining with me."

I didn't need visual confirmation that the owner of the deep voice was the man from moments ago, the one near the archway. I felt him around me—his presence—as well as within me, confirmed by the way my pulse raced.

I spun within the cage he'd created with his muscular arms.

This man, the one I didn't know, surrounded me, his height dwarfing me and his body electrifying me. The spicy aroma of his cologne mixed with the whiskey on his breath created a concoction that blended perfectly with the Hurricane's rum in my system.

He was so close that at first my eyes met his broad chest. Slowly, I brought my chin higher and higher. His wide neck came into view as his Adam's apple bobbed. Finally, my gaze met his. "I believe you have the wrong—"

The rest of my sentence disappeared into the black hole of his stare.

Such as with a true region in space exhibiting gravitational acceleration so strong that nothing can escape from it, I felt myself drawn into the depth of his nearly black eyes. In the crowded courtyard filled with stagnantly hot, humid New Orleans air, a chill covered my skin, bringing goose bumps to life and drawing my nipples taut.

Why hadn't I worn an outfit with a bra?

What would it feel like to fall into this mountain of a man?

Just another inch forward and my breasts and his chest would collide.

"Our table is waiting, Emma."

Releasing his grip of the bar, the man's large hand came to the small of my back.

My forehead furrowed as I tried to make sense of what made no sense. His touch seemed too intimate and his presumption without merit. "Perhaps I'm the wrong Emma?"

~

Watch for "FATE'S DEMAND" – Coming for #Free March 2021 (Text Aleathaɪd to 21000 for a text alert when Fate's Demand is live)

Pre-order the full-length NEW dark romance novel **DEVIL'S DEAL** today and be ready to fall in love with danger and mystery May 2021.

WHAT TO DO NOW

LEND IT: Did you enjoy DAWN? Do you have a friend who'd enjoy DAWN? DAWN may be lent one time. Sharing is caring!

RECOMMEND IT: Do you have multiple friends who'd enjoy my dark romance with twists and turns and an all new sexy and infuriating anti-hero? Tell them about it! Call, text, post, tweet...your recommendation is the nicest gift you can give to an author!

REVIEW IT: Tell the world. Please go to the retailer where you purchased this book, as well as Goodreads, and write a review. Please share your thoughts about DAWN on:

*Amazon, DAWN Customer Reviews

*Barnes & Noble, DAWN, Customer Reviews

*iBooks, DAWN Customer Reviews

* BookBub, DAWN Customer Reviews

*Goodreads.com/Aleatha Romig

BOOKS BY NEW YORK TIMES BESTSELLING AUTHOR ALEATHA ROMIG

NEW STORY COMING:

DEVIL'S DEAL

Coming May 2121

THE SPARROW WEBS:

DANGEROUS WEB:

DUSK

Releasing Nov, 2020

DARK

Releasing 2021

DAWN

Releasing 2021

WEB OF DESIRE:

SPARK

Released Jan. 14, 2020

FLAME

Released February 25, 2020

ASHES

Released April 7, 2020

TANGLED WEB:

TWISTED

Released May, 2019

OBSESSED

Released July, 2019

BOUND

Released August, 2019

WEB OF SIN:

SECRETS

Released October, 2018

LIES

Released December, 2018

PROMISES

Released January, 2019

THE INFIDELITY SERIES:

BETRAYAL

Book #1

Released October 2015

CUNNING

Book #2

Released January 2016

DECEPTION

Book #3

Released May 2016

ENTRAPMENT

Book #4

Released September 2016

FIDELITY

Book #5

Released January 2017

THE CONSEQUENCES SERIES:

CONSEQUENCES

(Book #1)

Released August 2011

TRUTH

(Book #2)

Released October 2012

CONVICTED

(Book #3)

Released October 2013

REVEALED

(Book #4)

Previously titled: Behind His Eyes Convicted: The Missing Years

Re-released June 2014

BEYOND THE CONSEQUENCES

(Book #5)

Released January 2015

RIPPLES

Released October 2017

CONSEQUENCES COMPANION READS:

BEHIND HIS EYES-CONSEQUENCES

Released January 2014

BEHIND HIS EYES-TRUTH

Released March 2014

STAND ALONE MAFIA THRILLER:

PRICE OF HONOR

Available Now

THE LIGHT DUET:

Published through Thomas and Mercer Amazon exclusive

INTO THE LIGHT

Released June, 2016

AWAY FROM THE DARK

Released October, 2016

~

TALES FROM THE DARK SIDE SERIES:

INSIDIOUS

(All books in this series are stand-alone erotic thrillers)

Released October 2014

~

ALEATHA'S LIGHTER ONES:

PLUS ONE

Stand-alone fun, sexy romance

May 2017

ANOTHER ONE

Stand-alone fun, sexy romance

May 2018

ONE NIGHT

Stand-alone, sexy contemporary romance

September 2017

A SECRET ONE

April 2018

~

ABOUT THE AUTHOR

Aleatha Romig is a New York Times, Wall Street Journal, and USA Today bestselling author who lives in Indiana, USA. She has raised three children with her high school sweetheart and husband of over thirty years. Before she became a full-time author, she worked days as a dental hygienist and spent her nights writing. Now, when she's not imagining mind-blowing twists and turns, she likes to spend her time with her family and friends. Her other pastimes include reading and creating heroes/anti-heroes who haunt your dreams!

Aleatha impresses with her versatility in writing. She released her first novel, CONSEQUENCES, in August of 2011. CONSEQUENCES, a dark romance, became a bestselling series with five novels and two companions released from 2011 through 2015. The compelling and epic story of Anthony and Claire Rawlings has graced more than half a million e-readers. Her first stand-alone smart, sexy thriller INSIDIOUS was next. Then Aleatha released the five-novel INFIDELITY series, a romantic suspense saga, that took the reading world by storm, the final book landing on three of the top bestseller lists. She ventured into traditional publishing with Thomas and Mercer. Her books INTO THE LIGHT and AWAY FROM THE DARK were published through this mystery/thriller publisher in 2016. In the spring of 2017, Aleatha again ventured into a different genre with her first fun and sexy stand-alone romantic comedy with the USA Today bestseller PLUS ONE. She continued with ONE NIGHT and

ANOTHER ONE. If you like fun, sexy, novellas that make your heart pound, try her UNCONVENTIONAL and UNEXPECTED. In 2018 Aleatha returned to her dark romance roots with SPARROW WEBS.

Aleatha is a "Published Author's Network" member of the Romance Writers of America and PEN America. She is represented by Kevan Lyon of Marsal Lyon Literary Agency and Dani Sanchez with Wildfire Marketing.

facebook.com/aleatharomig
twitter.com/aleatharomig
instagram.com/aleatharomig

Made in the USA
Middletown, DE
17 February 2021